To VALHALLA

TO VALHALLA

a novel

PIERCE KELLEY

TO VALHALLA

iUniverse books may be ordered through booksellers or by contacting:

iUniverse
1663 Liberty Drive
Bloomington, IN 47403
www.iuniverse.com
1-800-Authors (1-800-288-4677)

ISBN: 978-1-4917-6355-1 (sc)
ISBN: 978-1-4917-6354-4 (hc)
ISBN: 978-1-4917-6419-0 (e)

Library of Congress Control Number: 2015905957

Print information available on the last page.

iUniverse rev. date: 04/24/2015

Dedication

To the men and women of this country who fought in the Kamdesh, Kunar and Gowardesh Valleys of Afghanistan, a land so foreign as to defy the imagination of most Americans. Many of those soldiers now live with the scars inflicted upon them, both physical and mental, from those days, including my friend, for whom and about whom this book is written. Daringly, those brave men and women entered what were valleys of death, knowing that someone had blundered by sending them there.

Alfred Tennyson said it best in 1854 in his classic poem, The Charge of the Light Brigade:

> "Half a league, half a league, half a league onward;
> Into the valley of Death rode the six hundred;
> 'Forward, the Light Brigade! Charge for the guns,' he said,
> Into the valley of Death rode the six hundred.
>
> 'Forward, the Light Brigade!' Was there a man dismay'd?
> Not tho' the soldiers knew someone had blunder'd:
> Theirs not to make reply, Theirs not to reason why,
> Theirs but to do and die;
> Into the valley of Death rode the six hundred.
>
> Cannon to the right of them, cannon to the left of them,
> Cannon in front of them volley'd and thunder'd;
> Storm'd at with shot and shell, boldly they rode and well,
> Into the jaws of Death, into the mouth of Hell rode the six hundred.

Flash'd all their sabres bare, flash'd as they turned in air,
Sabring the gunners there, charging an army while all the
world wonder'd;

Plunged in the battery-smoke right thro' the line they broke;
Cossack and Russian reel'd from the sabre-stroke
Shatter'd and sunder'd, then they rode back, but not, not
the six hundred.

Cannon to the right of them, cannon to the left of them,
Cannon behind them,
Storm'd at with shot and shell, while horse and hero fell,
They that had fought so well came thro' the jaws of Death,
Back from the mouth of Hell, all that was left of them, left
of the six hundred.

When can their glory fade? O the wild charge they made!
All the world wonder'd, Honour the charge they made!
Noble six hundred!"

   The soldiers in the valleys of Afghanistan, much like the cavalrymen of old, did their duty, despite the obvious and apparent danger of being sitting ducks to a well-armed enemy hidden in mountains above them firing rifles, mortars, rocket-propelled grenades and other missives at them. Those valleys are in the northeast corner of Afghanistan amid the towering and majestic mountains of the Hindu Kush. Those soldiers understood, as did the entire world, why they were there, and that was to capture or kill Osama bin Laden and all terrorists who could be found there. That sense of purpose didn't make their jobs easier, because there were many in Afghanistan who sought to protect bin Laden and didn't want us there, most notably the Taliban.

   Forty years after Tennyson's poem was published, Rudyard Kipling wrote a poem entitled "The Last of the Light Brigade." His poem dealt with the plight of the veterans of the Crimean War, as he saw them, those many years after the war ended, and how the survivors of the

Light Brigade experienced old age. At the time, there was little public assistance offered to those wounded veterans. His poem is said to have been a plea for help.

The U.S. soldiers who survived the valleys of death in Afghanistan are, without doubt, receiving better treatment than soldiers returning from Viet Nam in the sixties and seventies did, or the survivors of the Light Brigade, but the respect, comfort, care, sympathy and empathy they receive is, in many cases, not enough, because of the severity of the injury or condition. They continue to suffer. This is a fictitious account of the life of one such soldier, and his life after his military career ended by way of a medical discharge. This book is dedicated to him, and to the men with whom he served in the Blue Platoon, Crazy Horse Company, 173rd Battalion of the United States Army.

"….though I walk through the valley of the shadow of death, I will fear no evil…"

Psalm 23:4

Other works by Pierce Kelley

A Deadly Legacy, (iUniverse, 2013);
Roxy Blues, (iUniverse, 2012);
Father, I Must Go, (iUniverse, 2011);
Thousand Yard Stare (iUniverse, 2010);
Kennedy Homes: An American Tragedy (iUniverse, 2009);
A Foreseeable Risk (iUniverse, 2009);
Asleep at the Wheel (iUniverse, 2009);
A Tinker's Damn! (iUniverse, 2008);
Bocas del Toro (iUniverse, 2007);
A Plenary Indulgence (iUniverse, 2007);
Pieces to the Puzzle (iUniverse, 2007);
Introducing Children to the Game of Tennis (iUniverse, 2007);
A Very Fine Line (iUniverse, 2006);
Fistfight at the L and M Saloon (iUniverse, 2006);
Civil Litigation: A Case Study (Pearson Publication, 2001);
The Parent's Guide to Coaching Tennis (F &W Publications, 1995);
A Parent's Guide to Coaching Tennis (Betterway Publications, 1991).

Acknowledgements

I THANK THOSE WHO HAVE supported and encouraged me on this and other projects. In preparing to write this book, I read a number of books to acquaint myself with Afghanistan and the battles fought there. Those books include the following: <u>The Outpost</u>, by Jake Tepper, Little, Brown and Company, 2012; <u>War</u>, by Sebastian Junger, Hatchett Book Group, Inc., 2010, <u>South of Heaven: My Year in Afghanistan</u>, by Daniel Flores, iUniverse, 2012; <u>Taliban, Militant Islam, Oil & Fundamentalism in Central Asia</u>, by Ahmed Rashid, Thorndike Press, 2000; <u>Afghanistan</u>, by Miriam Greenblatt, Scholastic Library Publishing, 2003; <u>Uncommon Valor</u>, by Dwight Jon Zimmerman and John D. Gresham, St. Martin's Press, 2010, 2011; <u>No Way Out</u>, by Mitch Weiss and Kevin Maurer, Penguin Group, 2012; and <u>Lions of Kandahar</u>, by Major Rusty Bradley and Kevin Maurer, Bantam Books, 2011, among others.

I also watched many movies on the topic, such as Lone Survivor and Restrepo, which were accounts of battles fought in the Kamdesh, Kunar and Gowardesh valleys in Northeast Afghanistan. I also watched Alive Day, an HBO presentation hosted by James Gandolfo, which was about survivors who recalled the day on which they could have, and possibly should have, died. That was the day on which they were badly injured. It is called "Alive Day" because they were, sometimes miraculously, still alive.

Another movie I watched to prepare myself to write this book was a movie called Black Tulip, filmed in Afghanistan with Afghan actors, which told the story of people who welcomed Americans into their country and appreciated what we, and our allies, did for them. They were happy to see our soldiers drive the Taliban from power in 2001, but they suffered and continue to suffer consequences for doing so. The Taliban often either killed or punished those people.

Yet another movie which influenced me in the writing of this book was one called Drones, which is a story about two drone operators called upon to kill a significant target, even though women and children might be killed as well.

More than anything or anyone else, however, I acknowledge and thank my friend, who will be nameless, who told me his story and related to me what it was like for him to be there and what it has been like to go forward with his life after being there. I could not have written this book without his assistance.

Preface

THE WORD VALHALLA COMES to us from the Vikings. The "Viking Age," as it is known, is considered to have been that period of time during which people from the Scandinavian countries of Norway, Sweden and Denmark ruthlessly looted England, Ireland, Scotland and various ports in Western Europe. It is said to have lasted for a period of several hundred years, beginning in 787, when history records the first "raid," until the middle of the eleventh century, when the Vikings were defeated in various battles and forced to retreat. Many settled permanently in the areas they had ravaged.

To the Vikings of old, Valhalla was heaven. The literal translation from the Norse language is "hall of the slain." It was believed by them to be a palatial building located in a mythical place called Asgard, which was ruled over by Odin, their god, reserved only for those who died gloriously in battle.

Once in heaven, their days were filled with fights to the death. Their wounds would miraculously heal in time for them to enjoy the nights, which were a never-ending series of drunken orgies. The myth was that deceased warriors who died valiantly in battle sat at long tables in that magnificent palace, together with Odin, and feasted on wild boar, with a roaring fire to warm them and beautiful women to serve them bottomless steins of beer. Death in battle was a much sought-after reward for heroism.

History regards the Vikings as a people who sought to gain riches by plundering those who lived within sailing distance from them. The word, "Viking," translates from the Norse language as "men who travel for adventure." The romanticized version conjures up images of giants, with long, flowing red or blonde hair, full beards, huge swords in one hand and large wooden shields in the other.

Vikings may best be known to Americans from the 1960 movie of the same name, starring Kirk Douglas, Tony Curtis and Vivian Leigh, or from the mascot of Minnesota's NFL team, with a helmet of gold and two large horns atop his head. A cartoon character, Hagar the Horrible, provides us with a daily reminder of them.

From all accounts, they were fierce warriors who put fear in the hearts of all who saw them. One can only imagine what it was like to see them menacingly approach, rowing their long-ships, with dragons on the bows. While much of Viking lore comes from historical facts, there is much mythology surrounding their culture as well.

But what of those valiant and courageous marauders of old who fought but didn't die from the wounds inflicted upon them in battle? What became of them? Denied the privilege of eternal life in Valhalla, those men returned to their homes and struggled with life as non-warriors. They had fought and come ever so close to achieving the immortality they sought, but they came up short.

And what of the modern day soldiers who don't die with their boots on and must deal with life after reaching the brink of Valhalla? Today's soldiers go off to war in foreign countries seeking victories in battles, much as the Vikings did, but they hope to return from the fray and live long, healthy and happy lives. They don't want to die gloriously on a foreign shore.

They know that Valhalla doesn't exist, and that their reward, if any, may be in heaven, or not, but their lives go on…and so does the life of one Christopher Paul Buchanon, one of those hundreds of thousands of soldiers who served in Afghanistan. This is a fictionalized account of his life. All names in this book, with the exception of political figures, historical figures, known Afghani terrorists, and U. S. soldiers who were awarded Medals of Honor for bravery in battle, are fictitious, including Mr. Buchanon's name.

Prologue

IN SEPTEMBER OF 2001, the Taliban ruled Afghanistan. It had subdued over 99% of the country by military force, after little more than seven years of civil war. Only one province in the northern part of the country held out resistance. The only remaining opposition, which was comprised of a variety of religious and political groups, was called the Northern Alliance.

The name, Taliban, comes from the Arabic word "talib," which means student. One man, who will be called Mohammad Mogabbi throughout this book, who was a "mullah," or one. trained in Islamic law to be a teacher, founded the group in 1992, three years after the Russians had withdrawn its troops from the country after ten years of occupation. His followers were said to be his students. He was, and remains to this day, the undisputed ruler of the Taliban in Afghanistan.

The Taliban are Sunni Muslims, and they speak Pashtu, one of the many dialects in the country. Under Mullah Mogabbi's leadership, the Taliban has forced its interpretation of the teachings of the prophet Mohammad upon all those whom they have conquered. The most controversial aspects of Sharia Law, as it is called, involve the submission by women to the rule of men in homes, politics, the workplace and every other aspect of life.

Women were not allowed to attend school or work outside the home. Women were required to wear clothing which hid their faces and their bodies. They were not allowed to wear perfumes or make-up.

Men were required to wear beards. It was forbidden to play or listen to music. It was against the law to play sports or fly kites, among many other restrictions and prohibitions.

Sharia Law is said to be God's law, the law of Islam, or the code of conduct for all Muslims to follow. There are many interpretations of the Quran, their holy book, just as there are many interpretations of the Bible, or the Torah. However, Mullah Mogabbi's interpretation of the Quran is considered to be the most extreme interpretation of Mohammad's teachings the world has ever seen, although Saudi Arabia has also developed an extreme version of Sharia Law over the last two decades.

The views of Shi'ite Muslims and all other religions were not and are not tolerated. Although the United States and other countries disapproved of the many human rights violations perpetrated by the Taliban upon the people of Afghanistan, nothing of any consequence was ever done to prevent the Taliban from doing as it pleased. All that changed on September 11, 2001.

On that day, al-Qaeda attacked the United States, destroyed the Twin Towers in New York City and caused damage to the Pentagon. Osama bin Laden was the founder of that group. He took credit for the loss of life and financial devastation he caused and vowed that more carnage would follow.

Immediately following the events of September 11, the United States sought to capture or kill bin Laden, who was believed to be living in Afghanistan. Mullah Mogabbi denied that bin Laden was in his country and he demanded proof that bin Laden had been responsible for the atrocities committed upon the United States. It was quickly established that he was, in fact, providing shelter for and protection to bin Laden and his followers.

Within a matter of weeks, after Mullah Mogabbi continued his refusal to cooperate and hand over bin Laden, the United States organized a military campaign to oust him from leadership in Afghanistan and to find bin Laden. On October 7, 2011, President Bush ordered air strikes against known al-Qaeda training camps and military installations of the Taliban regime. Many countries joined the U.S. in this effort, although the United Nations did not initially sanction those actions. The UN subsequently authorized the deployment of a UN International Security Force, however.

Mullah Mogabbi immediately fled the country. He was declared a terrorist and a $10 million bounty was placed on his head. In the years since, neither the United States nor any of its allies in the world have been able to locate and apprehend him. He is believed to be living in Pakistan, in a part of the country known as the Tribal Lands.

In the years since September 11, the Taliban, under the leadership of Mogabbi, has continued to fight and kill U.S. soldiers in Afghanistan, and it does so to this day. Whether or not the United States will continue to pursue the Taliban, despite the fact that it officially withdrew all combat troops from the country earlier this year, remains to be seen. Whether or not the United States will continue its efforts to locate, capture and/or kill Mullah Mogabbi remains to be seen as well.

CHAPTER ONE

A Soldier

"**G**ET YOUR SORRY ASS out of bed now!" I rolled over, rubbed my eyes, and saw my mother's face about six inches away from mine, screaming at me.

"Don't think you're gonna sit around this house, watch television and feed your face all day, because you're not!"

"What's wrong with you, Mom? Have a bad night at work?"

"What's wrong with me? She asked, as she slapped me upside the head. "What's wrong with me? There's not a damn thing wrong with me, you sorry-ass son-of-a-bitch. You're the one who has things all wrong!"

Before she could hit me again, I rolled off the other side of the bed and struggled to my feet. She wasn't done with me yet.

"What's wrong with me? I'm not the one who got suspended from school, again, am I? No, that's not me...I'm the one who worked all fucking night to make enough money to buy the food you eat and put a roof over your head! What's wrong with me..."

She started coming at me again. I blocked her slaps as I backed out of the room and headed in the direction of the bathroom.

"Alright, alright, alright, alright! That's enough! I get your point. So I can't go to school for a week...what do you want to do about it? Do you want me to do some chores? What?"

"I want you to get a job and get out of my house! If you don't want to be in school, get out! Find yourself a job! Find yourself a place to live!

Just get out of here! I'm tired of this! I'm tired of getting calls from your school! I'm tired of it all!"

"It wasn't my fault! That guy started it! I was just defending myself!" I yelled back at her.

"Yeah, yeah, yeah…just like the last five times, right?"

"That's right! Guys mess with me and they'll pay for it. I don't back down to nobody! Nobody!"

With that, I ducked into the bathroom and closed the door behind me, locking it as I did, but she stayed on me.

"Yeah, you're a tough guy alright. Why are you in school anyway? Your grades are awful! You're gonna get zeros in every class while you're suspended! At this rate, you're not going to graduate with your class and I sure as hell don't want you around here for another year!"

I turned on the shower and didn't respond to that comment, but that didn't stop her.

"Either you get a job or you go in the Army! I don't care which. I'm tired of this shit! You hear me? I'm tired of it!"

She banged on the door a few times and yelled some other things I can't remember. After a few more minutes, when I didn't respond, she went away. I stayed in the shower a while. When I came out, she was in her room with the door closed.

Once I was dressed, I went straight down to the Army Recruiter's office. That was the day when everything changed. That was the day I decided to join the Army.

It wasn't like I hadn't thought about it before. I had, but that was a pivotal moment in my life. I won't forget that day. It wasn't like we hadn't had similar conversations in the past. We had, but that was the last straw.

I was born in Tulsa, Oklahoma in December of 1982. My mother and her family were part Cherokee and, therefore, so am I. That's the part of Oklahoma where the Trail of Tears ended for the Cherokees in 1841.

The name on my birth certificate reads Lucian George Shepherd. My biological father was from Tennessee, I am told, and he must have been Irish, because I've got red hair and I have always loved to fight, and drink.

He wasn't a big man and I inherited his size, as well. I'm 5'6" tall and I weigh about 150 pounds. So I've got his red hair, his small body, a powerful thirst for the "holy water," and his pugilistic soul, I guess. That's about all I know about him.

My mother and father split up when I was an infant and I have no recollection of him. My mother told me, when I was older, that he had died in a fire while working on oil rigs, but then she told me while I was filling out to papers to join the Army that he was an alcoholic and died of liver failure a few years earlier. So I'm not sure if he's dead or alive and it doesn't matter. He hasn't shown any interest in me, and I have no interest in him.

My mother moved to Titusville, Florida when I was three. She didn't like the cold Oklahoma winters and had an opportunity to work in the medical field in a much warmer climate, which appealed to her. She was a nurse and she accepted a position at a center for mentally handicapped people. The job didn't work out and she ended up managing a local bar for the next twenty years. She didn't take shit from anyone, least of all me.

She met and married a man named Paul Buchanon not long after moving to Florida. He was a construction worker. He adopted me a few years after that and, when he did, I was given an entirely new name... Christopher Paul Buchanon.

For whatever reason, and I doubt that it would take a team of psychologists and sociologists to figure out, I was rebellious. The only organized activity I enjoyed participating in during my youth was karate. I became a black belt by the time I was 13 and won 3rd place in a State Tae Kwon Do tournament one time.

I learned how to fight at an early age, which was a good thing, because I got into fights all the time. My grades weren't good, and one of the many reasons for that was because I kept getting suspended for fighting. I wasn't a student.

The Army required that I obtain my GED to get in. I took the test and passed it on my first try, but they wouldn't allow me to join up unless my mother agreed to sign the papers, since I hadn't reached my 18th birthday. That wasn't a problem. She gladly did that. They didn't have to ask her twice.

I didn't join the Army because of any patriotic desire to serve my country, or because military service ran in the family. I did it, like many other men I met in the Army, to get out on my own and become my own man. The Army was going to provide me with an opportunity to make a better life for myself, and it seemed like my only way out.

I figured that I could obtain some skills and earn some money in the process, but mostly it was just about getting out of her life and making a life of my own. I also liked the idea of firing guns and using all of the other weapons the Army has. I signed up to be in the infantry.

I officially entered the Army in February of 2000, well shy of my 18th birthday. Once I had signed up, things settled down at home, but we didn't talk much about what I had decided to do. She couldn't wait for me to go, and I couldn't wait to get out of there. We were in agreement on that.

I was sent to Fort Benning, Georgia for basic training. At my request, I was put in the mechanized infantry and I learned how to operate vehicles. I received an additional 9 weeks of training for that.

The primary vehicle I was trained on was the Bradley. It was named after General Omar Bradley, who was part of the D-Day invasion. Those were the ones that carried troops to the beaches of Normandy. They were also used extensively in the Pacific for beach landings. It doesn't have wheels. It has tracks, like a tank. It carries 8 or 9 soldiers in the back, with a soldier on top, a radio man and one other soldier in the back seat, and an officer in the passenger seat.

As it turned out, I rarely had the opportunity to utilize those skills. I was sent straight from Ft. Benning to Korea. I had little idea of what to expect when I got there, but I found out quickly that I wasn't going to be transporting troops. I was going to be a sentry.

I became one of the 20,000 soldiers in the 8th U.S. Army unit stationed in South Korea. Our headquarters were in Yongsan, and it was the main military base in the country. The Air Force had about 8,000 Airmen stationed at Osan, 27 miles away, on the coast. The Navy had about 300 sailors in Osan, too, and the Marines had 100 men there as well. The primary function of the 20,000 soldiers in Yongsan was to guard against an invasion by the North Koreans.

Prior to WWII, Korea was a colony of Japan and had been since 1910. After WWII ended, the Allies met in summit in 1946 and decided to divide the country in half, putting the northern part of the country under the rule of the Russians, and the southern half under the control of the United States. General Douglas MacArthur, whose headquarters were in Tokyo, was in charge of the newly created nation of South Korea. The dividing point was at the 38th parallel.

Since the Russians, as enemies of the common enemy, were our "friends" and had been our allies during the war, they claimed entitlement to do so. It was much like what was done with the breaking up of Germany. It was an agreement entered into by the countries which had banded together to defeat Germany, Japan and Italy, the Axis powers.

In the north, the Russians established a communist system, with Kim Il-Sung in charge. In the south, Syngman Rhee was elected as the first president of the new democratic government. From the outset, Kim Il-Sung openly declared that his goal was to re-unite the country by force, if necessary. As a result, both sides were in a constant state of military readiness from the very beginning.

In June of 1950, the North Korean army invaded South Korea and caught the South Koreans and its allies, including the U.S., by surprise. The South Koreans offered little resistance. With assistance from the United Nations, the invasion was stalled in the area of Puson, a port city deep in the southern part of the country.

General MacArthur then put two divisions of U.S. soldiers in behind the North Korean army, thereby creating a vice. It caused the North Koreans to retreat back north of the 38th parallel, with the U.S. and its allies in pursuit. However, when we advanced too close to the Manchurian border, China took offense.

At that point, which was September of 1950, China joined the fray. It sent in hundreds of thousands of soldiers to not only defend its territory, but to regain the offensive. Together with the North Koreans, and the Russians, it crossed back over the 38th parallel, and back into South Korea.

The war raged on for the next several years. Basically, the United States and its allies were fighting against Russia and China, but soldiers from the two Koreas were active participants, as well. In July of 1953, a truce was negotiated which involved a return to the 38th parallel, where a de-militarized zone was created.

Ever since, soldiers stand behind two ten-foot high, barbed-wire fences, staring at each other. A narrow strip of land sits in between the two fences and runs the entirety of the country from east to west. On a near daily basis, hundreds of thousands of North Korean soldiers, literally, can be found at or near their side of the fence, whereas there were only twenty thousand U.S. Army soldiers on the south side of the fence.

I was put in the 9th Infantry Regiment, a distinguished unit with a history dating back to the earliest days of our country. For the next several years, except for the occasional R & R respite, I was never more than ten kilometers from the fence. There wasn't much for us to do except be ready for an attack.

We all knew that if another invasion took place our land forces would be easily and quickly overwhelmed. Despite that, our job was to defend the DMZ and that was our sole purpose. We were on "alert" at all times, never knowing when an attack might take place and there were many, many times when North Korea committed acts of aggression and threatened to take further military action. We continuously received training and did our best to be prepared for anything and everything, but things were always tense, even grim, actually, but I enjoyed it.

I found Korea to be a very beautiful and interesting place. I took advantage of every opportunity to leave the base and explore the country. I enjoyed it so much that when my first year of deployment ended, I agreed to serve the next three years in Korea. I could have asked to be sent elsewhere. There was nothing for me back in the States and I liked Korea, so I stayed there.

I lived in a JSA, or Joint Security Area, most of that time. That's an area right next to the DMZ. When I wasn't at the DMZ, my quarters were less than 10 miles away. I, like all other soldiers, except for the officers, was housed in the barracks. Both places were two story, concrete block buildings in which thousands of soldiers slept in bunk beds in open dormitories. In other words, I was in a large, open room with dozens of other men.

The worst part about being in North Korea was the non-stop barrage of propaganda coming from loud speakers. North Koreans would personalize their broadcasts with things like…"Private Buchanon, wouldn't you rather be back in Florida, where you belong? You could be driving down I-95 in a convertible, with the top down, on your way to the beach, enjoying yourself? Did you know that your girlfriend is running around with another man while you're here standing in the cold?" I never got used to it. It was a constant annoyance.

Every now and then we'd have a show of force at the training grounds, which was close enough to the Demilitarized Zone so that the North Koreans could see us. We'd have some equipment and weapons brought in to show off, including some tanks and the Bradleys, but that was a rare event. I think I only drove one time.

I was in Korea on 9-11. Life in the United States Army became much more focused after that day. Not only were we ready for action, we all wanted that action. We all wanted the opportunity to get even with the people who had done that to us. We were ready for combat, just itching to have an opportunity to make them pay for what they had done.

We expected something to happen and we were ready for it. The Army made sure of that. Discipline increased dramatically and every training event took on new meaning.

Fortunately, or unfortunately, nothing ever came of it as far as those of us stationed in Korea were concerned. The stand-offs and the stare-downs continued. After two years, I decided to join the airborne infantry. That meant that I received instruction on how to jump out of airplanes. Every now and then I would get to do a jump as part of a training exercise, but that was a rare event. I was still a soldier in the infantry and I was a sentry.

The most interesting and most physically challenging part of being in Korea was the Manchu Mile March. It was, and still is, a grueling test of endurance for soldiers. It consists of a 25 mile long trek across mountainous terrain, in full gear, following in the footsteps of what soldiers from the 9th Infantry Regiment did in 1900.

At the time, China was experiencing a major revolution. U.S. soldiers were sent to Korea on a mission to rescue American diplomats and others from the mayhem erupting throughout China during the Chinese

"Boxer" Rebellion. Troops landed and immediately proceeded to hike the 25 miles from their base at Taku Bar, where they disembarked the ship that transported them, to the city of Tientsin. Upon their arrival, they were in combat. They successfully accomplished their mission, but not without heavy casualties.

Soldiers who complete the Manchu Mile earn a buckle. It is a source of pride for all infantrymen, and all soldiers in the 9th are required to complete it. I did it twice. It was a painful experience, but I am proud to say that I accomplished that feat. It is intended only for the 9th Infantry Battalion and those who complete the challenge are part of what is called a Manchu Brotherhood.

After four years, I was ready for a change. When my time was up, I opted out.

CHAPTER TWO

A Brief Civilian Life

UPON MY DISCHARGE FROM the Army in February of 2004, I returned to Florida and went back to Titusville. My mother and step-father still lived there. I might have been allowed back in the house, but after being on my own for so long, and after going through the things I had, I couldn't stay with them. Besides, I didn't want to. I found a couple of other guys, like me, who were fresh out of the Army, and we shared an apartment in Orlando, about 50 miles away to the north and west.

At that point, I was still only twenty one years old and, although I felt much older, I was still a kid and had a lot to learn, especially when it came to the members of the opposite sex. I had been living with other male soldiers for years. Except for the few weeks spent here and there during R & R visits, I hadn't had much experience with women, and what experience I had wasn't something to tell my kids about. Although the number of women in the Army was growing, it was difficult to establish any meaningful relationships with them, and I certainly hadn't been able to do that, not even close.

I proceeded to do as any and every other red-blooded American boy would do, and that was to locate, befriend and then engage in sexual adventures with members of the opposite sex. Orlando was a target-rich environment and I made it my mission to find women. I had been deprived of female companionship for so long that it became an obsession.

While I was in the Army, I had few opportunities to spend the money I had earned. Therefore, I had four years' worth of savings at my disposal. Every night was spent at a bar chasing skirts and every day was spent in bed, sobering up in time for the next nocturnal adventure.

When I wasn't in a bar, drinking and carousing, I was at the movies or watching movies at my house. I wanted to see as many movies about war that I could. Arnold Schwartzenegger, Bruce Willis, Claude van Damm and Nicolas Cage were a few of the biggest action-hero movie stars of the day. I saw all of their movies and I rented as many war movies from Blockbuster as I could put my hands on as well. My thirst for movies about war was unquenchable.

After several months of debauchery and drunkenness, I decided I had to get a job and earn some money. My bank account was spiraling downward. Between rent, food, alcohol, insurance, movies and the rest, I was down to a few thousand dollars in the bank before I knew it.

As I quickly learned, standing on guard duty, knowing how to fire weapons and being able to march for hours at a time were not skills which transferred easily to civilian ranks. The best job I could find which matched those qualities was as a security guard. The pay wasn't great, and it was menial work, but it was a steady paycheck.

Although I worked long hours, often at night and on weekends, I continued to frequent the bars. I chased women every chance I could. I might have been dead-tired after work, but I would still answer the bell when it was time to go out, instead of just falling asleep, like my body was telling me I should.

But in the mornings, no matter how bad the nights before were, I reported for duty. The Army had instilled a number of things in me. The first thing I learned was to obey orders. The second thing was to get up early and report for work on time. I was always there when roll call was taken. Unless I was dead or dying, I wasn't going to miss a day of work, or be late.

After two years of civilian life, and after watching hundreds of movies about war, I decided that I wanted to go back into the military. My time spent in Korea, though at complete military readiness at all times, was, in retrospect, unsatisfying. I hadn't fired a gun at an enemy soldier once. I hadn't experienced combat. I hadn't satisfied my desire to be a soldier of war. I re-enlisted with a specific purpose of going into combat with a known enemy. I wanted to go to Afghanistan and engage Al Qaeda and the Taliban in battle.

I had been in Korea from February of 2000 until February of 2004, but I had made an eight year commitment, so after I completed four years of active duty, I was still required to remain in the Army for four more years. I became a reservist and I was assigned to a Military Police unit in Orlando, where I was required to report one weekend a month, which I did. I was also required to do two weeks of active duty per year, which I also did.

As a Reservist, I knew that I could be re-called to active duty at any time up to 2008, though I hadn't been. So I figured it really wasn't a big deal for me to go back in, since I was, technically, still in the Army. I requested to be put back on active duty and be sent to the front lines.

By March of 2006, I was back on active duty and the Army was glad to have me back. They gave me a pay increase and a raise in rank to Sergeant. I was required to extend my commitment an additional two years, which I gladly did. The time away from the military helped me decide that I wanted to be a soldier for life.

I was allowed to select my duty station, and I selected an Airborne unit, since I had been trained as a paratrooper. I wanted to fight. I wanted to experience combat. I wanted to be a soldier, not a sentry.

I was assigned to the 173rd airborne cavalry battalion, which was a part of a larger brigade. Its headquarters were in Vicenza, Italy, and that is where I was sent. Once there, I would receive orders as to what particular detail I would be assigned to within that battalion.

After a few months in Vicenza, I was put into a Special Forces unit. That meant I would receive training on virtually any and all assignments a soldier might be called upon to fulfill. I was transferred to Bamburg, Germany, where that unit of the 173rd was located.

When a soldier goes into the Army, sometimes he or she is allowed to choose what job they will perform, as part of the enlistment process, but most of the time a soldier is assigned to a post depending upon the "needs of the Army." In those situations, the soldier does what he is ordered to do. I didn't choose that assignment.

The Special Forces Unit I was assigned to was an elite group of soldiers, but there were various units within the Special Forces Battalion, not all of which were like the Navy's Seal Team Six which killed bin Laden. One of the job responsibilities of my unit involved providing security for high-ranking officers and government officials who might be traveling in high-risk areas. It was called the Personal Security Detail.

As part of that unit, I spent almost a year in Bamburg learning, among other things, how to speak the Afghan language. Since there are a large number of different dialects in that country and, depending upon what part of Afghanistan I would be in, unless I knew that dialect, it didn't matter much, but they taught me as much as they could.

We also learned how to assist the medics, the supply corps, and do a wide variety of things a soldier might need to do, if called upon to do so. We were more like reinforcements who could be thrown into any situation at a moment's notice.

The majority of my time was spent getting prepared for the many challenges that were specific to being in Afghanistan, in addition to the physical ones. We were going into a culture that was completely different from anything any of us were accustomed to. Plus, the rules of engagement were changing. The Army wanted to show that it had learned from some of the mistakes made in Vietnam. There was much discussion and training regarding how we could win over the hearts and minds of the people, not just militarily subdue them.

Within my brigade, there were three other combat battalions, which were the 502nd, the 503rd, and the 191st, which was also an airborne cavalry-scouts unit. There was also a supply battalion, and a headquarters unit attached to our brigade.

Fourteen months later, in May of 2007, my brigade received orders to go to Afghanistan. We flew on C-130 transport planes into Bagram, the main headquarters for the Army in Afghanistan, just outside of Kabul, the capital. It took a few planes to transport the entire brigade, since we numbered about 5,000 soldiers in all. In addition to most U.S. soldiers, all foreign soldiers, including Australian, German, Korean, British, French, Italian, Spanish, Canadians, and everyone else under the United Nations umbrella, were there, too.

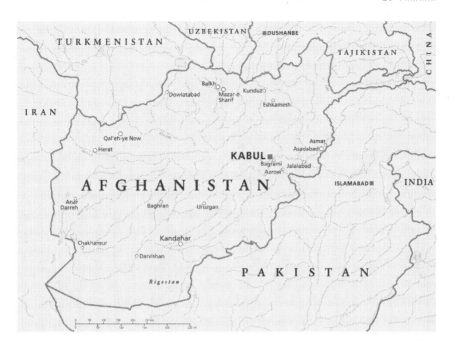

All other branches of the United States military were there, as well, including the Navy, even though there wasn't any access to a sea or an ocean. Afghanistan is a land-locked country. The CBs were there and the CBs are a naval unit. A number of the Naval Seal teams were there, too.

It was a huge base and there were tens of thousands of military personnel there. Many civilian contractors were based there, as well as the CIA. The main hospital complex was on the base and it had the capabilities to handle the most seriously injured soldiers, when necessary. Engineers were there, as were many Afghan military units.

While awaiting our orders as to exactly where we were to go within Afghanistan, we were put in massive tents, much like the "big top" circus tents. It was called tent city because there were these large tents as far as you could see in any direction. My unit, the Personal Security Detail, would be staying close to Bagram, since that was where the high-ranking officers and dignitaries would be.

Since the 173rd was such a large brigade, we were in quite a few of those extremely large tents. The Army assigned each battalion to a separate part of Afghanistan, and then that area would be subdivided further, with companies going to Forward Operating Bases, or FOBs. Platoons were then sent out from those Bases to even smaller locations, called Outposts.

Our brigade received orders to replace 10th Mountain at various FOBs and Outposts in Nuristan and Kunar provinces. Both provinces bordered Pakistan. On the other side of the border was the area of Pakistan known as the Tribal Lands, which was where many people believed Osama bin Laden was hiding out. Both provinces were hot-beds of activity. Our entire brigade, all four battalions, was to operate in those two areas.

While the other soldiers in the 173rd were in the process of replacing the 10th Mountain at the various FOBs, I was with officers and dignitaries, along with the other members of our Personal Security Detail. It was not where I wanted to be, but it is where the Army wanted me to be. Though it was nothing compared to what my fellow soldiers were doing in the mountains, what I was doing was not without peril. A mishap on our part in which a high-ranking officer or official was injured or killed would have been world news. We took our jobs seriously, and nothing bad ever happened on my watch.

There were many advantages to that job. I got to travel around Afghanistan in relative style, because of who I was with. I spent most of my time in Kabul and in Kandahar, but I was also in Jalalabad and other cities, too. There were paved roads in Kabul and Kandahar, but I didn't see many paved roads anyplace else.

When I was in that unit, I saw many men wearing western-style suits and driving fancy cars. I also had the opportunity to talk to Afghans who spoke English, and there were a surprisingly large number of such people in the cities who did. I learned about the religious diversity in the country. About 79% of Afghanis were Sunni's, 20% were Shi'ite's, and 1% were some other religious groups, like Buddhists. There weren't many Christians, Hindus or Jews in Afghanistan. Over 99% of Afghans were Muslims.

Differences between the Shi'ite and the Sunni Muslims weren't obvious. There was no way you could tell them apart, not by the way they looked, or dressed, or the way they talked. It was, however, an extremely important distinction to be aware of.

When Mohammad died in 632, he didn't name anyone to succeed him as the leader of Islam. Not long after his death, a division within Islam developed. One branch of Muslims, the Sunnis, believed that the successor should be the best person available to lead the Muslim community. The other largest branch of Muslims, the Shi'ites, believed that the successor had to be a blood relative of Mohammad.

The difference of opinion, or belief, between the two groups has caused hundreds of thousands, if not millions, of people to die over the years. The fighting in Iran, Syria and everyplace else between the two groups at the present time continues to involve that one specific issue. I avoided any conversations about that distinction. That was not my business. I just thought of it as being much like the difference between the Catholics and Protestants. Catholics believe that the Pope is the leader of the Christian world and Protestants do not.

Another divisive point within Afghanistan was the language. There are many different ethnic groups within Afghanistan, all of which having separate languages. The Afghan National Anthem mentions 14 separate ethnic groups, including the Pashtun, or Pushtun, Tajiks, Hazaras, Uzbeks, Aimaqs, Turkmen, Baloch, and Nuristani. Each of which speaks a different language. Well over half of the population speaks Pashtun. As a result, Pashtun speaking Sunnis dominate the politics.

After a few months of providing escort service for the muckety-mucks, I was ready for action. I hadn't joined the Army to be a sentry, and I didn't want to be a member of an Honor guard, either. What happened to change that was an unfortunate occurrence.

One of the generals for whom we were providing security lost a son in battle. Not long after that, a number of men, including me, were transferred from the Personal Security Detail to units in the field, which were under-staffed as it was. This general decided he didn't want or need the security, since he was always surrounded by soldiers wherever he was, and he wanted to put more soldiers on the front lines.

I was flown in, together with other soldiers, by a Blackhawk late one night to FOB Monti. By that time, which was almost six years after we first entered Afghanistan, helicopter pilots had been refusing to fly into those areas during the day due to the number of deadly attacks upon helicopters which flew into those tight areas, close to the mountains. From there, I would be transported to the Outpost where the platoon I had been assigned to was located.

FOB Monti was named after Jared C. Monti, who died as he ran to assist a wounded comrade in a battle known as Hill 2610, near Gawardesh, in 2006. He was leading a troop of fourteen soldiers when his group was attacked by a force more than four times as large. For his bravery, he was awarded the Medal of Honor for uncommon valor.

Only ten such medals had been awarded up to that point in time since the Vietnam War, and six of those were awarded to men who served in Iraq and Afghanistan. Four of those men received medals for their courage in battles in the northeastern area of Afghanistan, in the several valleys adjacent to the border with Pakistan, right where I was going.

He was the team leader for the 3rd Squadron, 71st Cavalry Regiment, 3rd Brigade Combat Team, 10th Mountain Division. On June 21, 2006. His assignment was to gather intelligence and provide support to other forces working in the area, which is what he was doing when attacked. My unit would be doing the same thing.

All of our Forward Operating Bases were named after soldiers who had been killed in action. They would often be re-named when someone else died in action later on. Most of our Outposts were named after soldiers who had been killed in battle, also. Some of those Outposts were quite small and contained only a platoon. Others were larger and might contain almost a full company.

I was assigned to "C" company. Each brigade usually had four battalions and each battalion had four companies, A, B, C and D. Most were called Alpha, Bravo, Charlie and Delta, but people could change the names, as long as they kept the A, B, C and D labels.

Platoons followed the same structure. There were four platoons to each company. My unit called itself the Crazy Horse company. It was made up of four platoons. I was being sent to the B platoon.

The 173rd was assigned to push as deep into the Hindu Kush mountains as it could. Our job was to capture and kill Osama bin Laden, if we could find him, and to destroy any members of Al Qaeda or the Taliban whenever engaged in battles by them. We wanted to keep the bad guys from entering Afghanistan and causing more problems than were already there, and to protect the local populace, build friendships and help them develop the infrastructure of the country as best we could.

Where possible, troops would be driven in, with equipment, materials, supplies and the rest. Where that wasn't possible, due to bad roads or no roads at all, troops were air-lifted in by helicopter. When that wasn't possible, troops marched to their bases, carrying what they could on their backs. Since I was going to an extremely remote area, I was one of those who walked in.

Most of the habitats I saw along the way were made of river stone. From what I saw, buildings throughout the whole country seemed to have been built in the stone-age. They were old and had no modern amenities such as indoor plumbing or electricity.

Just seeing how the normal, average Afghan dressed shocked me. Virtually all Afghanis in that part of the country wore baggy trousers, tied at the waist with a string, and a shirt that hung down below the knees. Some of the men wore caps made of karakul skin, which comes from the sheep found in the area. The rest of the men wore a cotton cloth around their heads which they wrapped into a turban.

I arrived in August. Most men were wearing vests. At night, when the temperatures dropped, they wore a heavy sheepskin coat. They would wear sandals during the day, usually, but when it got cold, and at night, they wore heavy boots lined with sheepskin.

About the only things I saw which looked like they came from the 20th century in this part of the country were the vehicles. I saw some pick-up trucks and older cars, not many, because most people still rode donkeys and horses. The trucks that were still operable were badly beaten up from driving in that tough terrain.

I was to join up with my platoon in the Kamdesh District of Nuristan province, at the bottom of a valley. After a full day's walk, I arrived at my destination and saw that the outpost was surrounded by three steep mountains that were a part of the five hundred mile long Hindu Kush mountain range.

In some ways, it reminded me of Korea. If the enemy chose to attack that base with overpowering numbers, like we feared the North Koreans might do, or like the Indians did to Custer, we would be in serious trouble. In fact, before I left Kabul, that's what some people called the base I was going to....the Custer Compound.

I had heard about how bad it was from men returning from the front, but it didn't hit me until I arrived. It was a shock. The base was basically unprotected.

The other thing that struck me about our post was how small it was. I saw a few make-shift buildings with HESCO barriers around them, and that was it. Our mortars, which were our primary offensive weapons, were right next to where we slept. I didn't believe it was as bad as I was told it was until I saw it with my own eyes.

Though I was full of machismo, bravado, testosterone, and a few other things, I also had a healthy dose of dread. It was immediately obvious that this was a dangerous place.... and it scared me.

CHAPTER THREE

The Blue Platoon

MY PLATOON WAS A light, scout cavalry unit. There were twenty of us. We had no vehicles, no armored personnel carriers, and no transportation options other than our own two feet. We were infantrymen, in the purist sense of the word.

When I arrived, I was the new kid on the block. The guys in the platoon had been together for a while. Most guys were in for their third or fourth tour of duty, and they, like me, planned to make the military their career. They were "lifers."

Since I wasn't new to Army life, I didn't have any problem fitting in. A few of the other guys had been to Korea, too, but most of the men hadn't, so they wanted to know what Korea was like, and I was happy to tell them.

Although I didn't know anyone in my unit when I arrived, it didn't take long for me to feel at home. I took an immediate liking to our Lieutenant, and that helped a lot, because he set the tone for the whole platoon. He was a hands-on leader and everyone knew that he was in charge.

He was a bit of a hard-ass, and he was stern, but he was also compassionate and very knowledgeable. He was from Texas and loved to talk about horses and country music. He loved the four Highway men… Willie Nelson, Johnny Cash, Kris Kristofferson and Waylon Jennings.

I think the thing I liked about him the most was that he made everyone feel that anyone could do what he had done, that we were all as good as he was and that he was no better than we were. He had come into the Army as an enlisted man, straight out of high school, like most of us, but after several years he went back to school and became an officer.

He loved to tell the young men in our Platoon, including me, to "Dream the Gold." He told us that when our time was up, we should go to college and become an officer, just like he had. I had no illusions about ever doing that, but I loved the fact that he made me think that he thought I could do it, and he made everybody feel that way.

We seemed to have a similar sense of humor and he laughed easily. I liked his leadership style. Like me, he'd served time in Korea and he was a lifer. He made it a point to have some kind of meaningful conversation with everyone, every day. I looked forward to those daily conversations.

I always knew who was in charge, and that he would always have my back. That's what I wanted in a leader…strength, with compassion. I didn't want to be best friends with my LT. I wanted him to be a good leader. My life, and everybody else's life, was in his hands.

His name was Michael McMullen, but his nickname was Dozer, as in Bulldozer. He was a big, strong man, and built like the proverbial brick shit-house. He would tackle every problem like he was driving a bulldozer right through it.

Over the course of the next year and several months, I bonded with every man in that unit. We all realized the dangers we were exposed to, and everyone handled their responsibilities as well as could possibly be expected. Everyone had a nickname. Mine was "Buck."

Next in charge was our Platoon Sergeant, First Class, Kevin McCarthy. He was a Special Forces operator before he came back to the infantry. Like our LT, he was both funny and intelligent. More importantly, he had an amazing sense of what to do in combat, especially when it came to anticipating what the enemy might do.

We were always talking about what to do if this happened or that happened. We felt as if we were prepared for whatever might happen. He was very down to earth and approachable, too, just like the LT. He also had a great leadership style. I had meaningful daily conversations with him, just like with our LT. He was from Georgia and had a big southern drawl.

With those two guys leading our platoon, we really didn't need much more in the way of leadership. We had a whole bunch of sergeants, though, including me. There were more sergeants in our unit than any other rank.

Our staff sergeant was Don Fletcher. He was in charge of keeping our firearms in good working order and making sure we were ready to fight at all times, which was important, because not one single day went by when we didn't have some exchange of gunfire with the enemy... not one.

Steve Goodbread, from Oklahoma, was also a sergeant, as was Billy Dubin, who was from Rhode Island. He loved his Red Sox. Alfredo Amaroso, or "El Saragento," was from Los Angeles. John Rafferty was a Baptist from West Virginia. He carried a Bible with him at all times and could be seen reading it whenever the opportunity allowed him to do so.

We had a number of specialists, who were men who had very specific skills and tasks. Dennis Gunther was our mechanic; Pepe de Merida, nicknamed "El Diablo," was responsible for firearms and weapons; Fernando Valentine's specialty was firing the mortars; Matthew Salmon was our communications guy; Cory Lunsford was also a communications specialist; Our medic was Henry Battle. He was from Texas and loved the Cowboys.

And then there were the six privates. Yoshi Toya from Taiwan; Sanford Jackson, or "Sandy," from Washington, D.C.; Justin Giambi, an Italian from New York; Willie Wilson from Louisiana; John Courtney from Miami; and Timothy Underwood from Minnesota.

Timmy was the youngest guy in our platoon. I believe he had just graduated from high school and was still 18. He was intimidated by everyone and laughed at everybody's jokes. He was a good marksman, our best, so he was put on the 50 mm gun whenever we were in a fight. We called him "The Kid."

Guys were from all over the country and they were of differing ages, backgrounds, levels of education and social strata. A unit, and this applies to all units in the Army, would have one CO, or commanding officer, which in our case was our Lieutenant, several Sergeants, several specialists, some Corporals and several Privates. There would also be men assigned to our unit who could speak the language and translate for us. These were always Afghans. We didn't consider them as part of our unit, though, because they came and went so often.

Before I got there, they had dubbed themselves the Blue Platoon. Our LT told us almost every day that we had to understand that we had no one other than ourselves to turn to if things got bad. Whatever help we might get from jets, helicopters or whatever, wasn't going to get there fast enough. We had to be ready, all the time.

Soldiers in the 10th Mountain had put up a HESCO barrier around the base, which was little more than a wire cage, and filled it up with sand. They had dug trenches, as best they could, which wasn't easy because of the rocky terrain. There wasn't much of anything there when they first got there, but they had to do something to protect themselves, and that was the best they could do.

For a home base, they had chosen a spot that was the closest thing they could find to flat ground. We were at the bottom of the valley, surrounded by the mountains. We set up a few points as high up the three surrounding mountain as we could, so we could over-see the base and, do our best to prevent our enemies from destroying us from above.

We had one particular spot overlooking the base, which we called Observation Point Delta, where a squad of four or five guys would stay overnight. Guys were there every night. While at the observation posts, nobody slept. They were there to protect us while we slept. They were guarding us.

However, nobody slept at the outpost, either. In fact, I don't feel like I ever slept during that entire deployment, once I got to that base. It was more like I passed out from exhaustion and woke up sometime after that.

The physical challenges were substantial. It was difficult to walk up and down those mountains with an 80 pound pack on my back. Worrying about being shot at while doing so made it even more of a challenge.

We were at that location for our entire fifteen month deployment.

We lived in squalor for all of those fifteen months. It was Spartan-esque, to say the least.

The food came from cans and was rarely heated. We had no heat. We had no spare time to sit around and get warm anyway. The only thing on our minds at all times was survival. Sleep was something you did when you were too exhausted to do anything else. We all knew that life could end in a moment's time.

No one wants to live in shacks, in sub-freezing temperatures, without any heat, in the winter time, as we did. We had no electricity, not even from generators. The FOBs and larger outposts had them, but not us.

We slept side-by-side, like logs, in our sleeping bags, on the ground, and tried to keep ourselves warm, which didn't work well. We slept in our uniforms all of the time. Even in the summer, and we were there for two summers, it was cold at night.

Our home sat on top of a dilapidated concrete slab which had supposedly been built by the Russians. The slab was all that was left of a compound that had been destroyed. We were told that the Afghans had slaughtered every single Russian soldier that had been there.

The Hindu-Kush mountains are higher than the Rockies. It wasn't unusual for temperatures to drop below freezing, even during the summer months. The summer season came late and left early. As I look back on it, I remember it as being always cold.

I don't know why my platoon called itself Blue. Maybe it was because the men were always so cold that they felt like they were turning blue. To me, a Florida boy, it was always freezing.

My platoon had been ordered to create a checkpoint beside what was considered to be one of the many routes from Pakistan into Afghanistan. It wasn't much more than a dirt path, really. No motor vehicles ever came by. We called it Checkpoint Delta.

It was right next to the Gowardesh River, which divided the two countries. We swam in it when the weather permitted, but it was too cold to swim most of the time. We dealt with mostly pedestrian traffic, a heavy dose of goat herders, and a few men on horseback. Goats are at home in the mountains and goats were big business in Nuristan.

Northeastern Afghanistan was the worst during 2007 and 2008

while I was there, as far as the number of firefights was concerned. Consequently, the number of casualties was the highest during that time frame. Ours was one of the smallest Outposts, since we were a platoon of twenty men.

Basically, we were behind enemy lines. The enemy was all around us and we weren't close enough to other units to be connected to any other base in any meaningful way.

It wasn't unusual for men in other parts of the country to go out in squads of four and not return. That never happened to us. I credited our Lieutenant for that. He didn't allow that to happen.

We were out of artillery range for any support from our big artillery guns, or for any immediate help from helicopters. They were based in Kabul, an hour away. The A-10 Warthogs and the bigger jets could be summoned, and they were on many occasions, but it took them an hour to get to us, too, because they were coming from the airport in Kandahar, which was even further away.

The enemy was on ridges above us. Every day, we would get an attack of some sort. Sometimes it would only be a matter of some bullets being shot at us. Other days it would be mortar fire, or maybe RPGs, which are rocket-propelled grenades. Most of the time, they hit us with 50 caliber shells.

One day, as I was coming out of the hut where we slept and about to walk into a meeting of all of the sergeants in another hut, I stopped to have a word with Sergeant Fletcher. We heard a tic-tic-tic sound, which we knew was the sound of bullets coming from an AK47. Before we were able to take cover, mortars and RPGs started landing around us. We dove for cover and avoided injury. Things like that happened fast and they happened all of a sudden.

Another day, as I was standing next to Sergeant Dubin, a mortar landed 10 feet away. It, literally, knocked us off our feet, sending us flying in the air about 10 feet until we crashed into the building we were about to enter. Neither of us thought we were hurt, because we weren't bleeding and no bones were broken. We just got up and walked into the meeting, like nothing out of the ordinary had happened.

People see movies in which they hear the sound of a mortar coming in and think that's the way it really is, but it isn't. The only warning we would get would come from the wind. It wasn't much, but if you were paying close attention, you could hear a disturbance, like the wind increasing just a little.

The point is we never heard it coming, never saw it coming and never knew it was coming. It was more like it landed without warning and fragments were sent flying in all directions at the same time. There was no time gap in between the two.

Another time, when I was in another part of the country, on my way for a two week R & R, the vehicle I was in was damaged when we ran over a bomb. It destroyed the vehicle, but I wasn't badly injured because the vehicle was designed to withstand such things. I had ringing in my ears and headaches for a long while. When asked if I was okay, I said that I was fine and went about my business.

Yet another time, while I was standing outside the building where we slept, having a cigarette, an RPG landed nearby. It knocked me down and I hit my head on the ground. I had bad headaches for months after that.

Again, it just happened, without any warning whatsoever, just like the mortars. We knew that it could happen at any time. We lived with that fear on a daily basis. The problem with that kind of thing was that it happened so suddenly...one minute, nothing was wrong and the next minute your whole world exploded. It made us jumpy, or on edge, all the time.

The constant threat took a toll on all of us. The bulls-eye was always on our back. That was stressful. Although it didn't leave a mark, it did cause damage. Even though I wasn't seriously injured by those mortar blasts or any of the other incidents, as I learned later, those hits took a toll on my body, and my mind.

Because we knew that we were always in the cross-hairs, and because of the fortifications we had, we rarely stood up straight. We were almost always crouched down, behind the HESCO barriers, so as not to give our enemy a shot at us. I don't think any of us realized the mental strain it put on us at the time.

As I look back, I think it took more of a mental toll on me than a physical one, although I sustained damage to both systems. I just always knew that death was right around the corner. We all did. Little did any of us know that problems would develop years later because of all of that.

Several months after I arrived, we received orders to participate in an offensive called Operation Rock Avalanche. It was a six day operation which involved our entire battalion. The purpose was to hunt for Taliban fighters in the Korengal Valley, which was known to be a Taliban stronghold. We called it the Valley of Death.

It was basically a "seek and destroy" type mission, similar to what soldiers in Vietnam did. It resulted in many skirmishes and several casualties on both sides. We didn't drive the Taliban from the area, but we let them know that we were there and that we could attack them, rather than just sit in our bases and wait for them to attack us. Fortunately, our unit didn't suffer any losses during that operation, but we did engage the enemy on several occasions.

Sebastian Junger, the author, was imbedded with the 173rd and spent some time with our platoon at our base, although he spent more time with other units than he did with ours. He and his camera man, Tim Heatherington, were with another platoon of the 173rd during that six day offensive. Together, they created the movie Restrepo, which was the story of how FOB Restrepo got its name and how Private Juan Restrepo died, which was during Operation Rock Avalanche.

It wasn't unusual for us to have visitors, but Junger was the most famous person to stay with us. Another time we had a German journalist pay us a visit. We also had a female journalist stay with us. I never read anything any of our visitors wrote, except for Junger's book and I did see his movie. He got it right.

We would take turns doing long-range advance scouting missions, or LRAS duty. We had a thermal-optical surveillance system that allowed us to see up to fifteen miles away. There were times when we were deep into the mountains of the Hindu Kush and the only things around us were the animals, and there were some strange animals there.

Rhesus monkeys, leopards, horned vipers, wild cats, six foot long lizards, porcupines, feral dogs, centipedes longer than a man's foot, scorpions, wolf spiders and giant red bees, to name a few, roamed the area. The most terrifying of all, though, were the enormous camel spiders, which were as big as a soldier's hand. They were brown in color and had metallic helmet-like bodies. They had long legs and could run up to 10 miles an hour. They ate lizards, scorpions and birds, among other things. Sometimes, when things were boring, just watching the animals, or watching out for them, was priority one.

Although it never happened to us, because we didn't have vehicles and couldn't drive in or out of our base, the two biggest causes of casualties for U.S. troops in that part of the country involved the use of vehicles. Because of the treacherous roads, vehicles would fall off the mountain. 10th Mountain lost about 7 soldiers who were in vehicles which, literally, fell off the mountain. The second leading cause of casualties in Afghanistan, much like in Iraq, was road-side bombs.

Because it was impossible to get supplies to us by vehicle, most of our supplies came from helicopters or planes, which just dropped them from a safe distance to a designated spot. Several helicopters were lost on their way to or from us either because of enemy fire, bad weather conditions, or for some other reason, like mechanical malfunction.

One time a Blackhawk was downed not far from us. The Army didn't want it to fall into enemy hands, because it was afraid someone would find something about the technology. I was one of the soldiers who located and protected the Blackhawk until some demolition experts came in and destroyed the bird. They tried a recovery, but it wasn't possible. The chopper had fallen in an area that was too remote. Some Taliban fighters attacked us, but we were able to fend them off.

An Apache was shot down not far from us, too, but we didn't have anything to do with that one. We heard that it was completely destroyed in the crash and a recovery of the helicopter wasn't possible. That happened when an Apache was coming up from an FOB and, as it was rising, it was hit with an RPG as it went by, way too close to the mountain. A rising helicopter doesn't go that fast, not nearly as fast as it can go when going forward, obviously, or down.

Another time we were ordered to retrieve a fallen drone. There, too, the Army didn't want our enemies to see the technology. We sent the guts of that drone back to headquarters.

During our 15 month deployment, men would come and go on R

& R. When they did, other soldiers would fill in for them. One time a female soldier was stationed with us, which was awkward, since we didn't really have separate facilities of any kind. Despite that, it worked out. She slept by herself in a place we created for her.

Our presence in Nuristan definitely bothered the Taliban and al-Qaeda. We heard that Osama bin Laden himself made a plea to the people of Nuristan province to declare a holy war, or Jihad, against our specific unit, the Blue Platoon, so we must have been causing some kind of problems for them. That heightened our concern for our well-being.

Because of the leadership of our LT, we were ready for them and they never attempted an all-out direct assault on us. We knew they were there, though. They loved to make sure we knew they were there. Every day, we would hear them shout "Allahu Akbar!" God is great!

There were almost ten times as many military personnel in Iraq than there were in Afghanistan at the time. Even though the action in Iraq was said to be a "peace-keeping" mission, soldiers were dying there, too, but those deaths were mostly due to suicide bombers and road-side bombs. The actual fighting was being done in Afghanistan, and over 90% of the fire-fights, as they were called, involving the exchange of fire, occurred in the mountains in northeastern Afghanistan, right where the Blue Platoon and all others in the 173rd were stationed.

There were actually far more Reservists in Iraq than there were regular U.S. Army enlisted men. There were few reservists in Afghanistan and those that were there weren't on the battlefield. Regular U.S. Army soldiers did the fighting in Afghanistan. Almost everyone I ever saw in Afghanistan was an enlisted soldier, like me.

The distance between our bases and our outposts was such that there was no way we could stop people who wanted to avoid us from getting through our defenses. Regardless, that was our job...to stop bad guys from entering the country.

The attitude of the people of that region towards Americans wasn't good. Many of the people didn't want us there. Both al-Qaeda and the Taliban used those routes to come and go as they pleased and most of the locals weren't willing to help us intercept those terrorists, for fear of being killed themselves. Since 90% of the province was in mountains, with caves built into the sides of the mountains where terrorists could hide, it was virtually impossible to ferret them out.

We always felt that a large percentage of the local population was either a part of the Taliban or that they sympathized with the Taliban. The Army went in with hopes of changing that. We understood that the locals may not have been as cooperative as we wanted them to be because they feared the Taliban, and what it might do to them for being too friendly with the American troops who were trying to befriend them.

There were mostly small villages dotting the countryside in both Kunar and Nuristan provinces, and both were extremely rural in nature. Asmar was, by far, the biggest city in Kunar province and there was no city nearly as big in Nuristan. Asmar had, at the time, nearly 15,000 people in it. It sat right on the border to Pakistan and it was believed to be one of the main avenues into and out of Afghanistan. The terrorists could easily make their way through the forests and into Asmar without us being able to stop them. We knew it, and so did they.

Nuristan, where the Blue Platoon was situated, was the least populated, and poorest, province in Afghanistan. The people there were Sunni Muslims. There were no Shi'ites, Hindus, Buddhists, Christians, Jews or any other denomination where we were. They all spoke Nuristani, not Pashton. Its remoteness, and lack of security, is what made it so desirable to insurgents. The Taliban, and their allies, had been able to do as they pleased in that area, until we arrived.

The Gowardesh River, which is in Nuristan Province, divides Pakistan and Afghanistan. Several of our platoons were stationed on the border, next to the river. My platoon was one of those units. The river flows south from there to Jalalabad, over a hundred miles away.

We could throw a stone and hit the Tribal Lands of Pakistan. Even though we were pretty sure that Osama bin Laden was hiding there, someplace, we knew that we weren't going to be the ones to find him. He was always on our minds, though.

In mid-December of 2001, the battle of Tora Bora took place, little over three months after 9-11. Not long after, the U.S. found out that we had bin Laden in our grasp but he was able to escape. Tora Bora is near the Khyber Pass, the most famous pathway between Pakistan and

Afghanistan. Tora Bora is in Nangarhar province, just south of Kunar province, not all that far from us.

In fact, he was found less than a hundred miles from where we were. He was out of the country, but not by much, and he was close to where we were, but not that close, and not close enough. We weren't allowed to cross over into Pakistan, and we never did.

We were there until August of 2008. I confess to being glad to leave by the end, although I had some mixed emotions as we packed up and walked out of what had been our home for over a year. Being as defenseless, and defensive, as we had been, it made us all wish we could have, just once, had a major shoot-out with them, with guns blazing on both sides, where we could see the whites of their eyes, but that never happened. It was a series of daily skirmishes, some of which were quite protracted, but never any real toe-to-toe gun battles. We all wanted that.

We were sent back, as a unit, to Bamburg. We received a Presidential Valorous Commendation for the way we handled Checkpoint Delta. We were one of the few units that had been hit hard many, many times, but never over-run, never even close. We achieved a degree of fame for what we had accomplished, at least within the military community, and we were proud of that.

Nobody outside of the military community ever heard of us. We never won any major battles, or killed any prize targets, but we did our jobs, defended our positions and we never let the enemy get the better of us...never, and we experienced no deaths or serious injuries. Looking back, it was quite an accomplishment, really, because Nuristan Province was the worst area in the country during that time.

While the Blue Platoon didn't suffer any loss of life, other platoons in the 173rd weren't as fortunate. In addition to Private Restrepo, who died on July 22, 2007, three soldiers from the 173rd received Medals of Honor. All four received those medals for their actions during the period of time I was in Afghanistan with them. Their battles were fought in the same provinces and in the same valleys where my platoon was stationed.

Staff Sergeant Salvatore Giunta was in the Korengal Valley, the valley of death, when his unit came under fire on October 25, 2007. He risked his life to prevent the enemy from taking one of his fellow soldiers captive. Because of his actions, and the bravery he displayed, the Army awarded him the medal. He was the first active duty soldier in 40 years to receive the award.

Specialist Kyle White of the 173rd was awarded the Medal of Honor for his actions on November 9, 2007. He risked his life to save fellow soldiers and prevent the bodies of other soldiers from being taken by the enemy. He was hit by shrapnel from two RPGs and sustained two concussions during the day long battle. The worst part of that incident was that it was an ambush orchestrated by people who had invited us to a meeting.

Another soldier, Robert James Miller, received the Medal of Honor for his actions on January 28, 2008, while working with a unit from the 173rd in Kunar Province. He was leading a team of approximately a dozen soldiers when they became engaged in a battle with over 150 insurgents. He risked his life, and ultimately lost his life, in that battle, in an effort to save the men he commanded.

When you consider that over 2.5 million Americans have served in Iraq and Afghanistan since 2001, and only twelve medals of honor have been awarded over that period of time, it is remarkable that four were given to soldiers who were either in the 173rd or fighting with us. I am proud of that fact and it goes to show how dangerous, and deadly, the fighting was in the northeastern corner of Afghanistan during the time I was there.

CHAPTER FOUR

Back to Bamburg

GOING BACK TO GERMANY wasn't like being back in the states, but if felt like it. We were no longer in the gun sights of our enemies. Nothing was likely to happen to us back on base, but it took a while before any of us felt safe sleeping in a bed, even if it was just a cot. Life in the Army doesn't involve luxurious accommodations, no matter where you are.

Most of the time spent in the Army, outside of a war zone, was tedious. There was always the element of discipline…time to wake up, time to eat, time for training, time for lights to be out, and men barking orders at you constantly. After being in a war zone, though, nothing on base could compare to what life was like in Afghanistan.

Also, life on base, after being in combat, was different from what it was like before going to Afghanistan. Maybe it was because I had become a true veteran. I had been G.I. Joe. I had seen combat. I had fired weapons at the enemy and they had fired their weapons at me. I had experienced life and death situations. I was a different person after that experience, and so was everyone else who had been there with me.

Many of us in the Blue Platoon had every intention of re-enlisting, including me. We expected that we'd return to Afghanistan, or some other theater of war. We were battle-tested and, as a result, we were different from those soldiers who had yet to have those experiences. Some, like Privates Wilson and Courtney, were planning to go back to civilian life. They had experienced enough of the Army and combat.

I was playing a numbers game with the Army. My term of enlistment would be up in another year or so and, though I had every intention of re-enlisting, I wanted to do it at exactly the right time to maximize the benefits I could realize by doing so. If I played my cards right, I would get a larger signing bonus, an increase in rank, plus more options with regard to what I wanted to do by way of an assignment. There is a right time to make that election and I had to be patient and wait for that time to arrive.

In the meantime, we were given a whole lot more slack on base than I had ever experienced. The Army knew that guys like us needed some time to adjust after being in Afghanistan as we had been. Besides that, there were only about 150 of us from the 173rd who were stationed in Bamburg, so we really had much more freedom than a soldier at a larger base would have. We had time almost every day to get off base, get into town and enjoy a life outside of the military.

Since it was so small, there wasn't much to do on base anyway. There wasn't much more than about 20 barracks, a Px and a gas station on the base, so soldiers would go into town to have some fun when not on duty. There were several pubs and clubs to go to.

Bamberg was, and still is, a beautiful, little, historic town that hadn't been bombed out during WWII, like many other German cities had been. Because there hadn't been any military presence in the town during the war, the Allies had left it alone. It has three cathedrals and other buildings that go back to the Middle Ages.

Since I had been stationed there before going to Afghanistan, I knew the town to some extent, and I had made some friends and acquaintances in the community. I had a few places I liked to go where soldiers and the locals would mix. One such place was called the Rathskellar.

I met my wife, the former Ingrid Knopfler, at that establishment. That was when I was first in Bamburg. She and her friends frequented that place and she had become friendly with some of the guys who were in the military police unit on base. I went there with all the other guys and, since I was new to the Army and one of the youngest guys in the group, I didn't talk too much.

Besides that, she was and is a very attractive woman and all the guys were attracted to her, so she wasn't particularly attracted to me at first. She's about 5'5" tall, with light brown hair and green eyes. She's very thin, almost anorexic, actually, but athletic looking and she liked to go on hikes and things, like us soldiers did. She liked to dye her hair frequently which used to make me laugh, because it would change her appearance so much when she did. She was interested in another soldier at the time, anyway.

We didn't have too much to do with each other during that first stay in Bamburg, but people did things in groups and I was part of the group she was in. The most memorable thing we did together that took place before I left for Afghanistan was when I asked her to fix me up with a friend of hers that I was interested in, and she did. Nothing came of the date, but that was the beginning of a relationship between the two of us. We knew each other.

When I came back, the other soldier was gone and she wasn't in a relationship with anyone. She remembered me and wanted me to tell her what it had been like for me in Afghanistan. We started doing things together and that's when our relationship really began.

She liked snowboarding, skiing, white-water rafting, hiking, cycling…all kinds of outdoorsy things, and so did I. We would do those kinds of things with friends, at first, and then we began to do things together, just the two of us. Slowly, over time, our friendly relationship developed into a romance.

Since I hadn't re-enlisted yet, and I still wasn't ready to do that, the Army decided to send me back to the States. I didn't have any problem with that, because I still had every intention of re-enlisting, except that I didn't want to leave Ingrid. I had never been with another woman who I cared for as much.

When it came time for me to go back to the States, we both agreed that a long-distance relationship wouldn't work and we would just end it when I left. However, since she had never been to the States, we decided that she would come back with me for a vacation. I was being sent to Fort Stewart, Georgia, but I would have at least a month to travel about with her before reporting for duty, so that's what we did.

We flew together from Bamburg to Orlando in June of 2009. We rented a car and began traveling about. I was the tour guide. I took her to Disney, Universal Studios, a few of the theme parks like Sea World and Water World, then down to Miami and to the Seaquarium, to the Keys and swimming with the dolphins, among other places.

We watched the sun set in Key West, and spent many happy days on the beaches, in the water, and at bars along the way. The life she saw in Florida was much different from the life she was used to in Germany, and she liked it. During that vacation, our relationship grew stronger and, when she saw what the United States was like, she wanted to stay. She didn't want to go back.

When she came over, neither one of us knew what would happen between us. I think we both realized, in the back of our minds, that our relationship might blossom, but we really hadn't talked about it or given it a lot of thought. But, it did, and before she left to go back to Germany, I asked her to marry me and she accepted.

When it was time for me to report to Fort Stewart, she boarded a plane and went back to Germany. She had to terminate her lease, close out her business affairs and pack all the belongings she could take on a plane into boxes and suitcases. She planned to come back as soon as she could. She obtained a 90 day visitor's visa and came back several weeks later.

Fort Stewart is located in southeast Georgia. It's the largest military base in the eastern United States, in terms of acreage. It has about 40,000 troops on base and it's primarily for infantrymen.

I was enrolled in a training program called the Warrior's Leader Program. All sergeants are required to take it and there are five separate courses to be taken. Sergeants are considered to be non-commissioned officers. Much is expected of them and much is required of them, as well.

By completing the course, I would be given a higher rating and better pay. It was a full-time job for me and it wasn't easy. The Army still owned me. I was busy, but my heart wasn't in it. While she was gone, I was pining for Ingrid to get back so that we could begin our lives together as a married couple.

When she came back, we couldn't live together at first, since we weren't married yet, so we got married as soon as we could. On August 24, 2009, a Wednesday, on my lunch break, I came into town, met her at

City Hall, raised my right hand, swore to love and honor her until death, signed the papers, and went right back to work. Ingrid is still waiting for the honeymoon.

Since we were married during her 90 day visa period, she was able to apply for permanent residency. Once she did, because we were married, and because I was in the military, she was going to be allowed to remain in the country while her application was pending. She was granted residency, but only on a temporary basis.

There is a two year probation period during which time the residency could be revoked. One reason to revoke the residency status would be if we divorced during that two year period. Another would be if it was really a sham marriage that they wouldn't recognize or honor.

After we were married, we were allowed to live in the married quarters. For several months, things were as good as could possibly be for two newly-weds. We were as happy as we could be, but then something unexpected occurred to change all of that.

As part of the program I was enrolled in, I had to pass extensive physical tests. One day, while I was doing some sit-ups as part of a routine physical, my back locked up on me. It was frozen. I couldn't move.

I was immediately taken to the hospital on base, where all kinds of tests were performed, including x-rays and MRIs. The results weren't good. I had no idea that I had any medical problems at all, but they told me that I did.

The doctors found herniated disks at L4-L5 and L5-S1. That was a serious medical problem which would likely require surgery to correct, and it definitely would affect my ability to do my job as an infantryman in the Army. My life was changed dramatically in a matter of moments.

After being released from the hospital, I met with my commanding officer, who wanted to talk about life after the Army. I told him that wasn't an option as far as I was concerned. I wanted to remain in the Army. He said, and I remember his every word,

"Sergeant, you're not going back into the infantry in this condition, so if you want to stay in the Army, we have to decide what, if anything, you can do in the military. Otherwise, you will be discharged from the

Army for medical reasons. What jobs are you interested in doing, outside of being an infantryman?"

"I don't know, sir," I responded. "I'll do whatever is asked of me. All I know is that I want to stay in the military. I know there must be some jobs I can do that don't require me to carry 80 pounds on my back and climb mountains. What do you suggest?"

"I've been giving it some thought, Sergeant, and I was thinking that you might be well-suited for our Unmanned Aerial Vehicle Operator unit."

"Drones?"

"That's right."

"I know nothing about them, sir, other than watching them. I recaptured a couple in Afghanistan, after they were downed."

"We'll teach you."

"If you say so, sir."

"If you want to stay in the military, Sergeant, I think this is your best bet. It may be your only chance."

So I told him, "I do want to stay in the military and I will do exactly what you suggest. Thank you, sir, for giving me this opportunity."

"It will take a few days to do the paperwork, and find out when the next class starts, but you can expect to receive transfer orders shortly. Corporal Reilly will explain the details of the program to you, Sergeant. That will be all."

The Captain stood and extended his hand, saying,

"Good luck, soldier. I wish you well."

I was escorted out of the office and into another room, where Corporal Reilly met with me to explain the program.

"You'll be transferred to the Creech Air Force Base in Nevada where you will receive 23 weeks of training, which will include performing intelligence surveillance and reconnaissance simulation missions; preparing maps, charts and intelligence reports; analyzing aerial photographs and using computer systems.

"Your job duties, once you complete the training, will be to conduct air reconnaissance, surveillance, targeting and acquisition missions; plan and analyze flight missions; perform preflight, in flight and post-flight checks and procedures; launch and recover aircraft from the runway; and perform maintenance on communications equipment, power sources; light and heavy wheeled vehicles and crane operations. Do you have any questions, sir?"

"It didn't say anything about firing weapons. Am I going to learn how to do that, too?"

"I can't answer that question, sir. I can give you this pamphlet and maybe it will provide some further details."

"Thank you, Corporal. I guess I'll find out all about it when I get there."

When I was in Afghanistan, I could have charged up a mountain with an 80 pound pack on my back, carrying my weapon in hand, and not thought a thing about it, right up to the very day we packed up and moved out. I had no idea that I had anything wrong with me. If asked, I would have said there was absolutely nothing wrong with me from a physical point of view.

I truly couldn't believe what had happened to me, and the suddenness of it all. It was as if a mortar had landed at my feet that I didn't see or hear coming, or a vehicle I was in suddenly exploded. It was just as dramatic. I had no choice. I was going to Nevada and I was going to learn how to operate drones.

CHAPTER FIVE

Fort Creech, Nevada

Two weeks later, I was on my way to Indian Springs, Nevada, leaving Ingrid behind. We decided that it would be best if I went first to see what the program and the area was like. Once I got the lay of the land, she could join me. I wasn't sure that I would be able to do what was expected of me. This was all happening fast.

En route, I learned as much as I could about my new assignment. The base was huge. It had a 15,000 square mile bombing range. It was established in 1941, after Pearl Harbor, as a military training camp for the Army's Air Force, as America went to war.

In 1947, after the war ended, it was shut down, only to be reopened a year later when the United States found itself in what was called a "Cold War" with Russia. Nevada, with its wide open spaces, provided airmen with the opportunity to learn how to drop bombs in a realistic field operation. It was used to train aviators in all branches of the service, not just the Army or the Air Force.

It was at Creech Air Force Base in 2001 that the first successful firing of a Hellfire missile from a drone was accomplished. It was then that these reconnaissance aircraft became offensive weapons. An RQ-1 Predator drone was the first one used.

In 2005, the base was named after Wilbur L. Creech, a veteran of over 275 combat missions in Korea and Vietnam. He was called the

Father of the Thunderbirds. He had been the commander of the famous demonstration team that he founded.

I reported for duty and began my training immediately. This was more like being in school than it was like being in the Army, and I had never been all that good in school. This was different. I was there for a reason and I had a purpose. I needed to make this work and I was determined to give it my best shot.

I read all the materials provided to me, and more. I especially liked the fact that drones represented an entirely new weapon in the military's arsenal because it was a risk-free, remote form of killing. It allowed precision as to the selection of the target without the risk of loss of life on the part of the operator.

The drones were to do the killing, while the person who actually caused the killing was never known, and certainly not by the victim. The operators are insulated from risk, unlike pilots or the soldiers loading pieces of artillery, and in this case, the hell-fire missiles. I liked that part, too.

I noticed the cautionary warning that operators of drones could experience a form of operational stress, much like post-traumatic stress disorder. There was a danger to watching too much video of the kills and spending too much time in front of these machines of destruction. A drone operator was required to spend time away from the computer screen.

I read where the two most commonly used drones were the MQ-1B Predator and the NQ-9 Reaper, which were the newer models of both. The Predator had the capability to destroy a target from up to five miles away. It could carry two Hellfire missiles. It traveled at approximately 135 miles per hour.

The Reaper could carry four Hellfire missiles and laser-guided bombs. It could travel faster than the Predators, and reach speeds of up to 150 miles per hour. A third type of drone, called a Hummingbird, with superior sensor-equipment, was to be placed in operation soon. There was also a Sentinel drone, called an RQ-170, which had jet engines, not propellers like the Predator and the Reaper, and it was more difficult to detect on radar than the others.

The Predator was 66 feet long and 36 feet wide and could carry a payload up to 3,750 pounds. They were much, much bigger than the others. I had seen several drones while in Afghanistan, but they were nothing like these bad boys.

Drones were usually flown at altitudes above the range of the hand-held weapons. At 20,000 feet, the drones could cover a 65 mile range, with excellent vision, due to state-of-the-art 1.8 gigapixel color cameras. With that degree of clarity, the operators would have a much better ability to clearly see the intended targets and thereby avoid the killing of innocent civilians. There had already been much criticism of drones by the time I got there because of the number of women and children who had been the unintended casualties of some strikes.

I was particularly excited to read that technology was being developed which would allow drone operators to see individuals on the ground at night.

I wondered about how easy it would be to shoot down a drone, if it flew too low. I was somewhat relieved to read that even though drones could be killed by planes fairly easily, since planes travelled much faster than drones did, and they were much more maneuverable, they were rarely shot down. Since neither the Taliban nor al-Qaeda had an air force, that wasn't going to be a problem in Afghanistan.

I read where fifteen drones were shot down during the Bosnia-Serbia conflict. One had been shot down by a machine gun, but that was in the early 1990s, when Clinton was President. Drones had come a long way since then.

The Pakistanis were the ones to fear. They had the capability to destroy the drones flying over Pakistani air space. Although they threatened to do so, they had never shot down a drone, yet. They didn't want us violating their sovereignty.

I read in earnest everything I could about drones. I wanted to learn this stuff so that I could stay in the Army. I didn't have a clue what I'd do if I wasn't able to do the job. I hadn't even considered it. I was going to make this work.

Before September 11, the drones were unarmed and used only for surveillance purposes. The first recorded use of an armed drone occurred in February of 2002, in the Paktia province of Afghanistan, near the city of Khost. A number of Afghanis were killed, including a few unintended targets.

At that time, Donald Rumsfeld, the Secretary of Defense, said that he, together with other unnamed persons within the Bush Administration, had made the decision to unleash the Hellfire missiles. I remembered that being a controversial issue, but getting bin Laden was the goal and there was very little that wasn't fair game in that process. Nobody voiced too much concern, other than that we hadn't found and killed bin Laden.

Once the decision to use drones in warfare was made, all branches of the military, as well as the CIA, began using them. The interaction between the CIA and the military was always unclear to me. I knew that they all worked cooperatively on various missions, but I never quite understood how the decision-making process worked. I often wondered why the CIA was involved if the military was in control of things. Who coordinated things between them?

The idea of using un-manned aircraft to strike enemy targets came into existence during the first World War, but they were never actually used in battle. During the second World War, the idea was to use remote control devices to guide un-manned B-24 bombers, loaded with explosives, to selected targets in Germany. It was tried, on several occasions, but no success stories were reported.

The most famous, or infamous, use of a "drone" B-24 involved Joseph P. Kennedy, Jr., the older brother of John F. Kennedy, who died while piloting the aircraft. He was to parachute out after getting the plane in the air and to a cruising altitude. It was a dangerous mission.

Kennedy volunteered for the assignment. He wanted to be a hero, I'm sure. He died when the plane he was flying exploded not long after take-off. The program was considered to be a disaster as that was not the only loss of life and property. Rockets and long-range missiles were used instead.

The long-range missiles, called Cruise missiles, were like drones in that they could be shot into the air and guided in flight. Some of the missiles had cameras. Rockets and missiles could not, however, do what drones do, and that is hover over a given location or return to base with pictures of the battlefield or whatever terrain was being viewed. Also, the rockets and missiles carried one explosive device, not several, as modern-day drones do.

The idea of using remotely controlled planes to do surveillance and carry weapons didn't come back into existence until the 1980s, when vast improvements in electronics and computers were realized. Members of the Air Force were the first to begin experimenting with the idea of having remote controlled planes do both surveillance and carry bombs. It took years, but the process paid off and now everyone was in on the action.

The training was hard on me. I wasn't used to sitting in a chair for long periods of time. I was an infantryman, a guy who liked to jump out of airplanes, drive Tracs and hike mountains. My back wasn't happy. I had to get up and move around every so often, which other people in the class didn't seem to have to do. I wasn't sure this was going to work.

After spending all day in a classroom, I went back to the barracks and studied until I fell asleep. I called Ingrid every night. I told her to stay where she was. I explained how hard the training was and how busy I was from the time I woke up until the time I went to sleep. I wasn't sure I was going to make it. She agreed to stay in Georgia for a while longer. I needed the time to be by myself and study.

Half way into the 23 weeks, I knew that I was going to make it. I told Ingrid to pack her bags and make plans to get to Nevada. There were married dorms available, and we could stay in them until we could find someplace off base. She was going to have to take care of that when she got here. Fortunately, or unfortunately, we didn't have that much stuff, but it would still be a challenge for her to get everything packed up for the move.

It took her a few weeks to get things together and, when she did, I flew back to Atlanta on a Friday after finishing training for the day. Together, we drove straight through to Nevada. It took us the full two days of driving to get there and I was a tired puppy going back to training the following Monday. She was there when I received a medal and another patch for completing the course.

I learned how to operate all of the drones the Army had, which were the same drones operated by the CIA and the other branches of the military. The first drone I learned on was like a miniature airplane. It had a 10 foot wingspan and was 4 and half feet long. It weighed 44 pounds and it could fly at an altitude of up to 19,000 feet. It could stay in the air for over 24 hours. We also had one that had a four foot wingspan and weighed only 5 pounds. We used those for surveillance. They weren't big enough to carry any weapons, obviously.

It wasn't long before I was allowed to work with the Predators. They were still the most commonly used pilotless drones. They were equipped with ultra-sensitive cameras and spying equipment. They had some limitations, though, such as they were only good in daylight hours and only on days with no rain or excessive turbulence.

The Predator MQ-1 drones were also relatively slow, they couldn't evade radar detection, and they were noisy. People on the ground could hear them and then look up and see them. Improvements were needed and improvements came, but that's where I started out, on those Predators.

I was then qualified to operate a Sky Warrior drone, which was smaller than the original Predator, but it could fly higher, up to 29,000 feet and go faster, 150 miles an hour, and stay up in the air longer, for up to 30 hours.

Drones kept getting bigger and better. The newest model of the Reaper was a turbo-prop plane which could stay up in the air for up to 30 hours on a 4,000 pound fuel tank. It could travel up to 240 miles an hour and carry up to 4,000 pounds of missiles and bombs.

For me, the most amazing thing about those Reapers was how high they could fly yet still provide such incredibly clear pictures. They were able to fly up to 50,000 feet in the air and still deliver a missile with pinpoint accuracy, plus provide amazing video evidence of what it had done. It amazed me.

Then came the Global Hawk. It first went into service in 2007. It had a wingspan of 116 feet, a payload of 2,000 pounds and it could fly at over 300 miles per hour. It was able to stay up in the air for somewhere between 2 and 3 days. For me, the most unbelievable part was that it could fly at 65,000 feet! That was about 12 miles into the air. It astounded me.

And it went on and on. More and more drones were being built by more and more people. Many countries and many different agencies, including police and border patrol, started using drones. More and more manufacturers, from many different countries, started making them, and all were just a little bit bigger and better than the ones before.

Everyone wanted in on the action and I was at the center of it all, together with my fellow operators. We were at the heart of things. The military wasn't about to let some other country, or any other entrepreneur, get ahead of it on this, and I took it all in.

I learned to operate every drone, and I, together with my fellow operators, was called upon daily to provide my input on how to make the drones better. They wanted to know of any defects, any problems, and any issues we could identify. They wanted to know about anything that went through our minds about operating a drone.

However, as proficient as we were in doing our jobs, and we became very good at doing our jobs, we couldn't do it alone. We were safely ensconced at a secure military facility in the U.S. of A. Men on the ground had to get the birds in the air and land them for us. They had to be relatively close to the target area.

For us, that meant the men on the ground were in Afghanistan, primarily, but we covered the globe. At times, it was inconvenient to coordinate things with people all over the world. They were working on getting things more efficient so that operators were able to make the drones take off and land by themselves. I received training on how to do it, but it wasn't perfected by the time I left.

I was a particularly desirable source of information to other operators because of the fact that I had been an infantryman in country. I told them stories of what it was like for us in those valleys. I also told them stories about the Nuristanis and the Taliban and how they set us up, took our money, lied to us and did their best to kill us.

I know there were others who disagreed with me, but I didn't trust any of them. I had heard too many stories of betrayal, and many of the Afghans who did help us were tortured and killed for doing so. Therefore, the way I saw it, the only ones left in Nuristan province were those who wouldn't help us, or would only pretend to help us.

Although I operated drones with the Hellfire missiles and bombs while I was at Fort Creech, I never actually dropped any on anybody or anything, except on bombing ranges. I dropped some in the barren areas of Afghanistan, too. Guys all around me were firing weapons and killing bad guys, and some made mistakes and killed some innocents, or so the Pakistanis and others said.

I never believed any of those reports. I would wait to see the hard evidence before I believed any of it, especially when they said women and children were killed. I never saw a woman or a child on a battlefield in Afghanistan, though I heard many stories from the Vietnam days about how women and children were used by the Vietcong to kill our soldiers. Some of those shepherd boys were young, but I didn't consider them to be children. They were old enough to carry weapons and fight.

I always felt badly whenever we killed any of them. We all did. with the improved technology of those things, even from that altitude, we could be very accurate. The problem was that oftentimes the bad guys weren't completely alone, or by themselves. So things like that occasionally happened. They were the innocent casualties of war. We tried hard to avoid it, but sometimes innocents died, that was true.

I settled in quite nicely to my new life in the military. Ingrid wasn't all that happy with our new digs because of the heat and terrain. It was nothing like Germany. It was mostly desert, and there are no deserts in Germany. She and I were still in love and this was all still a big adventure for us, so she put up with it.

We were going to be there until we were given orders to go somewhere else. I was thinking I was going to be there a long time. I thought about buying a house. Fortunately, I didn't. I was wrong. Just when it seemed like I had dodged a bullet by finding a home as a drone operator, and just when things settled down and seemed to be going fine, life threw me another curve.

Barach Obama had become our new president in January of 2009, replacing George W. Bush, who had been the one to get us into Iraq and Afghanistan in the first place. Among Obama's campaign promises was a promise to get us out. He also promised to reduce the level of spending on the military as quickly as possible.

As long as we were still at war, and we were, I wasn't too concerned about losing my job. Politicians make promises like that all the time. I didn't expect much to come of it. It had been two years since he took office and we hadn't captured or killed bin Laden and, until we did, I knew we weren't going anywhere. If we moved out of Afghanistan before finding bin Laden our chances of getting him would have been greatly reduced. Everyone knew that.

I also knew that we needed to be in Afghanistan or else the Taliban would be back in control in no time. We had entered Afghanistan in late 2001 and quickly helped the Northern Alliance to get rid of the Taliban and install a democratic government, but the Taliban didn't go away. They were still there. They were our biggest enemy. They fought us every day. I was still angry over what had happened in Nuristan after we left, as well as what happened while we were there.

A year after the Blue Platoon pulled out, in October of 2009, Camp Keating was attacked. Camp Keating was actually called a Command Base, not an FOB, and not an outpost, like we were. It had more men but, even then, it was way under-protected. Men in five guard stations and four Humvees were all that watched over the U.S. soldiers sleeping at Camp Keating that morning. It was located in Nuristan, not far away from where our base was. Like ours, it was within a few miles of the Pakistan border.

They had three mortars on the post, which was more than we had. One was a 60 millimeter and the other two were 120 millimeter mortars. Other than that, the soldiers had only the weapons they could hold in their hands.

Just prior to dawn, while most of the base was sleeping, approximately 350 Mujahadeen, or holy warriors, attacked the 60 soldiers at the base, which sat at the bottom of a valley, next to a river. Over the next twelve hours, many of those soldiers died or were seriously injured defending themselves against the attack from the enemy, who were equipped with state of the art RPGs and AK-47 rifles.

The camp was over-run and the fighting was, at times, hand-to-hand. The barracks were destroyed. The men who survived were able to do so because of the heavy support given them by Apache helicopters and A-10 Warthogs, which came in at close range, plus the jets which came to the rescue from higher above. The camp wasn't lost and the soldiers weren't massacred. In the end, we won the battle.

Everyone involved sustained some injuries, though. No one was unscathed. As many as 200 Taliban fighters were killed. As a result of the battle, 27 Purple Hearts, 37 Commendation medals, 9 Silver Stars, 21 Bronze Stars and one Medal of Honor were awarded to the soldiers engaged in that event.

Within days of the battle, Camp Keating was closed. Forward Operating Base Fenty and a few others were closed, too. Little more than a year after we left, the Army had basically abandoned Nuristan province altogether.

Soldiers, like me, had been killed constructing that outpost and others were killed while stationed there. We had died clearing the paths to those outposts. We had died patrolling the areas around those outposts. We had died driving to or from those outposts. We had died in the air getting to and from the post and, ultimately, many died and many more were injured within those compounds. We had fought hard in Nuristan province to rid it of the Taliban and al-Qaeda and to make it a safer place for democratically minded Afghans to live.

Shortly after the closure of those bases, I read that the Taliban retook complete control of the province. I was not happy when I read the news. I knew that if we left Afghanistan, the same thing would happen all over the country. I was sure the U.S. wouldn't leave Afghanistan and allow that to happen.

On May 2, 2011 Osama bin Laden was killed. I remember the day well. I was on duty at Fort Creech and I, along with all other soldiers, watched the news with delight when reports came in that Seal Team Six had killed him. I immediately knew, and so did all the others, I'm sure, that there would be some changes as a result of that happy event.

Within a short period of time after that, President Obama declared that all U.S. combat soldiers would be out of Afghanistan as soon as possible. A drawdown was to begin. The Taliban greeted that news with glee, I am sure. I did not. I felt like we needed to stay there and finish our mission by ridding the country of all the bad guys.

Shortly after the death of bin Laden, less than two years after I had learned, and mastered, my job of operating drones in and around Afghanistan, I was notified that I was to be discharged from the Army due to medical reasons. I knew it was just part of the process of reducing the size of the military and, accordingly, reducing the amount of money spent on the military.

I still wanted to remain in the Army. For reasons beyond my control, I would no longer be able to do that. I was sure that my medical condition wasn't the real reason they were letting me go, but that was the Army's official justification for letting me go.

Ingrid and I talked about what we should do. Part of her wanted to return to Germany. She missed her family, but she loved living in the United States. We talked about where to live within the U.S. We could go anywhere we wanted to, but we had something else to consider... Ingrid was pregnant.

After weeks of thought, we chose Greenville, South Carolina.

CHAPTER SIX

Greenville, South Carolina

WE CHOSE GREENVILLE FOR a number of reasons, but the most important factor was probably that a large percentage of the population was German. While we were driving around the South to places not too far from the base, after we were married, and while we were living at Fort Stewart, we had visited Greenville. We found a restaurant owned and operated by Germans and had a nice meal there. The owners were delighted to talk to Ingrid because, among other reasons, one of the owners was from Bamburg and still had family there.

They had told her that she had a job waiting for her if she ever came back. Many of their customers spoke German and it was important to them to find waitresses who could speak the language. Since my prospects for work weren't too good, we figured that it was definitely a plus that she had a place to work if we moved there.

There is also a BMW plant, a Seiman's Medical equipment company and a Michelin Tire plant in Greenville. Although Michelin is a French company, it hires many Germans. That appealed to Ingrid a whole lot more than it did to me, but I liked the area, too.

We had gone camping in areas not far from Greenville, in primitive areas, where only hike-in tent campers were allowed. That was the type of camping I was most interested in, not being in a campground with a whole bunch of people around. Plus, it was free.

On top of that, not far away from Greenville were some great white water rivers. The Chattooga River, made famous by the movie *Deliverance*, is less than an hour away. We went down Sections III and IV together several times. We liked to rent small, inflatable rubber duckies and do Section III one day, and then go down Section IV in a raft, with a guide, the following day.

The Chattooga is probably the biggest white water river on the East Coast, next to the Gauley in West Virginia, which is the best. An outfitter named Chattooga Wildwater hooked us up. We hadn't found the time to do the Gauley when we were there before, but we had every intention to do it this time. There are other good rivers in the area, too, such as the Ocoee, the French Broad, the Nolichucky and the Neuse.

I liked that part of the country more than I did Florida, which was beautiful, with the Atlantic Ocean and the beaches, especially during the winter months, but the Carolinas offered such diversity. Surprisingly, or at least it was to me, Ingrid preferred the cold weather. I thought she would love the Florida sun, and she did, but it was too hot for her. She wanted the change of seasons, and she liked the cold.

Greenville, although it is relatively small, has a decidedly European flavor to it, and that wasn't just our assessment. I read that the architecture isn't like anyplace else in the country. It's modern, not post-Civil War, like most historic things are in Charleston, Savannah and numerous other cities across the South. Many of the buildings in Greenville were designed by European architects.

It's about an hour west of the State Capital, Columbia, and an hour and a half from Myrtle Beach and the coast. So we could still get to the beach with a short ride, as well as to the mountains. It has a moderate climate with four three-month seasons. It seemed like a perfect choice.

Since I was going to be out of a job, and Ingrid wasn't going to make too much as a waitress, the best we could do was find a place to rent not far from the restaurant. However, since Ingrid was pregnant, she wasn't going to be able to work too long before having the baby. We knew that this was a temporary thing and were hoping to find a house to turn into a home.

Fortunately, once I was officially discharged from the Army, the checks from the VA began coming in the next month. I was entitled to those benefits because I was discharged for medical reasons. It wasn't enough to support the family, and pay child support for the two children I had fathered during my two year hiatus from the Army, but it was enough as long as Ingrid was able to work. I began looking for work, too.

I found a job as a security guard at a hotel in town, but that didn't last too long as it required me to stand and walk continuously for ten hours. I could hardly stand for ten minutes without the problem in my back becoming excruciatingly painful. Although I needed the work, I just couldn't do it.

Next, I next took a job at a manufacturing facility. Because of my experience in the Army, they made me a manager, but that didn't work out too well, either. In the Army, when I gave an order, it was immediately carried out or I was going to know the reason why not. In civilian life, it doesn't work like that, as I soon discovered. I wasn't politically correct with some things I said and did and I offended too many people in a short period of time. They said I had a "poor attitude."

Things weren't great, but we were getting by, and the excitement surrounding the impending birth of a child overshadowed everything. It was a tough pregnancy for Ingrid, and she was ready for the baby to be born long before her water broke. I supported her through all of that, including going to all of the classes at the local hospital, and all of the pre-natal check-ups.

Our daughter, Darla, was born on July 20, 2012, with no complications whatsoever. It was a relatively easy childbirth, according to the doctors, but I wouldn't dare tell Ingrid that. To her, it was the most difficult thing she had ever done in her life.

It was a Monday. Ingrid had worked that Saturday night, and she took Sunday off once the contractions started. Her water broke about twelve hours after the first contraction. We called the doctor's office first thing, and got their answering service, but they called us back and said to wait until the contractions were more regular and to let them know when they were starting to come about five minutes apart.

They wanted me to measure how much she was dilated, but I couldn't do that. I just couldn't do it, so we didn't. We made a list, just as we had been taught to do, of every contraction, when it started, how long it lasted, and what the severity was.

The weather was perfect. It was a beautiful summer day. The temperature was in the high seventies and the sun was out. After making sure that the car was packed and that we had everything we needed for the trip to the hospital, we took a walk around the neighborhood, not straying too far from home.

After a couple of hours, the contractions started coming in every five minutes. We called the doctor's office and they told us that the doctor would meet us at the hospital. I drove her to the emergency room entrance, where an orderly with a wheel chair was waiting. While I parked the car, he wheeled her into the hospital and up to her room. She was in the birthing room, in the chair, by the time I got there.

Within an hour, Darla Dianne Buchanon came into the world weighing 7 pounds, 11 ounces and measuring 21 inches long.

I bathed her, with a nurse watching over my shoulder, and put her in a blanket after doing so. The nurse then gave Darla to Ingrid. After that, we were alone to enjoy our new baby. They would come back in to check on us every so often, and finally came and took her away after an hour or so for more testing.

I have been with her, and able to enjoy her, every day since. If I had still been in the Army, I wouldn't have been able to do that. Within a few weeks, Ingrid was back to work at the restaurant.

With Ingrid working, and me being unable to work, I became a stay-at-home Dad. It was difficult for me. My tolerance levels needed adjustments. I had been a soldier, sleeping in the one of the most primitive areas in the world with a bunch of other soldiers, just a few years prior to all this.

I was really hands-off with the baby as far as changing diapers, feeding, and the rest, at first. It was even more difficult for me, in the beginning, because she was a girl. I was used to dealing with guys...rough guys...and guns, bombs and the rest. This was a whole new deal for me.

But I had wanted a daughter, and I could not have been happier with Darla. Maybe part of the reason I wanted a little girl was because I really didn't have a warm and fuzzy relationship with my mother. I don't know.

That was something one of the shrinks told me later on. My mother had been a bartender. She talked like a bartender, even to me. She was a tough woman. And this was a tender, little, helpless human being who was my flesh and blood.

A special bond was created between me and this little girl right from the start. I had no idea what to expect. I didn't know how I would react. This experience was completely different from the first two children, for a number of reasons.

I can honestly say that I not only didn't mind being the stay-at-home parent, I enjoyed it. For the first time in my life I deliberately conceived a child. It was also the first time when I was able to go through the whole process of birthing. It was the first time I was ever even around a baby.

I saw the first baby I thought I had fathered maybe four times before I asked for DNA testing. After that, I wasn't able to see him again. I haven't seen him since. Even though it turned out I wasn't his father, for six or seven years I thought I was.

With my other son, Cliff, I didn't get to see him as a baby. He was born in May of 2006 and I was overseas in Germany at the time, getting ready to go to Afghanistan. I found out via a Red Cross message when he was born.

When you want to get in touch with a soldier who is away, it's better to use the Red Cross than the military. It's reserved for important things, like serious injuries or deaths, or for a health and welfare message, just to make sure that the soldier is okay. The birth of a child was an important message.

I knew the baby was coming. I knew it right after she became pregnant. The mother called me and asked if I wanted her to abort the pregnancy. I am against abortion and told her no, even though I really didn't want to be a father at that point in my life, and I knew then that the relationship with the mother wasn't going to last. Despite that, the two of us agreed to have the child.

I didn't actually see him until I got back to the states, after my time in Afghanistan, which was in 2009. By then, he was a little boy, walking, talking and riding a tricycle. It was nothing like what it was with Darla.

So Darla was a whole new adventure for me, and I liked it, once I got used to the diapers, the feedings, the baths and the rest. I was trying to get the military out of my mind, but I kept an eye on what was happening. I read the Stars and Stripes regularly.

I was happy. Things were pretty good. Money was still an issue, but we couldn't complain too much, but then another mortar shell exploded right in the middle of my sand box. Some problems from my days in the military came to the surface and, like a bomb or a bullet, they snuck up on me. I didn't see them coming.

CHAPTER SEVEN

Post-Traumatic Stress Disorder

THE INITIAL DIAGNOSIS WAS "an occupational and social impairment with reduced reliability and productivity." That was a fairly accurate description of my condition. After a few months of being out of work, and taking care of Darla, my mental condition was in poor shape, and I definitely wasn't reliable or productive.

As happy as I was with Darla when she was awake, it was boring when she wasn't. She slept most of the time and it drove me crazy with nothing to do. I had too much time on my hands and I had nothing of interest to do with it. My mind began to play tricks on me. It got so bad that I went to the VA for help.

I had sought help before, while still in the Army, but one thing that the shrinks and all the people within the Army focused on was that I didn't have a TBI, which is a traumatic brain injury. I hadn't been the one who was grievously injured, maimed or otherwise damaged, even though I had witnessed such things. They dismissed my complaints and told me to buckle up, take it like a man, and do my job. It was never taken seriously by them.

To a soldier, it's a sign of weakness to admit to being less than perfect. No matter how bad you were hurting, when asked, you were expected to say, "No problem, sir!" and do whatever you were ordered to do. The mental problems I was having were much like the physical problems I had previously experienced. I didn't realize that I had a problem while I was still in the Army.

As a result of the initial evaluation, my problem was reported as being that I had "recurring and distressing recollections of the events, including images, thoughts or perceptions," and that I had "recurring dreams about the events," all of which was true. It was also reported that I experienced "intense psychological distress at exposure to internal or external cues that symbolized or resembled an aspect of the traumatic events." No shit. I had nightmares, not dreams. They are not the same thing.

The initial report reflected that I had "experienced, witnessed or was confronted with events that involved actual or threatened death or serious injury, or a threat to the physical integrity to myself or others." No shit. Our unit was involved in events on a daily basis in Afghanistan when shots were fired at us. We killed people and I saw dozens of dead people.

I told them about the nightmares I had been having and about the beheadings that I witnessed, though I wasn't present when they actually happened. Even though I didn't know the people who were beheaded, nor was I close to them, I came upon those situations a couple of times, not long after they had occurred. I kept seeing those people in my dreams. When I did, I might wake up screaming, or bolt upright, wide awake.

In real life, some of the people who had been beheaded were people from nearby villages who we had met while on routine patrols and befriended. In most of my dreams, it was someone I had never seen before. In some, I might be the one who was about to be beheaded, or it could have been one of my brothers in the Blue Platoon who was about to die a horrible death.

We all knew, or we believed, that what the enemy wanted to do was to capture one of us, torture us and then behead us. Then they would post a picture on the internet. That wasn't our imagination at work. Those things happened, and we were well aware of it.

I think the United States Army knew that the Taliban, or al-Qaeda, or both, wanted to capture U.S. soldiers and use them for propaganda. If you look at all the Medal of Honor recipients, many received the medals for their bravery in trying to keep a fellow soldier from falling into enemy hands, even if the soldier was already dead. The phrase "no soldier left behind," really meant something to us, and it was drilled into us at every opportunity. Preventing the body of a dead soldier from falling into enemy hands was almost as important as saving the life of a fellow soldier.

I had seen enough to know that was their way. The villagers who saw their fellow villagers beheaded after those people had offered any assistance to us, or after they had cooperated with us in any way, were certainly less likely to want to have anything to do with us after something like that. It scared them, which was the intent. It scared us, too.

The truth was that those villagers were, as far as I could tell, simple people who didn't necessarily agree with the Taliban and Sharia law, but they had to take sides, whether they wanted to or not. Those who didn't take the Taliban's side might be killed just for not taking the side of the Taliban. Some were beheaded as a warning to others.

Sharia law basically means the law of Islam, but that depends upon who is interpreting or applying the law. All Muslims have a core belief system, based on the teachings of Mohammad, as found in the Qur'an. But there are different interpretations of those teachings. The interpretation given by the Taliban is the harshest and most stringent the world has ever seen.

The ironic part about us being in Nuristan was that the people in Nuristan weren't really a part of the group of people who were causing all of the problems. They were Sunni Muslims, but they weren't jihadists. They were just defending themselves against people who had come into their territory. They just happened to be in the wrong geographic place on the globe.

They were a totally separate ethnic group. They were Nuristanis. Now the al-Qaeda fighters were an entirely different breed of cat. They weren't Afghans. Nuristan has its own language. Actually, it has five languages, all different, and Pashtun wasn't one of them.

Historically, it was a separate country, called Kafiristan. It was the land Rudyard Kipling wrote about in his book, <u>The Man who would be King</u>. It was made into a movie starring Sean Connery and Michael Caine.

The people of Nuristan were converted to Islam in the late 19th century at the point of a sword, but not everyone was converted. People in those mountains were the poorest and lived in the most remote area in all of Afghanistan. They knew very little of what was going on in the rest of the world, but they were ferocious fighters. After the Soviets invaded in December of 1979, some of the bloodiest battles were fought in Nuristan.

The Nuristanis in those remote villages were simple peasants. They really weren't our enemies. They weren't the ones we were after. They just lived in the wrong place. The Taliban and al-Qaeda, were trying to kill us, not them.

As hard as it was for us to believe, some of the people we met in those remote villages actually asked us who we were and where we were from. They didn't know if we were Russians, Americans or Martians. They truly lived in a part of the globe which was isolated from the rest of the world for a number of reasons. Their life was a day-to-day struggle for survival.

But I grew to hate some of those people. I saw so much corruption and deceit that it made me sick. The ordinary people weren't the problem. The people who sought to profit from what was going on were the problem, and there were plenty of them.

The United States poured money into that area, created sources of water for them, built schools, roads and gave them jobs, money, training and a whole bunch of other things they never had. Truth was, if not for us, they never would have had any of those things for a long, long time. We were trying to win the hearts and minds of the people, but it didn't work. I don't think it ever had a chance of working. I saw that most of the money went to a few dishonest people, and the rest really weren't all that interested in becoming a part of the 21st century.

I saw where promises made weren't kept. I saw people who told us they were our friends, and we later found out that they had been the ones to set us up for an ambush. I knew several of the soldiers from the 173rd who died while I was there, because of them.

In my nightmares, the faces of many of those Afghani men kept appearing. One minute they would be all smiles and as friendly as could be. The next minute they would turn into ugly, terrifying, menacing people threatening to kill me.

I tried hard to avoid any thoughts about what I had seen and been through, and I refused to talk about it to anyone. I didn't even tell my wife. I stayed away from my fellow soldiers or people who had been where I had been. I no longer watched war movies. I tried to keep those thoughts and dreams away, but they kept coming back.

The nightmares were the worst. It got so bad that I couldn't sleep. I couldn't, or wouldn't, let my feelings out, and that affected my relationship with my wife. I wasn't able to love her as fully as I wanted to, or she wanted me to, because I was holding back. I had these pent-up emotions that were inside me, and not too far from the surface, either. They were tearing me up.

I was always irritable and I'd have occasional outbursts of anger. The person who would be the recipient of those outbursts was my wife, who I loved more than anyone else in the world. I don't know how she put up with me as long and as well as she did, but she did, thank God.

I had trouble falling asleep, and when I did finally fall asleep I'd wake up after a short time and then I couldn't get back to sleep. When the sun came up, and Ingrid and Darla were waking up after a good night's sleep, I was groggy and irritable. So when the psychologists said I had trouble concentrating on the tasks at hand, I told them, "No shit! You would be, too! Who wouldn't be?"

Darla was my only source of joy. She was a complete innocent. She was pure. I could never lose my patience with her. She saved me from sinking further into the depths of despair, but she wasn't there all the time. Since she slept most of the time, I was dealing with monsters a large part of every day.

I was spiraling downhill and I knew it, but I did have some kernel of something left in me...I had enough wherewithal to know that I had a problem, and that is why I sought help. Again, I think Darla saved me. I wanted to be there for her, and for Ingrid.

I can't take all of the credit for that. In fact, I probably don't deserve much credit for it at all. It was my wife who made me do it. If I didn't, I believe she was going to leave me and she was the last thing in the world I could afford to lose. If I lost her, I lost Darla, too. I knew that much, and thank God that I did.

When I applied, I wasn't sure that I would be eligible for assistance because I had requested treatment while still in the Army, but those requests had been denied. I didn't know what to expect when I went to the VA for help that first day, but I wasn't optimistic. I was surprised when I was officially diagnosed with PTSD and found to be eligible for treatment.

Once I was approved, I didn't know what, if anything, they could do to make it all go away. I expected medications, bull-shit counseling sessions, maybe some group sessions, like in AA. I actually expected them to tell me the same things the Army had told me when they turned me away, but PTSD had grown into something much bigger over the years, and I wasn't alone.

In the words of the shrinks, "all of these problems caused clinically significant distress or impairment in social, occupational, or other important areas of functioning," as in my marriage, my employment and friendships. I asked myself "What friendships? What employment?"

I had no friends, because I wouldn't let them in. My only friend was my wife. I had no job, because I behaved inappropriately, at times. Most importantly, they confirmed that I was truly disabled, from a clinical point of view. So they were right…this condition adversely affected my life in significant ways…really significant ways.

Once the counselling sessions started, after I was approved, I told them everything. I told them about me yelling at my wife, about losing jobs, about having no friends, about my nightmares, about my childhood and all the rest. I had nothing to lose at that point. I wasn't in the Army and they weren't taking me back. It made no sense for me to be heroic at that point.

Ultimately, they determined that I had a 90% service connected disability based on depression and post-traumatic stress disorder, in combination with the medical issues involving my neck and back, and the migraine headaches. I still had chronic neck and back pain. Even while at Fort Creech, and afterwards, many times a day, most days of the week, my heart would start pounding and I would have trouble breathing.

I immediately applied for Social Security Disability benefits. If I was 90% disabled, then I figured I should have been declared eligible for Social Security Disability benefits. After trying to work as I did, I realized I really wasn't able to work, for either physical or mental reasons, or both. I was hoping that I would be declared eligible, but I wasn't optimistic.

After the diagnosis was made, the counselling sessions became more intense. I told them how I felt emotionally numb, unable to have loving feelings for anyone other than Darla, not even my wife, who I knew loved me, or else she would have left me long before, I was always super-alert, watchful and on guard, like I was on duty. I was jumpy, easily startled. I told them about the angry outbursts I had on a regular basis. I didn't hold anything back.

I told them about the many incidents where RPGs struck near me and how I hit my head on rocks and the ground, about the mortar rounds landing nearby to me, about the mishap on an airborne jump when I landed badly, and about the incident with my Humvee hitting a road-side bomb. I told them about everything.

Even while I was going to counselling I was drinking more than I should, and I admitted it. I wasn't doing any drugs, other than those prescribed for me, but between the drugs and the alcohol, I was a mess. They could tell I wasn't faking it.

The collective diagnosis of the several psychiatrists and psychologists who I eventually saw was "a) depressed mood; b) anxiety; c) chronic sleep impairment; d) mild memory loss, such as forgetting names, directions or recent events; e) flattened affect; and f) disturbances of motivation and mood."

Again, I have to say that their assessment was fairly accurate. I was severely depressed, and it worried the shit out of me. I couldn't sleep worth a damn. I was forgetting all kinds of things and I was doing it all of the time. As for that flattened affect, I think it played into the last notation about disturbances of motivation and mood, which could both be summed up in one short phrase...I didn't give a shit!

I was put in a research project that was described as being a "New Treatment for Combat PTSD." I had to consent to the protocol, because it was somewhat experimental, and I had to agree that I was volunteering to be in the project. I needed help. I knew it, and I knew I couldn't do it by myself, so I readily consented to whatever it was they were going to do to me or for me.

They explained the program to me and gave me an opportunity to ask questions. I signed up. That was October 17, 2013, over five years after I left Afghanistan.

They asked a lot of questions about my life before I went in the Army. They said that some of my problems were because I hadn't received enough nurturing and love from a completely absent father and a mother who neglected me. Since she was a bartender, she wasn't around much, especially at night, and she slept most mornings. She was a hard-ass, pissed-off person when she was awake. I could never do anything right with her. The best thing I ever did, as far as she was concerned, was get out of her life and into the Army.

Some of that was true, but I didn't think it was the cause of my problems. I thought that was just a bullshit way of saying what happened to me while I was in the Army wasn't the cause of my problems. I thought they were still trying to find a way to say that the Army wasn't to blame and, therefore, I wasn't entitled to benefits of any kind. I didn't trust them at first.

That assessment didn't explain the nightmares and the PTSD. I really struggled not to get upset when they asked questions about all of that. I didn't have dreams about my family. They weren't in my nightmares. As far as I was concerned, those issues had nothing to do with what I perceived my problems to be.

Things started to get better when I was assigned to one specific psychologist. She was my savior. She didn't want to let me off easy on anything, but she believed me and she knew that I wasn't making that shit up. I trusted her.

She said it was best to deal with the emotional issues, no matter how long ago they occurred, and no matter how serious they might be, and to come to grips with the problems on an intellectual level. By doing so, she said, it would promote healing. She also explained that was the way for me to deal with more recent problems, and it would teach me how to deal with problems as they developed in the future as well. I accepted that and went with the program.

She told me that in order for this program to work, there had to be three things present: 1) I had to realize that I had a problem, and I did; 2) I had to have the physical and mental capability to deal with the problem, which meant that it wasn't a medical or mental situation that was truly beyond my control, and it wasn't; and 3) which they said was the most important ingredient, I had to want to deal with the problem, and I did.

I had a young daughter to care for. That was a job I would not let myself fail at. I was determined to succeed at this.

They gave me some medications. I expected that going in. I had never heard of any of the drugs they prescribed for me...Esomeprazole Magnesium, EC Cap, Tramadol and Acetaminophen, among others.

I started to see things improve fairly soon after I began working with her. Progress was slow, but I could see some progress. I think just finally dealing with the issues, in a positive way, instead of letting them control me, was a big help. I still had nightmares, but I began feeling as if I was going to beat them, and that they weren't going to beat me.

Some good things happened to us, too, completely unrelated to the counselling. With the 90% disability rating, I was found to be eligible for Social Security benefits. We started receiving a monthly check shortly thereafter. That helped.

With the additional income, and with help from the VA, we were able to get a loan and buy a new home. We were first time home-buyers and they had a special program for me. As a soldier recently discharged from the military due to medical injuries sustained while in the service of the Army, I was eligible for much needed financial assistance.

Things changed when we moved into our new house. It was beautiful. Ingrid loved it. It was nothing like what I experienced growing up and nothing like anything I had ever experienced anywhere I had ever lived. It took some adjustments.

The sessions were one-on-one with my psychologist, just the two of us. I was required to maintain eye contact with her as best I could and we talked about the things that were bothering me. Basically, we identified the problems I was having and we talked about the cause of those problems and what I could do to make the problems go away, or at least make them less of a problem.

After a while, Ingrid would join me for the sessions. My psychologist wanted her to understand what PTSD was all about. That gave my wife an opportunity to meet my psychologist and ask her questions, which made her feel better about things. Also, my psychologist felt that meeting Ingrid helped her understand me better. I think it helped me, knowing that Ingrid would have a better understanding of what I was going through.

Psychotherapy. The word still scares me. I guess it comes from when I was a kid. When we thought somebody was weird, or really crazy, we called them a psycho. I didn't want to be one of them. I didn't want my wife, or my daughter when she was old enough to know what it meant, to think I was a psycho.

What it means, though, or at least the way my therapist explained it to me and my wife was this…it just means treating mental health problems with a psychiatrist, psychologist or other mental health provider. It was supposed to teach me coping skills so I could deal with my problems myself. I was the one who was going to make myself get better. They were just helping me figure out how to do it. I knew that was true…nobody could change me except me, and I was changing. And we dealt with every issue I could identify.

Regarding the issue of childhood neglect, there was nothing I could do about that. It happened. There was nothing I could do to change that. I had to be more mature about it and just accept that as a fact, not as a cause of any more hurt. It might explain why I felt the way I did, but I couldn't let it destroy my life for the rest of my life.

As far as the illusions, delusions, hallucinations, and dissociative flashbacks, which are the terms she used, we talked about them at length. We discussed the fact that I knew that most of those nightmares hadn't really happened and were nothing more than my over-active imagination. I had to tell myself they weren't true and to let them go. It was easier said than done, but it helped, because when they happened, I told myself that they weren't real, and to get back to sleep.

Regarding the fact that I had no friends and felt isolated, she said those feelings of detachment and estrangement from others wasn't abnormal, especially since that was me doing it to myself for the most part. She made me go out of the house more. I had to take my wife and child out to dinner at least once a week. We also started to go to church. That was important for social reasons more than religious ones.

By going to a church, and there was a Catholic Church just down the street we could walk to, we became part of a social network. It made me feel more normal, not like an outcast. It was weird for me to walk into that church for quite a while. I hadn't spent much time in a church before in my entire life. Ingrid wasn't all that religious, either, but she was a Christian, like I am, and the Catholic Church was something we both had some familiarity with.

As far as me being worried about a career, being afraid my marriage would fail, that I would lose Darla, and that I wouldn't have a normal life, she explained that everybody has those fears. I wouldn't be human if I wasn't concerned about those things. The important thing was that I knew that I didn't want those things to happen and that I, and only I, had the power to make sure those things didn't happen. There was nothing she could give me to prevent that from happening. I had to do that.

About the frustration I experienced and continued to experience because of being released from the Army, through no fault of my own and against my will, that, too, she explained, was normal. Who wouldn't be concerned about that? I had planned on that being my career. It wasn't my fault that it didn't happen. I hadn't done anything wrong to make that not happen. I shouldn't blame myself for what happened to me. I had to be thankful for what I had and move on. It was more about me growing up and being more mature.

Regarding my complete lack of energy and desire, she made me promise to start exercising just a little every day, and to increase a little every day. Again, Darla helped me. As she was getting older, she was getting more active. Once she could sit up and her neck was strong enough for her to hold her head up straight, I bought a bicycle with a kid seat on the back.

I rode all over the neighborhood with that. Darla loved it. The more I exercised, the more energy I had. I also made some friends with people in the neighborhood, especially at the playground with parents of other kids Darla's age.

And the part about me yelling at my wife, that was, probably, the easiest to address. She was the one person I loved the most, and the only person I· had ever really loved in my whole life. She was the very last person I wanted to hurt, other than Darla, of course. And that was the problem…I wasn't mad at her, I was mad at myself.

I didn't like the person I had become. I wasn't the person who I wanted to be, and it made be angry. Ingrid was the only person I could take out my emotions on. I didn't want to do any of the things I was doing. That was the last thing I wanted to do.

It wasn't a quick fix, and it's still a problem for me. There were times when I threw things around the house and I broke them, and some of those things were things that I liked. After I did it, I immediately regretted it, but it was too late. I just couldn't control my emotions. I stopped yelling at Ingrid, but I broke things instead. I wasn't cured, but I was getting better.

As my sessions continued, my face-time with my counsellor increased, not decreased. I was up to well over an hour of face-to-face, eyeball to eyeball, with my shrink, and it wasn't easy. She asked probing questions, and wouldn't let me avoid issues.

One thing she recommended was for me was to get a pet, so we got a puppy. She said it would keep us company, and it would help settle me down. We got a male German Shepherd, of course. He was eight weeks old when we got him. We found him at a Humane Society kennel in Columbia. We named him Dusty.

When I was a kid, one of my favorite characters was GI Joe and he had a dog named Dusty. That didn't work out so well, since Darla was allergic to the dog hairs in the house. We had to get rid of him after a couple of months, but it helped for a while.

It took me months, three days every week, to get through all of that, and I'm constantly aware that it might recur at any moment. I didn't want that. I fought against that. I had learned the coping skills and I was better, but not completely well. I knew that.

During all of this time, we were having financial problems, with me being unable to work and my wife not making too much money waitressing, and me paying $600 for my son in Daytona Beach and another $800 for my son in Suwannee. Although the VA checks and the Social Security checks allowed us to pay the mortgage and put food on the table, there wasn't much room for anything else.

At some point in late 2013, I decided to contact a lawyer about my son in west Florida. He was almost eight years old now, and I hadn't seen him in years. Even though I hadn't ever done anything to pursue DNA testing before then, I decided to give it a try. I had reason to believe the child wasn't mine. I went on line and researched the issue of whether or not I would be allowed to do anything about it after all those years. It didn't look all that good, but it seemed as if I had a chance.

I contacted a number of lawyers, and they all wanted too much money. There was no way I could afford what they were asking for, but I found this one lawyer who agreed to work with me and allow me to make payments of $150 a month, or less, if I had to, and I retained him. He filed some papers requesting DNA testing and set a hearing for a few months later.

I attended the hearing by telephone. My lawyer was in the courtroom, together with the judge and the lawyer for the Department of Revenue, which became involved when the mother applied for benefits from the State of Florida at some point in time. Once that happened, the State of Florida wanted to collect money from me, and they made sure I paid. I never saw an income tax refund check from 2008 through 2013.

My lawyer convinced the judge to have a DNA test performed. The mother vigorously opposed the motion, saying I had waited too long and that I had signed the birth certificate, but the judge agreed with me. She had to submit to the test, which I had to pay for, but I was more than willing to do that. I went down the next day to a laboratory which has offices all over the country and did what I had to do, which was to give them a blood sample. Reluctantly, she did the same.

A few weeks later, the results came back that said there was a zero percent chance I was the father. She was pissed and I was as happy as I could be. I was going to have to pay that lawyer for the next year or more, but it lightened my financial load by $800 a month. It made a huge difference for us and the extra money helped us out in a lot of ways.

With my medical condition improving and my financial situation improving, my mood improved. I was less irritable, even though I still had moments of extreme anger. I knew it was going to take years to fix the financial problems that we were having. Even with the $800 per month for child support being eliminated, we were still spending more than we were making, since Ingrid wasn't making that much money at the time, but we were happy.

Our relationship was much better. Darla was a healthy and happy little girl. Our marriage had made it through a storm. Things were getting better for us on all fronts.

And then another mortar came out of nowhere and exploded in the middle of my house...there was a fire at the restaurant where Ingrid worked, and she lost her job. I really didn't know how I was going to ever get out of debt, or how we would pay bills on my disability checks alone. I could feel myself slipping back into a state of despair and depression, and then I received a phone call...

CHAPTER EIGHT

Captain McMullen

"**B**uck!"

"Dozer, is that you?"

"Hell yeah, it is. How the hell are ya, man?"

"I'm hangin' in. Can't complain too much."

"You doin' alright? Really?"

"Yeah. The wife and I had our first child this year and things are pretty good. It was a little rough there for a while after they put me out of the Army, but I'm still here. I'm a family man now."

"Yeah? You're still married, got a kid, that's good to hear."

"Yeah. We've been married for over four years now, Dozer."

"Damn! Has it been that long since we talked?"

"Afraid so, man."

"I'm sorry about that, Buck. I think about you and all the guys in the Blue Platoon all the time. Time flies, doesn't it?"

"That it does, Dozer."

"And you workin'? Making money?"

"Not really. I get disability benefits. That's about it."

"That's from the back problems you were having, right?"

"Yeah, and then I had some problems with my head, too."

"No shit? You got PTSD or what? What's goin' on with that?"

"It's a long story, Dozer. It started with my low back…"

"And that's when they sent you to Arizona, right? I remember that much from our last conversation."

"Yeah, but that only lasted for a couple of years, and then they let me go not long after we got bin Laden, and that's about when the PTSD kicked in."

"So you got all that shit all figured out?"

"I'm working on it. I'm much better, but I'm probably going to have to deal with those issues for the rest of my life."

"And your finances? How's all that working out for you?"

"My VA benefits were taken care of before I left the Army, actually. That surprised me. The checks started coming in as soon as I got out, and between that and my Social Security checks, I've been able to pay all my bills, so far."

"So far? What do you mean?"

"My wife lost her job here recently, so things are gonna be a little tighter for us than they were before that happened."

"Are those disability checks all you've got to live off of?"

"Yeah. That's about it at the moment."

"You can't work?"

"I'm disabled, man. If I did work, I'd lose my disability."

"But you can work if you had to."

"Yeah. I've still got my brain. It's my body that prevents me from working. That's what's causing me most of my problems. They rated me at 90% disabled."

"But you could work if the circumstances were right?"

"Yeah, if I could be stand up and move around whenever I need to, and lay down if I had to. There aren't many jobs out there that will let me do that."

"But if the job allowed you to do that, you could work, yes?"

"Well, yes, but I can't lift ten pounds, so it would only be a job where I use my brain, and I need to improve my skills some to be able to get any of those jobs, like working with computers and all."

"And you could use some extra money, right?"

"Of course. Who couldn't?"

"That's true. No matter what you have, it's never enough."

"Dozer, you didn't call to check out my financial situation, I know. So what's up, man? What's goin' on?"

"Yeah, you're right, Buck. I didn't call just to say hello. I can't believe it's been four years since we last spoke. I've just been so busy since we came out of those mountains in Afghanistan that I lose track of time."

"A lot of those guys from the Blue Platoon are still in, aren't they?"

"Yeah, quite a few, actually. Some guys have been transferred to other units, but the last I heard the 173rd was on alert to be sent back to Iraq."

"I've been reading about that. I hope that doesn't happen."

"So you keep up with all that's going on, do you?"

"Yeah, I read the Stars and Stripes all the time and the local paper most every day. Where are you? Are you still with the 173rd?"

"No. I've moved up the ranks some."

"Yeah? What's that about?"

"I'm now a Captain and I'm in Military Intelligence."

"Captain! Congratulations, Dozer! Dream the Gold, right?"

"That's right, Buck. Keep dreamin' your dreams, too, man."

"Be all that you can be."

"Roger that, soldier. Always!"

"So what's goin' on? What do you want to talk to me about?"

"I'd rather not talk over the phone. Can you meet me someplace?"

"Sure. Where are you?"

"I'm in the Atlanta airport at the moment, on my way back to D.C. later tonight."

"So you want to meet today?"

"If that's possible."

"That should be okay, now that my wife doesn't have to go to work. Where would you like to meet?"

"Ever heard of the Dillard House?"

"Clayton, Georgia?"

"Yeah."

"I've heard of it, been by it, but I've never eaten there before."

"It's about an hour from where you are and it'll take me about an hour to get there, too, so it's about halfway in between. Could you meet me two hours from now?"

"Sure. This must be something important, yes?"

"It is, and it'll be good to see you, Buck. I think it might be worth your while."

"It will be good to see you, too, Dozer. I will always be willing to listen to whatever it is you have to say."

"There's money in it for you."

"Yeah?"

"Good money."

"Like I said, I will always listen to whatever you have to say, Dozer. You know that."

"See you in a couple of hours. Drive safe."

"You, too, man."

After I told Ingrid about my conversation with Captain McMullen, she said,

"Go see your friend, Chris, but don't make any promises without talking to me first, okay?"

I gave her a hug, kissed her, and then told her,

"Of course I won't."

"Promise?" she asked, with a knowing look in her eye. "I know how you guys get when you get together...all that boorah stuff."

"I promise. I promise. I have no idea what he has in mind."

"Not a clue?"

"Not a clue."

"Well, you be careful driving and have fun. We'll talk when you get back."

I knew the road to Dillard well, having traveled it many times on camping trips to the Lake Jocassee area. I took State Road 64 through Clemson and Westminster, past Longbranch and the various companies which put rafters on the Chattooga River, and into Clayton.

Then it was six miles north on 441 to Dillard, and then, just as I entered Dillard, which was a few miles south of the North Carolina line, I turned right, drove a few hundred yards towards City Hall, took another right, and then entered the parking lot to a large, one-story building with a huge front porch area, with wooden rocking chairs lined up from one end to the other.

As I walked toward the entrance to the building, I heard a familiar voice exclaim,

"Incoming! Hit the ground!"

It made me laugh. I faked like I was going to dive to the ground, and then continued walking towards the chair on the front porch of the restaurant where Captain McMullen was sitting.

We embraced.

"You look good, Dozer, you really do."

"Thanks, man. I wish I could say the same. You still look like shit."

We laughed, and then Captain McMullen continued,

"You're out of uniform, though, soldier. I'm not used to seeing you without your cammies on."

"Yeah, those days are gone, my friend."

"I was sorry to hear about those problems you had. You'd still be in the Army if they'd let you, I'm sure, right?"

"Absolutely. It wasn't my decision. I wanted to be a lifer, like you."

"Yeah, that's a shame. Let's go inside and I'll tell you what I've got on my mind."

We followed the hostess through several rooms with clothing, gifts and country crafts, into the dining area, where over a hundred tables filled the spacious room. Large plate-glass windows filled two sides of the room. The kitchen was behind the third wall. Bathrooms and offices lined the fourth wall.

"We'd like a table where we could have some quiet conversation, and not bother anyone else, Captain McMullen told the woman.

She took us to a table in the corner furthest from the window seats, which was where everyone else wanted to be.

"How's this?" she asked.

"Perfect," he responded.

"Your server will be with you in just a moment," she said, with a slow, southern drawl.

"I love that accent," Captain McMullen told her. "I could listen to you talk all day."

"I have an accent? I thought it was everyone else who had the accents, not me. Imagine that."

We all laughed politely and she continued,

"Enjoy your breakfast. Emily will take your order."

A petite, perky, young girl, with blonde hair and blue eyes, who looked to be a junior or senior in high school, spoke up and said,

"Good afternoon. My name is Emily and I'll be serving you today. Is this your first time here?"

"I've been here several times, but it's the first time for my friend," Captain McMullen responded.

Turning to me, Emily said,

"Breakfast is served at any time of the day or night, and..."

"And that's what we're going to have, Captain McMullen interjected.

"I've traveled 50 miles just to have this meal. It's the best breakfast in the country. Trust me, Buck. You're going to love this meal."

"Two for breakfast then?" Emily asked.

"Yes, ma'am," he affirmed.

Emily looked at me, and I told her,

"I'm with him. If it's half as good as he says it is, it will be the best I've ever had."

"Everything is served separately and you are welcome to as many helpings as you please," Emily explained.

"All you can eat?"

"That's right," Emily confirmed.

"Great! I'm hungry and he's buying. That's a great combo."

"Coffee, Gentlemen?"

We turned over the coffee mugs in front of our place mats, and said, "Yes, please," at the same time.

"I'll be right back."

"This place is great. You've been here several times?" I asked.

"Well, maybe three times. My brother has been at Fort Benning for six weeks now and I come down to see him as often as I can."

"I remember how close you two are. So he's going into the infantry, like we did?"

"I tried to talk him out of it. I wanted to see him learn to fly planes or choppers, but he wouldn't listen."

"He wanted to follow in his big brother's footsteps, right?"

"Afraid so, and he's a fine young man, Buck. You'd love him. He's a soldier to the core, like us."

"I'm sure he is. You set a good example for him, Dozer."

"Thanks, Buck. I appreciate that. You're gonna love this breakfast. Just wait. It's better than good. It's the best. I hope you're hungry. Thanks for coming to meet with me."

Within minutes, two young men carrying large trays appeared and, after setting them down, proceeded to put plates on the table.

I watched in absolute awe as a plate of eggs was followed by a separate plate for the bacon, a plate of pancakes, bowls of grits and potatoes, cinnamon rolls, pastries, sausages, gravy, thinly sliced pieces of chicken, sliced apples, biscuits, jams, butter, and glasses of orange juice and water.

"Can I get you gentlemen anything else?" Emily asked.

"I can't think of it," Captain McMullen responded.

"Enjoy your meals. I'll be back to check on you shortly."

"Nothing like those packaged meals we got in Afghanistan, is it?" I said. The Captain just laughed.

We exchanged information about all of the other men in the Blue Platoon and where they were and what they were up to, while enjoying the sumptuous meal spread before us. Half an hour later, after a few helpings of seconds on the eggs and bacon, I sat back in my chair and exhaled.

"That was as good as you said it would be, Dozer. I'm stuffed."

"And you can take all that is left on the table with you. If you don't, it will be thrown away."

"Ingrid would like that, I'm sure. Darla will, too, especially the rolls and pastries."

"We'll get a to-go box."

After the plates were cleared, I took another sip of coffee and asked, "So what's this all about, Lieutenant? I mean Captain?"

"Did you see this article?" Captain McMullen asked, as he handed me a copy of an article from the Washington Post from a few days earlier.

I looked at the article, which read,

July 27, 2014   Washington, D.C.

Obama announces U.S. Combat Operations
in Afghanistan to end in December.

President Barack Obama announced today that U.S. combat operations in Afghanistan would end in December of this year. This confirms previous reports that such action was to occur. A residual force of less than 10,000 troops would remain in the country to train Afghan security forces and support counterterrorism operations against the Taliban and remnants of Al- Qaeda. By the end of 2015, that number will drop to less than 5,000 troops. All U.S. forces, except for those required to staff the embassy, are to be removed from the country by the end of 2016.

However, that plan is subject to the approval of the incoming Afghan government. Outgoing President Hamid Karzai refused to sign the agreement, saying that a new president should do so. One of the key provisions in the agreement is a bilateral security agreement which provides for immunity for U.S. troops serving in the country, which outgoing President Karzai had refused to sign.

"I didn't see this particular article, but I heard that he's going to do that."

"Okay, here's the deal," Captain McMullen said, as he scooted forward in his chair, looking around to make sure no one was paying any attention to us and that no one could hear anything that he was about to say…

"Because of what Obama's going to do, what with the debt crisis, the sequester, Congressional deadlock, and the constant fight over the budget, the Army is going to lose billions of dollars by way of government cuts once we get out of there. They are going to reduce the size of the military. There is absolutely no doubt about it. Before too long, there won't be as many soldiers on active duty. The Army is going to have to find a way to keep its defenses up, despite the decrease in money. So they have decided to use independent people and groups to do some of the things that soldiers have been doing…"

"Outsourcing?"

"Yeah, I guess you could call it that."

"Like what they've been doing in Iraq for years?"

"Well, let's make sure we're not talking apples and oranges here…I'm not talking about the civilian contractors who are getting rich off of government contracts by supplying material, supplies, services and those kinds of things, I'm talking about people who perform missions that were formerly being performed by military units, like ours, and are now going to be performed by someone other than personnel within the military."

"But it's all still under the command of someone in the military, right? The Army is still in charge. That would be crazy otherwise."

"Yes, of course, but there is going to be more independence, more opportunities for creativity for those of us who are still there."

"In the Army?" I asked, incredulously.

"Hard as that might be to believe, the answer is yes."

"Are you talking about things like what the CIA and Seals have been doing for years?"

"Yeah, that's closer to what I'm talking about."

"But more covert?"

"Well, a lot of those things were covert, so it's more about autonomy, really."

"Really? That doesn't sound like the Army, Dozer."

Captain McMullen laughed and said, "Things are changing, Buck. The Army isn't like the Army used to be when you were in it. There are people snoopin' around everyplace so much that you just about can't go to the bathroom without somebody wandering in and wondering what you had for lunch! It's gotten that bad."

"Come on. It hasn't changed that much, has it? Really?"

"I'm not shitting you, Buck, and the Freedom of Information Act is being interpreted to mean that non-military people are second guessing the military about every decision that is made, no matter when it was made. It could be something that happened twenty years ago or something that happened last week. It's gotten awful and it's gonna get worse."

"That's hard to believe."

"And this business of having journalists 'imbedded' with our soldiers has gotten completely out of hand. There can be a guy, or a woman, with a microphone in her hand during the middle of a fire-fight asking someone what's going on. Now we had some of that when we were over there, to some extent, but we had more control over things. Now, it seems like they're in control, or at least they think they are. It's bad!"

I shook my head, laughed, and said "You've got to be kidding, right?"

"I'm dead serious, Buck! I mean it wasn't bad enough with having journalists imbedded in our units, like we had, and before that was the 'Don't ask, don't tell' stuff, and then it was women in combat units and now we've got people up our asses asking about transgenders….I'm mean…really? What is the world coming to?"

"No question about it. The world is changing, Dozer, but where does any of this involve me? Where do I fit in with all this?"

"Where do you fit in? Here's where…I've been assigned to lead one of those type units and I want you in on it with me."

"Me? How, Dozer?"

"Because of what you can do for me, Buck. I need you. I really do."

"How so?"

"Because of things you and I did together in Afghanistan for one."

"What kind of things?"

Captain McMullen smiled, looked me straight in the eye and said, "You're gonna love this….you're gonna operate your own drone and you're gonna have a chance to get back at those mother-fuckers who shot the shit out of us back when…"

"My own drone?"

"Yeah."

"You're serious?"

"I'm as serious as a heart attack."

"I'm surprised, Dozer. I mean, I had no idea why you wanted to see me, other than to say hello and stay in touch, but you did say it might involve a job and some money, so I guess I just didn't think it would involve working with drones. I didn't know what to expect, but I didn't expect that."

"Well, the fact that you know how to operate those drones, and you know that part of Afghanistan as well as anyone else, makes you an ideal candidate for my mission."

Then Captain McMullen looked me in the eye and continued, "Plus, I know you and I would trust you with my life, Buck, and that means more to me than anything else."

"I appreciate that, Dozer, and I appreciate you. So tell me what you have in mind? What is it you're thinking I can do for you?"

"You know that many of the people operating the drones are sitting in Arizona or Nevada, thousands of miles from the war zone, just like you were a couple of years ago, but the use of drones is rising so rapidly that we just don't have enough qualified operators and we can't train them fast enough. So my project is really pretty simple as far as you are concerned. I'm just going to have you, a civilian contractor, do some of that work, instead of having it all done at Fort Creech or some other military base by a soldier, that's all."

"So where will I work? I don't want to move. My wife definitely won't like that."

"No, you won't have to move. You'll be able to work from your home."

"But what about getting the birds in the air and all the technology? There's a lot of hi-tech shit out there at Fort Creech, Dozer."

"I've got that taken care of. I'm still in the military, remember, and now I'm a Captain. I do have some rank, plus this wasn't my idea, or at least it wasn't entirely my idea. There are some people further up the food chain than I am who think this is an extremely important mission we'll be on."

"So can you tell me more about it or is this not the right time for that?"

"You don't need to know any of the details just yet. Once you agree to become a part of this, I'll fill you in on everything. For now, I just need to know if you are willing to become a part of this.

"I don't know, man," I said, "you make it sound so simple, but there's a lot to it. You know that, right? There's a lot more to operating a drone than me sitting in my house. It takes a team to make it all happen."

"Buck! This is me you're talking to...I'm not just another pretty face...I have approached this project the way I do every other project. You just have to do your job and let me take care of the rest."

"Who will I be reporting to, Dozer? Who else is involved? Anyone I know? Anyone else from the Blue Platoon?"

"You'll be reporting to me, nobody else."

"Really?"

"Really."

I took a deep breath, and said, "So basically you've got your own drone you can put me in and you can use me to help you operate outside of the view of the civilian population, if necessary. That's what I'm hearing."

"That's about right. I'm still in the chain of command, though, Chris. I've still got people I report to. There are times when we, and by that I mean the United States Army, don't want to be....." and Captain McMullen hesitated, while carefully choosing his words, then he continued,

"...constrained by others. Understand? Think of it as being more out of the line of sight. How's that? Better?"

"Off the books, then."

"That's right. Off the books. Exactly. We don't want to be second-guessed by the press..."

"or Congress..."

"You won't get me to say that, but I think you understand what I'm saying, Buck."

"Dozer, I trust you more than anyone else in the world, and that counts for a lot. I'm just going to be following orders given to me by the United States Army, right? This isn't anything more than that, right?"

"That's right. This is completely legitimate. You can trust me on that. I wouldn't jeopardize my career for anything. You know that. This is my life. Buck, we will be part of that 'residual force' President Obama was referring to in that press release."

"So there will be some people who won't know about what we're doing, like some Afghans, maybe? Is that it?"

"You get the idea, Chris. I don't want to put too fine a point on this whole thing just yet, but most of our military forces will be out of Afghanistan soon, and we don't want the whole world to know exactly what we're leaving behind. Does that make better sense to you?"

"And you're the one who's going to be giving me my orders, right?"

"That's right."

I thought about it for a few seconds and then told him, "That's all I need to know. If you think I can help you, and you tell me that I'll be answering directly to you, that's good enough for me. Count me in."

Captain McMullen extended his hand and said, "Thanks, Buck. I knew I could count on you."

We shook hands, and then I asked,

"So can you tell me anything more about what I'm going to be doing with a drone, Dozer? My wife is going to grill me on all of this."

"You can't tell her much of anything, Buck, and I mean that. This really is a top-secret operation. The less you know, the better, and I don't want her to know anything about this. As far as she is concerned, you can tell her that you will simply be performing surveillance inside the United States. That should be good enough for her. That's all she needs to know."

"Okay. I can do that, but can I tell her about the money? That will make her happy, I'm sure."

"Buck, I'm going to want you to spend eight to ten hours a day, four to five days a week on this. I will expect you to put in a good forty hour week for me. No one will be there to look over your shoulder, but I trust you. I have no doubts whatsoever about that aspect of things."

"Being able to work at home, lay down when I need to, move around when I have to…all of that will definitely make it possible for me to work with you, and the money will be a huge help for us. Darla is growing and getting more active by the day and the expenses are mounting…new clothes, new shoes…you name it, she's got to have it all. Whatever she needs, we're going to do our best to get it for her."

"Yeah, I'm sure she's special. I'll bet she's beautiful, yes?"

"We think so. Here…," I pulled a picture out of my wallet and handed it to him. "That's her."

"She's beautiful alright. Good thing she took after her mother, right?"

"That's for sure."

We laughed, and then Captain McMullen continued,

"It doesn't look like I'll ever know what that's like. I always thought I'd have a family, but unless something changes, that's not going to happen."

"No women in your life, Dozer?"

"No time for that, Buck. The military is my life. I'm on the move so much I just don't have time for a woman right now. My relationships are measured in hours, if not minutes. All I've got is my brother. He's my family, now that our parents are gone. He means everything to me."

"Well, who knows…maybe one of those female officers will make you change your mind."

"We'll see. That could happen, but I'm not seeing it right now, but let me tell you about the money that I can pay you, because I know that's important to you."

"It is, and it's even more important to my wife, I'm sure."

"I can give you $5,000 a month, no deductions, no pay stubs….you pay all taxes and everything. You'll be an independent contractor and I'll give you a 1099 at the end of the year. It's that simple."

"$5,000 per month! That's pretty good. I've never made that much in my life! That'll help. My wife will be real happy about that."

"I'm glad. I want you to be happy with this whole thing. That's about $27.50 an hour, or something like that, and people who can operate a drone aren't that easy to find. You have a special skill the Army is looking for."

"Who will be my employer?"

"I don't know that right now. It will be some company that the Army hasn't created yet, but this is all going to be on the up-and-up, Chris. All branches of the military are doing these kinds of things these days."

"Like the CIA has been doing for years."

"That's right, and Chris, I assure you that I'm not going to do anything to get you, or me, in any trouble. You know that's the truth. I promise you that. I've worked too hard to get to where I am to allow something like that to happen."

"Oh, I'm sure of that, Dozer. I didn't mean to suggest anything by my question. I just knew it wasn't going to be the United States Army, that's all."

"Have you ever heard of Alarbus?"

"Can't say that I have."

"Check it out. They've been in the news lately. It's a front company for the Army. It's just one of a number of such companies created by the military to allow them to act like the CIA does all over the world. This is legitimate, Chris. We do it all the time."

"Okay. I just didn't know. I'll check it out."

"But that's not the best part, although the money is important…" Captain McMullen said as he inched closer to the table, bringing his face closer to mine, while continuing to scan the room to make sure no one was paying any attention to them.

"You're gonna be able to get a few of the mother-fuckers who got Juan Restrepo, Robert Miller, the Cowboy and all those others from the 173rd at Camp Keating…and all the rest of those guys who died over there…"

"I'd like that," I told him.

"Once we get this thing cooking, your drone is going to be flying in and around the Kunar, Kamdesh and Gorandesh valleys."

"Which is another reason why you want me."

"That's right. You're perfect. You know the area. You know the players. You know the history, the culture, what went on over there and," he hesitated, lowered his voice, and added, "you're not afraid to pull the trigger."

"You've got that much power, Captain? You can make all that happen?"

Captain McMullen nodded his head up and down and said, "I do and I can make all of that happen."

"That's some heavy-duty shit, man."

"It is, but remember…not a word to anyone about that. Have I made myself clear on that?"

"Absolutely, Captain. But I thought that since we're pulling all our combat troops out of Afghanistan altogether later this year, we're only going to have one base near Kabul, but even that's in some doubt because Karzei has refused to sign the Treaty allowing us to keep any military bases in Afghanistan at all, right? And one of his biggest complaints was about drones killing civilians, right?"

"Karzei refused to sign a Treaty, and you're right, he and others, including the Pakastanis, are upset with our drone strikes, and some want us out of the country altogether, but the truth is he's afraid of what would happen to him if he signed the treaty and allowed us to stay in. But he's gone now and his two replacements are in favor of the Treaty. They need the U.S. to keep a small military presence in the country or else they know, or fear, that the Taliban will be back in control in no time. The U.S. is confident that there will be a Treaty signed. Either way, this project I'm talking about is going forward. Trust me on that."

"Even when the Army pulls out of the country?"

"That's right, Chris. That's the plan. We haven't agreed to stop going after the Taliban."

"But they've closed down most, if not all, of those bases and outposts in Nuristan and other parts of the country, right? They've given back all the ground we won, right?"

"I'm afraid that's right, Buck. That's what we did, but there are those in the Army who want to make sure that we keep our eyes on the parts of the country we've given up. That's why we're doing this."

"It disappoints me whenever I think about it."

"That's still one of the main avenues for people to go from the Tribal Lands into Afghanistan. We want to keep our eyes on that area."

"That makes sense."

"Now that we're not there, the Taliban is using it as a safe zone, and al-Qaeda is still there, too, though many of them have gone over to Syria and back into Iran at this point."

"That makes it even worse."

"And there are people in high places who still remember what happened in Somalia, and with the U.S.S. Cole, and the Embassies, not to mention 9/11, who don't want us to just walk away and let those guys get away. We know they're still there. This gives us a chance to still get them."

"I'd like to be a part of that, Captain. I've still got some bad feelings from those days. That's unfinished business as far as I'm concerned."

"Buck, since you have given me the green light, I'll get to work immediately. I'll get things arranged on my end. You'll need to provide me with a completely secure room in your house that only you can have access to. How long will it take for you to get your part done?"

"We've got a room in the back that we're not doing anything with right now. We've been thinking about having another child, but with finances the way they are right now, we can't do that, so that room should be perfect."

"The rest is easy. I'll just need to link you up to a satellite, assign you to a drone, and you'll be up and running in no time. I'm thinking we can put you to work in a few weeks. How does it sound?"

"I could sure use the money, Dozer." Then I remembered that I had promised Ingrid not to accept any offer until I talked it over with her, so I told him, "I'll have to talk to my wife before finalizing this, Captain."

"Buck, I hope that's not going to be a problem."

"I've got to tell my wife something. I can't set up this secret room in the house and not tell her what I'm up to. What do I tell her?"

"You tell her that you're a regional security specialist and you're job is to make sure that there are no terrorists within 300 miles of your home. Tell her that the NSA is going to rid itself of the data it collected and get out of the spying game, so the Army is going to take over that responsibility from the NSA, and it will continue to monitor things. And you tell her that nobody can know about it. She'll believe that, and she'll be happy to know you're protecting her neighborhood…and once you tell her about the money, she'll like that part the best, I'm sure."

"Interesting, Captain. Very interesting."

"And you can't call me Captain anymore when we're out in public. I don't want anyone to think that what we do has anything to do with the military."

"So what shall I call you?"

"Steve."

"Steve?"

"That's right. Stephen Johnson."

"That's not your name."

"It is now...look here, Captain McMullen pulled out a credit card and showed it to me. "See? It says Stephen Johnson, just like I told you."

"How much time do I have to think this over?"

"Today's Friday...how's Monday?"

"Monday! That's only two days!"

"Monday, Buck, and if you can't, or won't, do it, I'll have to find someone who will. You know how the military is...they wanted this done yesterday."

"How can I get in touch?"

"You can't. Once I get things set up, we'll have a secure line and we can talk freely, but until then, I'll have to call you."

"Okay."

"Give it some serious thought, Buck. Talk it over with your wife all weekend, if you want. I'll get in touch with you on Monday. This is important, but it's time for me to go. I've got to catch a plane later tonight and I'm going to meet up with my kid brother for a few hours before then."

"So where is he headed?"

"He's not going anywhere for now. Once he finishes basic training, he'll go to paratrooper school, which is at Fort Benning, too."

"What unit?"

"173rd. What else?"

"Following in big brother's footsteps...that's cool."

"I'm proud of him."

"So Fort Benning is a good hour drive southwest of Atlanta. You've got some driving to do."

"Yeah. I'd better be on my way. You'll be hearing from me."

We stood and walked towards the parking lot, after paying the bill.

"I appreciate the confidence you have in me, Dozer, and..."

"Steve. Remember, from now on it's Steve..."

"Steve, it's been good seeing you."

"Same here. Talk to you on Monday."

CHAPTER NINE

Drones

"H E WANTS YOU TO do what?"
"Make that back room into a place that's to be used exclusively by me to do surveillance within a 300 mile radius of our house. I'm going to do what I can to make sure there are no terrorist attacks in this area, kind of like what the NSA was doing before Edward Snowden became a traitor."

"And how are you supposed to do that?"

"With a drone."

"A drone....really?"

"That's what he said. He couldn't tell me too much, and he told me not to tell you anything about what I do, other than what I just told you. This is a top-secret kind of thing."

"Top secret...so what are you going to be? A 007 kind of guy? You? A secret agent?"

"No, no, no! He said I'm not going to have to leave the house. I won't have to do any traveling at all, but I kind of like that 007 thing. Yeah, maybe you should think of it like that...I'm going to be a secret agent...a cool guy."

"That's you alright...Mr. Super-Cool!"

We both laughed at that, and she continued,

"So is this going to be dangerous? Am I going to have to worry about somebody breaking in to kill you? Or worse yet, me? Or Darla?"

"Nobody is going to know about any of this except the Captain and me."

"Captain? I thought he was your Lieutenant."

"He was. He got promoted. I'm gonna be working for my old Lieutenant from the Blue Platoon of the 173rd. He's still in the Army and says my orders will come straight from him."

"The Army? I thought that domestic surveillance stuff was the National Security Agency, isn't it? They're not the military, right?"

"Yes, but the NSA is under enormous scrutiny because of Snowden and all that shit about spying on the German Chancellor and all. They're losing control over some of the things that the United States really doesn't want to lose control over, so the military is going to take over some of the domestic things that the NSA was doing, or that's what I understood him to tell me."

"The Army is going to be in charge of domestic spying?"

"With all the things that are going on in the world involving Islamic extremism, I think they're worried about another 9-11, or some more acts of terrorism."

"That's understandable, but if the military is supposed to be involved, then why do they need you?"

"For a couple of reasons...first, because they don't have enough drone operators. They're using drones more and more these days and there aren't that many people who know how to operate them...and secondly, because of all the cuts to defense spending, they're down-sizing the military, so they're out-sourcing some things to civilian contractors."

"So if the military is out-sourcing stuff, then it's not the military anymore, right?"

"Well, the military is still going to have control over it, but it's not going to be handled by military personnel. My Captain is still in the Army, so I guess you could say it's still being handled by the military."

"It sounds to me that you're going to be like those guys who killed all those people in Iraq? Who were those guys?"

"You're thinking of Blackwater."

"Yeah, that's right. Those guys. What were they doing?"

"They were providing security, among other things, and some of the guys got a little over-zealous and people got killed."

"Over-zealous? They shot and killed innocent civilians."

"No they didn't. They were under attack and fired back."

"That's not true. If that was true there wouldn't have been such a huge outcry over all of that. Those guys were like hired assassins. You're going to be like them?"

"No! I'm not going to be anything like them. I'm going to be right here in that back room looking at a computer screen. I won't leave the house!"

"And this is legal?"

"Yes, it's legal! My Captain assured me of that."

"And you believe him?"

"Yes, I believe him! I trust him more than anyone else in the world."

"Really? Even more than me?"

"No, no, no. That's different. You know that. That's why we're talking about this. You're my partner. I won't do this if you don't agree."

"So who are you going to be working for?"

"I'm going to be working for my Captain. That's it. I'll get paid in cash."

"That's got to be illegal."

"Not cash, although it might be. I don't know. I meant that I won't be working for the Army. There won't be anything taken out as if I was an employee. I'll get a 1099 as an independent contractor, and I'll have to pay all the other stuff, like taxes, social security and the rest. What can I tell you, Ingrid? That's why we're talking about all of this. That's what my Captain told me."

"So why you?"

"He said the government doesn't want to give up all of its spying operations around the country because of what that Snowden guy did, so they're going to do things more discreetly, and he wants me because I know how to operate a drone and he knows me."

"Discreetly...I don't like the sound of that, Chris."

"What? I'm just operating a drone, keeping my eyes on suspected terrorists within this country, keeping our neighborhood safe. What's wrong with that?"

"I don't know. It just sounded funny the way you said it...spying on people in this country who are suspected of being terrorists, but not wanting people to know what they're doing? That doesn't sound legal to me. Aren't they supposed to get a warrant or something?"

"I don't know. My Captain is taking care of all of that. I'm just supposed to operate a drone and keep an eye on things. That's it, and everyone is concerned about terrorists coming into this country now, after what's going on all over the world."

"That's true, but you still have to follow the law, right?"

"True, but no one wants another 9-11. I think we need to obey the law, but be as watchful as possible. My Captain says everything I'll be doing is legal."

Ingrid was quiet for a few seconds, and then she said,

"Sometimes I think we should just pack up and go back to Germany."

"You don't want to do that. You know you don't."

"Unless our financial situation improves..."

"You'll find another job! You know you will. You love it here. You said so. And you know that the Hoffakers expect to open another restaurant within the next year, right? So they'll give you your job back if you haven't found one by then."

"Within the next year...maybe. What are we supposed to do between now and then?"

"My Social Security checks and the checks I get from the Army are paying our bills. We just have to ride out this storm."

"Your checks barely cover our expenses, and we just bought this new house! And you want another child! How are we going to do that?"

Ingrid started to weep. I put my arm around her and said,

"I haven't told you how much he's going to pay me."

She sniffled and asked, "So how much is he going to pay you?"

"Five thousand a month."

She brightened a bit and asked, "Five thousand a month? Really?"

"Really."

Ingrid wiped tears from her eyes and said, "Really?"

"Really."

That changed her mood considerably, and she said, "I still don't like the sound of it. You're not telling me everything and something just doesn't sound right. There's more to it than what he's telling you, or more to it than what you're telling me. I'm sure of it."

"I'll tell you what…let's do this…let's give this a try and see how it goes. I'm going to be making a hell of a lot of money, which we'll put aside, and if this doesn't work out, at least we'll have some money if we decide to go back to Germany. We might even have enough to buy a house."

Ingrid liked the sound of that, and asked,

"So how often will you get paid? Every week? Once a month? What?"

"Once a month. That's what he said."

We sat in silence for a few moments and then she said,

"We could use the money, that's for sure, but I don't want you going to prison or getting your name in the newspaper like that guy who wants to be a woman. What's his name?"

"Bradley Manning, but now he calls himself Chelsea."

"So is he a man or a woman?"

"I don't think he's had the operation yet, but he wants to have it done and then serve his time in a prison for women."

"That sounds just like a guy to me…"

"Except he won't have his male organ, so what's the point?"

"I don't want to even think about that. What did he do anyway?"

"He spilled military secrets, a whole bunch of them, and that guy Julian Assange published them for the world to see on wikileak. I'm not doing anything like that. I'm just supposed to monitor activity in our little area, that's all. Not the whole country or even a large part of it, just a few of the surrounding states, and nobody is going to know about me."

"I still think that this has got to be illegal, Chris."

"Hey, you're not naïve. We both know that our government has been sending soldiers and the C.I.A. into other countries and into places we're not supposed to be, telling them that if they get caught they're on their own, that the country would disclaim any knowledge of their actions. I know that. You know that, but I'm not going to be doing that kind of stuff. I'm going to be sitting in this house the whole time!"

Ingrid became quiet again, still sorting out the information she was being provided.

"So what all are you supposed to do with that room anyway?"

"It's just gonna be me and a desk and some computers, I think, but some more electronics than that, probably. I don't know. He's taking care of all of that. We don't have to do anything except clear some space and make sure it is completely secure. Nobody except me is allowed to go in there."

"You're kidding, right? Not even to clean? That place will be a disaster in a week."

"Hey, hey, hey! I resemble that remark. I think I'm doing a pretty good job at being Mr. Mom!"

Ingrid looked at me with a quizzical look on her face and said, "You're kidding, right? I still have to follow around behind you picking up crumbs. You don't want me in there at all? Really?"

"That's what he said, and it's extremely important to him that we do it that way."

"Seems silly to me, unless there are things he doesn't want me to see, and that's what worries me."

"I understand, but if I give him my word that I'll do it the way he wants, then I've got to do exactly what he wants. More importantly, I've got to do exactly what I promise him I'll do. I wouldn't want to let him down."

"Five thousand dollars a month?" Ingrid asked again. She still couldn't believe it. "Are you sure?"

"Maybe I could get more…" I offered.

"You think you could?" Ingrid asked.

"Maybe. I can ask, if you agree to let me do this. That's over twenty five dollars an hour. Maybe I can get him to give me thirty five or forty dollars an hour. That doesn't sound too unreasonable to me. There aren't many people out there who know how to operate a military drone, so it's a good market for me right now."

"Do you want to do it?"

"I'm happy right now. Other than the money stuff, things are good for us. We've got a new house. We've got our baby. I'm getting the benefits I'm entitled to. I'm getting better. If it weren't for the fact that you lost your job and we need to make more money, I might not even think of taking this job. But it's a job I can do, Ingrid. I can get up when I want, lay down when I want, move around whenever I want…I'm not going to find a job like this ever again, I'm sure. You know that's true, and I'm kinda tired of laying around with nothing much to do. This could be exciting for me. I think I'd like to give it a try."

"I could get another job."

"And make what? A couple hundred dollars a week, maybe? I can make over a thousand dollars a week, almost five times as much as you can."

"You think he'd pay you seventy five hundred a month?"

"I can ask. I can tell him that I won't do it for less. He seems to want me bad."

"When does he want you to let him know?"

"Monday."

"Monday! That doesn't give us much time to think about it, does it?"

"We're thinking about it now. What do you think?"

"My gut tells me that I don't want you to do this. It reminds me too much of what was going on in Germany before I was born."

"You mean the Nazis? How is this like the Nazis?"

"From what my parents tell me, their parents were so patriotic and so proud of their country that they would do whatever they were told to do, no matter how bad it was. They did awful things, as we all know."

"So how is that like what the United States is doing?"

"Everybody wants to join the Army! Everyone in the military is a hero now…everybody. Men, women, married, gay, straight…it doesn't matter…everyone who comes home in a uniform is called a hero, and…"

"And you don't think they are?"

"That's not the point. What I'm saying is that it sounds like what was happening in Germany in the late '30s, according to my parents, or that's what my grandparents told them it was like. They had the Youth Corps and all of that…the German people, or most of them, really believed in what Hitler was doing."

"Hard to believe now, isn't it?"

"It should have been hard to believe then. The Germans are an extremely intelligent group of people, and yet they were so easily deceived. How did that happen?"

"But we're not burning books, rounding up Jews and loading them into box cars, or invading other countries like Hitler did!"

She looked at me with a questioning glance.

"Really? What was Gulf War I all about? Or Gulf War II? And why is the U.S. still in Afghanistan? Or Iraq? And who knows where else? Pakistan? The Middle East? Africa? Central America? Somalia? Syria? The Ukraine?"

"With what ISIS is doing, and al-Qaeda and all of these new terrorist organizations, I think we need to be all over the world, don't you? They don't wear uniforms anymore, you know."

"The U.S. is everywhere and people in the U.S. have no idea what the CIA or the NSA or these covert organizations you're talking about are doing."

"They've got to keep that stuff secret."

"I guess that's my point. Do you trust that your government enough to say that whatever it does to fight terrorism is okay? Even if it means breaking a few laws in the United States?"

"Come on! This is the best country in the world! You know that! We help everybody who asks for our help. Nobody else does what the U.S. does around the world. We're the good guys! Yes, I trust that my government is doing the right things! Actually, I wish they'd do more. It's not fair that our enemies get to do whatever they want and we have to make sure we don't break any laws."

"You're a good guy, Chris, and I love you very much, but I don't see things the same way you do sometimes."

"Why? Because you were born in Germany?"

"Yes, that's part of it, and I think all Europeans, except maybe the English, think that way. They see the U.S. as imperialistic, with their economy, their social ways, the way they dress, the movies they make, the products they make...everything. I think, and I think most Europeans would agree with me, that the U.S. is out to gain a financial advantage over every other country on the planet, and if that isn't imperialistic, what is?"

"Come on! Just because we're the biggest kids on the block doesn't make us bad. We're the movers and shakers on the planet. Our innovations and the imagination of our entrepreneurs is what makes us the wealthiest nation on earth, and people everywhere are looking to make money. Everybody on the planet is. We're pouring money into places where there is no money! Those countries are delighted to have us there, aren't they?"

"The United States of America is gaining an advantage and, even though it's not like it was in the colonial days, it's using financial might, and military might, to accomplish that. Nowadays, it's all about money, and you know that's true."

"So what's wrong with making money?"

"I'm saying it's a form of imperialism."

"So if making money is being imperialistic, then maybe we are, but that's not what the Nazis were doing."

"And your military?"

"Hey! The Soviet Union collapsed because it was a failed economic system. The cold war ended because the U.S.S.R. couldn't support its people and keep building ships and planes and everything else to keep up with the U.S. We didn't defeat them militarily, but it's a good thing there is no more United Soviet Socialist Republic, right?"

"It's better since the Soviet Union collapsed, that's for sure. Countries that had been completely overtaken, and had lost their identity and national pride, are now restored. Most of those countries are now prospering, as best I can tell."

"And Germany is better! No more wall!"

"And Germany is better, but you miss my point. My point is that the United States thinks it can do whatever it wants and doesn't have to answer to anybody! And this job this Captain of yours wants you to do sounds just like that…the Army is going to do whatever it wants, even if it's wrong, to make sure it knows what everybody on the planet is doing, and why? To make more money for the rich people in this country. That's why!"

"That's what creates jobs and helps people to have better lives."

"So you say. From what I see, and what I read, it's all about the upper 2 percent, or 1 percent, or less."

"You really think that? You loved it when you came to this country with me. You loved it! And you still love it here, don't you? Don't you?"

"I do, that's true. I never imagined all the things you Americans have which you take for granted, like this house. Nobody but very rich people own houses in Germany. You remember where I lived, before I came here with you? It was a little town-house which I rented. I never dreamed that I would ever make enough money to get my own house. This is better. We have our own house, with a big back yard. I love that."

"But you say you want to move back to Germany?"

"Sometimes. I miss my family, and I like the way things are in Bamburg."

"Everybody there is German! You've got no diversity at all! Here there are people from all over the world, all makes and models, that's what the U.S. is all about!"

"Some of what you say is true, but that's who I am."

"But if you didn't lose your job, through no fault of yours, you wouldn't even be thinking of moving back to Germany. That's true and you know it."

"That's true. I admit it. If Mr. and Mrs. Hoffaker hadn't been forced to get out of the building they'd been in for twenty years because of the fire, I might not be thinking that way, but they did and now they have no place to go and I have no job."

"But they'll find something. You know they will."

"They're getting old. Maybe they will and maybe they won't."

"But you'll find another job. You know you will."

"That restaurant was perfect for me. I speak German most of the time in there. I won't find anything like that again anytime soon."

"And we can go back to Germany to visit, if we want. I'm going to be making some good money by doing this job."

"That's true. I'm just saying…"

"We're getting way off the point here. Are you going to agree to allow me to do this or not? I won't do it unless you agree to it…and you've got to agree not to say a word to anyone, and I mean anyone…this is top secret stuff. I wasn't supposed to tell you any of this but I told my Captain that you wouldn't think about letting me do this without knowing what it was all about."

"I don't like this, but…"

"But you'll agree to let me do it?"

Ingrid heaved a sigh of resignation and said,

"On two conditions…"

"What are they?"

"One, you get paid seventy five hundred dollars a month, not five thousand…"

"And the other?"

"You will agree to move back to Germany with me if this doesn't work out and I say so."

I thought about this for a few seconds, and then told her,

"But you've got to agree to give me some time to see if it will work, not just say we're leaving after a few months…"

"How much time do you want?"

"At least a year, maybe two."

"Let's say a year. That's fair. That will give the Hoffakers time to find a new place for their restaurant and time for you to see if this is a good idea or not."

"I'll never have an opportunity to make this much money ever again in my entire life. I'm sure of that, but I don't want to do anything to mess up our life together. I love you, Ingrid. You know that."

"I know you do, and I love you, too."

"So I promise that if this gets too dangerous, or if I don't like the way things are working out, I'll go back to Germany with you, like you just said. Agreed?"

Ingrid stuck out her hand and said,

"Agreed! Let's shake on it."

"Shake on it nothin'. Give me a kiss."

We embraced, hugged each other tightly and kissed.

"You know I don't like this, but I trust your judgment, and I am trusting that you will do the right thing, but I don't trust your government and I definitely don't trust your military. I don't know this Captain of yours, so I don't know what to think about him, but you trust him with your life, and so Darla and I will, too."

"It's our government, and our military. When you married me, you married a soldier who was an American citizen. Because of that, you can become an American citizen, too, if you want."

"But I want to keep my German citizenship, and they won't let me. I'll have to give up my German citizenship. I'm not ready to do that."

"I understand, but this is still your country, too. It's our country. It's Darla's country. She's an American citizen."

"That's true, but like I said before, it reminds me of what Germany was like seventy years ago, so strong and so powerful that they thought they could do whatever they wanted to do, and that nobody could stop them…"

"And nobody did…until the United States entered the war…"

"This is a great country, but in this country money is more important than anything else…everything is about money…"

"Money makes the world go round, world go round, world go round…" I sang.

"You make a joke, but I am serious. I agree to this, but I am very suspicious."

"I hear you, and I don't want anything to come between us. I love you. And you've got to promise not to go into that room…ever. Right?"

"I agree, but I'll have my antenna up."

CHAPTER TEN

The Deal

"**S**o your wife gave you the okay?"

"With one condition…"

"Before you say another word, tell me if you can meet me today."

"Same place?"

"Yes."

"Yeah. I can do that."

"Great. See you in an hour or so."

An hour later, we were sitting at a table in the Dillard House. After ordering sandwiches, instead of the all-you-can-eat breakfast special, the Captain asked,

"So what's the one condition? More money, right?"

I stared back at him and asked, "How did you guess?"

"I may not have a wife, but I have had some experience with women. Is that it?"

"Yes."

"So what does she want? Fifty dollars an hour? Forty? What?"

"Seventy five hundred a month, whatever that works out to."

"And she thinks that what you'll be doing is illegal, right?"

"Right."

"And she isn't sure that she wants you to get involved in any of this, right?"

"Right."

"But the money changed her mind…"

"Right."

"And I told you it would."

"No, you didn't."

"Well, maybe I didn't tell you that, but that's what I expected."

"Are you okay with that?"

"I could negotiate with you, I know, but I won't. I want you with me on this. What we're doing means a lot to me, personally, and it means a lot to the country as well. Forty something an hour isn't unreasonable. That's about what crane operators make. I shouldn't have any trouble selling that, but don't push it. Remember, this is the United States Army."

"So you'll agree to that, Captain?"

"Steve."

"Steve."

"Yes. I agree."

"She's going to be so happy."

"I'm happy for the two of you, Chris, but you have a job to do and you're going to earn that money."

"I'll do the best I can, sir. You know that."

"Yes, I do. That's why I'm here. Any questions on your end?"

"I'm a little more than curious about this really top secret thing. I mean, other people are going to know about this, right?"

"Not many."

"But people are going to know when a drone kills some Afghans. That's news. People will know."

"You're going to be given very specific targets, and if you eliminate one of your targets, that will be news, but people won't be wondering who, within the United States, did the killing. The focus will be on who was killed by the U.S. So the focus will be on the Army, or the military, or the government, not you and me."

"And if I don't do my job right and I fuck up?"

"Then I'm on the hot seat and I'll have to explain things as best I can. Either way, you aren't identified, and you can't be traced."

I was a little uncomfortable with that explanation, but I told him,

"Okay. So what's next?"

"I've got to get your house wired and get you hooked up. That's the next step, and then I've got to train you on how to operate your new best friend. It's been a couple of years since you've been at the wheel of one of those things."

"Say when. We're ready on our end. The room is yours. Once you get things set up, I'm ready to go to work."

"You're ready to start collecting a paycheck, that's what you are."

"Captain…"

"Stephen…"

"Stephen, I know what I'm getting myself into, and I've got no problem with it. What my wife doesn't know won't hurt me. How are you going to do this so she won't know?"

"You and your family will have to be out of the house when I go in to get things set up."

"You do this yourself?"

"I have some helpers."

"And you don't want us around. Okay, I have no problem with that. Just let me know when and we'll take a little vacation. How long is it going to take you?"

"Two, maybe three days, to get it wired. Training you, or re-training you, won't take long. I've got a video that explains the procedure, and you'll pick it up quickly. Basically, it's not much different from the way you did things at Fort Creech. You'll do pretty much the exact same thing. I'll take care of the rest."

"You've got men on the ground in Afghanistan?"

"Yes. In fact, I have a picture of our facility. It's in the middle of no place," Captain McMullen responded. "Here, see? Nobody is going to find that place."

While I was looking at the photograph Captain McMullen added,

"But you'll be doing take offs and landings without them. They'll be there when it's time to load and unload missiles, do maintenance and the rest. You did that at Fort Creech, didn't you? Take offs and landings?"

"We were just starting to learn how to do them by ourselves when I left, but I'm sure I can learn how to handle it pretty quickly. I got all the training on how to do it, and there will be guys on the ground if I need them, yes?"

"Of course. You'll have everything you need. There are a few more whistles and bells with some of these newer drones, but you'll start with the ones you're familiar with, and then we'll give you something different once you're safely back in the saddle."

"Works for me, and you'll give me specific instructions about what I'm supposed to do, right?"

"You mean your targets?"

"Yes."

"Of course, but let's not get ahead of ourselves. One step at a time. Next step is to get you hooked up and in the air."

"When do you want me out of there, Stephen?"

"How about in a week?"

"Fine with me."

"Alright. Let's plan on a week from this coming Monday. That'll give us both plenty of time to get this done. Sound good?"

"Sounds good with me. I haven't seen my oldest child in quite a while, so I'm thinking a trip to Florida might be in order. That will give me a chance to see him but, just in case, check with me in a day or two. I want to clear it with Ingrid."

"Okay, Buck. I'll do that. Alright then," he said, as he smiled broadly, "I think we're about ready to light this candle. Are you excited about this?"

I was in…lock, stock and barrel. I smiled, extended my hand, and said,

"You bet your ass I am, Stephen! This is a great opportunity to make some money and do some good. I miss being in the Army. I'm a soldier who just isn't physically able to fight anymore. I'm looking forward to going back to doing what I love to do!"

We shook hands, and Captain McMullen added, "We're gonna have some fun with this, Buck. I aim to kick ass and take names, but there will be times when we might not even stop to take names," and he busted out a hearty laugh.

"I'm up for it. Bring it on!"

"Oh, by the way, here's an advance on your salary." Captain McMullen said as he took an envelope out of his coat pocket and handed it to me.

"In fact, that's not an advance. That's your first paycheck. It's yours. That should make her happy. It will give you some money to make that trip to Florida."

"Thanks, Stephen. We need it, and I know that she'll appreciate it. I do."

"You're welcome. Trust me, this isn't a charitable organization you're working for. We're gonna get our money's worth from you. You're going to be great at this. You're the perfect man for the job."

Later that night, when I told her of the trip we would need to take, she wasn't happy about it.

"We don't have the money, and I really don't want to go to Florida right now. Why do we have to do this, Chris?"

"Because we have to be out of the house when this place is transformed from a semi-normal house, where a small, happy family lives, into some super-sleuth kind of place, so yes, we do, and," I said, as I took a wad of hundred dollar bills from the back pocket of my jeans, "to help us do this, I got my first month's pay…"

Ingrid snatched the money from me and started counting.

"Wow! That's more money than I've ever seen in my entire life… okay, those are a lot of good reasons."

"He said it would only take him a couple of days."

"Alright then. It's decided. We're going to Florida. Darla hasn't been to Disney World yet. She'll be so happy."

"You think she'll know? She's barely two years old."

"Of course she'll know. She watches those shows all the time. That stuff penetrates into her brain. No doubt about it. She'll know Mickey and Minnie, Goofy and all the rest. Absolutely she will."

"That's for you, isn't it, Ingrid, not for Darla. Admit it."

"Maybe, but Darla's going to love it, too."

"I wasn't planning on Disney, Ingrid."

"You've never been, have you, Chris."

"No, and that's because I hate it. I always have. Ever since I was a little kid living less than fifty miles away from it. I never wanted to go."

"You were a strange child, weren't you, Chris?"

"I had a few challenges, but I turned out okay, right?"

"Right, but we're going to Disney and Darla will absolutely love it."

"But Ingrid…"

"Don't Ingrid me…this is all about you and your new job. It's the least you can do, and now we have the M-O-N-E-Y to do it," she added, with a gleam in her eye as she re-counted the money in her hands, holding it in front of her eyes.

"I'll want to take Cliff with us," I responded.

"He's how old?"

"Seven, but he'll be eight soon."

"I have no problem with that? He'll like it, too, and it will give me an opportunity to get to know him better under pleasant circumstances. That's good."

"That's assuming his mother will let us."

"Why wouldn't she?"

"Who knows. She doesn't let me see him whenever I want. She always makes it difficult for me."

"Why? What did you ever do to her? Other than impregnate her, leave her, reject her and otherwise ruin her life?"

"That's not funny, Ingrid. I was just a kid, doing what every young American boy thinks about doing 24 hours a day."

"So what have you done to her lately?"

"Nothing, except pay her child support. It's like that Puddle of Mudd song…she fuckin' hates me."

"I like that song."

"You're not helping here, Ingrid."

"You ought to have that lawyer help you on that."

"He's told me that I need to file something with the Court and get the judge to set up a Parenting Plan for me, and then she couldn't refuse to let me see him."

"So do it."

"It costs money and we don't have any…or at least we didn't until quite recently. So I will, but that takes time and we're talking about a week from now."

"Just ask and see what she says. Maybe she'll be nice to you for a change. Maybe she'll agree. She gets that check for child support every month, right? She doesn't want to lose that. You're entitled to something. That's not right. You need to stand up for yourself, soldier."

"I know, but it's not cheap. It'll cost well over a thousand dollars to do it."

"And you pay how much per month?"

"Six fifty."

"Call and see. That's a lot of money."

"So since you agree to do this, should we leave first thing Monday morning, or when?"

"Fine with me. Whatever you say."

"It'll take us a good ten hours to get there. I'm thinking maybe we should leave Sunday night. I'll drive through the night while you and Darla can sleep. With luck, the two of you can sleep the whole way. I'll sleep when we get there. That way, you can do Disney on Monday, maybe the beach on Tuesday, and we can head back Wednesday afternoon or evening."

"Sounds good to me," Ingrid responded, but then I thought to myself about the long drive, and going to Disney, and I got to thinking it might not be that great of an idea after all, so I said to her,

"That's a long way to go for a short period of time, don't you think, Ingrid? Wouldn't you rather just go to Myrtle Beach? Or maybe just stay at a motel in town?"

"No. We're going to Florida," she said, emphatically.

"You're sure."

"Yes. Darla is going to love Disney."

"And so are you…so you won't mind taking her on Monday, while I sleep, and…"

"No way, cowboy! You're doing this, too! You think I was born yesterday? I know what it's going to be like. Disney is going to be swarming with kids, and it's going to be hot. I'm going to need your help, especially if Cliff is going with us. You're goin'!"

Late Sunday night, with Ingrid and Darla tucked under covers in the back seat, I began the long trek to Florida.

CHAPTER ELEVEN

The Plan

As soon as I turned off the engine, upon arriving home, after a long drive and a short, but happy, visit with Cliff and the mouse, Ingrid darted into the house, with me right behind her. She wanted to see what had happened to what had been the messy back room. I knew what she was up to, but I would have none of it.

"You promised!"

"Oh, come on! Just a peak!"

"No! Now go get Darla out of the car. I knew you were going to do that."

When I tried to open the door, I couldn't, because it was locked. I looked around and couldn't see a sign of where a key might be. Then I thought to myself that the Captain must have figured that might happen, and then I went back outside to help unload the car. I was ready to begin this new adventure, but it would have to wait until morning.

The next morning, Captain McMullen was on the phone.

"Okay, the key is taped underneath the mailbox. There are two keys, actually. Keep one on your person at all times and hide the other one very well."

"Will do. Want me to get it now, or wait and talk later?"

"It can wait. I left a disk on the desk, so watch the video and then we'll talk later. I'll call sometime mid-afternoon tomorrow. I figure you'll need some time to recover from that trip."

When Ingrid left the house to go to the store, I opened the door... slowly. My eyes lit up when I saw the array of screens lining two walls. There were a dozen or more on each wall. There was a chair and a large, triangular desk, with a keyboard and two telephones on it in the middle of the room, facing the two walls with the screens on them.

The third wall had shelves from floor to ceiling with supplies, a photocopier and a fax machine on them. It reminded me of Fort Creech. It wasn't too different from the rooms I had worked in while in the Army, except that I would be alone, not sitting side by side with other operators.

I sat down in the chair and visualized what it would be like once I was up and running. I knew it wasn't an easy job. Sitting and staring at screens, even large ones, took a toll. I remembered the bad days, boredom, eye strain, headaches, back aches, and countless hours where nothing too interesting or exciting happened.

At Fort Creech, at least I could take breaks and converse with other soldiers, men and women, about things. I wouldn't be able to do that this time. This was going to be difficult.

I remembered running the Manchu Mile and thought to myself that I had to approach this job like I approached the run...knowing it was going to be long, knowing it was going to be hard, knowing that I had to do it, and knowing that I would have to steel my mind and do my job. We needed the money. I couldn't fail.

I turned off the lights, locked the door and walked into the living room to watch some TV until Ingrid and Darla returned.

When they did, Ingrid started in on me.

"So what's it like?"

"It's like it was at Fort Creech, not much different. I'm the pilot of a plane and I push buttons and make the thing go where I tell them to."

"So how does it get in the air? You can't make it do that, can you? It's not like it was for you in Fort Creech in that way, is it? It can't be."

"Some things have changed. Operators are now able to do take offs and landings by themselves, but I'll still need help from people on the ground."

"But someone is there when it lands to put it back where it belongs?"

"I'm sure, but you're right, it takes a team. I'm not the only one involved in this project."

"But you don't know anybody else on your team, right?"

"No. I don't know anyone else who is involved other than my Captain."

"So what are you looking for again?"

"I don't know yet, and even if I did, I wouldn't tell you. This is top secret stuff. I'm not supposed to tell you anything, remember?"

"But I'm your wife. You're supposed to tell me everything...no secrets, remember?"

"You promised, Ingrid. Don't do this and, besides, you never asked me all these questions when I was at Fort Creech. Why now?"

"Because now you're in my house! It's a little closer to home."

"That's true."

"So how long can a drone stay up anyway?"

"It depends. Some can stay up for days."

"What about yours?"

"I don't know which one is going to be mine yet."

"So how long are you supposed to work? Will you have regular hours or what?"

""That's something I'll need to talk about with my Captain. He might want me to work some nights, but I know he expects me to work a 40 hour week. What do you think we should do? Four 10 hour days or five 8 hour days?"

"Depends on what hours I'll be working, if and when I get my job back. I think we'll have to coordinate our schedules when that happens, but for now, you can do whatever you want. That's entirely up to you."

I knew that I would probably be working nights, because that's when it would be daytime in Afghanistan. There's an 8½ hour time difference, so when it was 6:00 a.m. in Afghanistan it would be 9:30 p.m. on the east coast of the United States. I was trying to figure things out in my head while talking to Ingrid, making sure not to blurt out anything that would alert her to what I was really doing.

"I'm thinking I'll be working at night."

"If that's the case, I think we're going to need a sitter or two as back-up. You know we're going to have conflicts and neither one of us can miss work. Once I get back to work, I think we should put her in day care every morning. You'll be tired from the night before and so will I. That may be the only time the both of us can get some sleep. We'll need a sitter at night, too, probably, but if we do it right, maybe the nights you work won't coincide with the nights I work anymore than necessary."

"That makes sense."

"Why would they want you to work nights? Ingrid asked. "You can't see anything at night, can you?"

"Oh, yes I can. Night vision is pretty standard with these things. It's amazing what you can see."

"Really? That doesn't make sense to me. What's going on at night? People sleep at night. None of this makes sense to me. I think military intelligence is a contradiction in terms."

"But it pays well, right?"

"That it does, and if they're gonna pay you $7,500 a month I don't care if they tell you to clean out the elephants' cages at the zoo! You're gonna do whatever they tell you to do."

"Good! Does that mean you won't ask any more questions?"

"Of course not! That's half the fun…trying to figure out what the hell you're doing."

Just then the phone rang. It startled us. We didn't get too many calls, usually.

I answered it. It was Captain McMullen.

"Can you go inside your room now? I'm going to call you and make sure we're up and running."

"Sure."

Minutes later, when I was safely inside my cave, in my chair, the phone rang.

"Ready to go to work?"

"Yes, sir!"

"Okay. Well, let's decide when that will be. When do you want to work? What days are best for you?"

"If it's okay with you, I think the first part of the week would probably be best. That way I'd have the weekends off to be with my family."

"I'm fine with that. I want you to be airborne during the daytime hours in Afghanistan. So I'm thinking 10:00 at night until 6:00 in the morning, which is an 8 hour day, but I'm also thinking that four 10 hour days might be better for you. What would you prefer? Four 10 hour days or five 8 hour days?"

"I'd say the four 10 hour days."

"That's what we'll do then. 10:00 p.m. until 8:00 a.m. I can be flexible on the days of the week, but that's the way it's gotta be as far as the time of day is concerned."

"Ingrid and I talked about it, and we're going to put Darla in day care, if necessary, and we're going to line up some sitters for nights when we both have to work. We know that there will be times when something big, really big, comes along, and this has to be the most important thing in my life right now. I understand that, Captain."

"I can't allow you to let anything interfere with the mission. This is job one. Everything else is secondary, just like when you were in uniform and on duty. Are we clear on that?"

"Roger that, Captain."

"Good. Now, I've got a package on its way to you. It will be delivered by a man in a FedEx truck, but that's not a FedEx employee, so don't worry about that. I cannot emphasize enough how sensitive the material you're about to receive is, and I'm sure you can understand why. You have to assure me that what I give you will not fall into anybody else's hands, especially your wife's."

"Why, because she's German?"

"No, because she is the one most likely to find it. The only way she is going to see it is if you aren't careful and you allow her to see it."

"I'm not going to do that, Captain. I told you I wouldn't and I won't."

"I'm talking about little things like leaving the door open when you take a break and go to the bathroom, or to have lunch...things like that. I don't want this mission to fail."

"So if it's so super-sensitive, why me, Captain? Why not just have soldiers do this job at a secure base? If you need security so badly, which is understandable, why not keep it in the hands of the military?"

"I thought we went over this already...Buck, listen to me...the United States is being criticized from inside and outside of this country over our drone policy. Everybody, with a few exceptions, is tired of hearing about innocent women and children being killed by drone attacks. The Army doesn't want things to get to the point where it would take an act of Congress to fire a missile. They are not going to allow that to happen. That is the primary reason we are doing this."

"The Army is succumbing to all that pressure?"

"You bet your ass it is. The press is on all of us over this. The international community is getting in on the act, too. It's no longer politically correct to kill bad guys without a judge and jury ruling on it first."

"It's not that bad yet, is it? There's more to it than that, isn't there, Dozer?"

"No, it's not that bad, but it's getting worse, and you're right, there is more to it. The Afghans are really up our ass about these drones, as are the Pakistanis, so we're being more secretive than usual. It's really more about them than it is about us here in the U.S."

"I can understand that. That makes sense, and there are those in the military who don't want anyone outside of an inner circle to know what we're doing, I assume."

"You got that right. Chris. There are leaks the military, too. Not long ago, Congress was debating a bill which required anyone who operates a drone anywhere in the U.S. to register. We don't think that includes us, but you never can tell with the politicians. New regulations are being implemented every day, it seems. Hell, Amazon is planning to use them to deliver packages, for God's sakes! Think of it like this...we are trying to stay under the radar and out of sight."

"So is this is a 'black op'?"

"Not really. We're just not at Fort Creech. We're still within the chain of command."

"Okay. That's better. I think I know as much as I need to know. It makes sense to me. In the back of my mind, I still wonder, why me?"

"Remember, the less you know the better, and you're dealing with me, and only me. No one else. Got it?"

"Roger that, Captain."

"Now that we have a completely secure method of communicating, we will we be communicating only by phone."

"I'm going to miss those meals."

"Me, too. We'll probably meet face to face every now and then, but it's going to be mostly over the phone from now on."

"No problem."

"You'll be getting a list of assignments in that package and once you start, you might not hear from me for weeks at a time. The important thing is that you now have a way to contact me if you see something and need to let me know about it pronto."

"No one else will be on this line but the two of us?"

"That's right, and you're not to talk to anyone else but me about this. If I don't answer, all you have to do is say Omaha, and give the coordinates for what you see that is suspicious. Nothing else. Mistakes will happen, and that's understandable, but until you've got a drone with a hellfire missile attached to it, you're not going to be able to do anything other than be on the lookout for our targets. We'll pull up what you're seeing and give it a second look."

"So I'll have a spy drone?"

"That's right."

"So no E-mails? Text messages? Twitter? Nothing?"

"None of that stuff. This phone line will be the only way I communicate with you and that will only be for me to call you and you to call me. That's it. Nothing else. No more conversation on this line other than that. You are to use this line for no other purpose.

"Understood. So what if I have trouble with the drone? Or the machinery?"

"Then you call me. You let me know, and you're down until I get things fixed. If you can't get the bird home, or if you get shot down, or you lose your ability to see anything, something like that, you call that in. If I don't answer, just says the word Omaha and say XXXX if it is a serious problem, or Omaha X if it is more of a minor mechanical issue. If you say Omaha XX that's less serious, and Omaha XXX is more serious. Don't use the four X's unless it is damn serious, though, and then it's my problem, not yours. Again, you won't be dealing with anybody but me. Got it?"

"Roger that."

"And I mean if anyone calls and tells you that I told them to call, don't talk to them. Tell them they have the wrong number and hang up. That's for your protection, and mine."

"Whatever you say, Captain. I'm ready to go to work. I'm excited. Paybacks are hell and I'm ready to pay some people back for what was done to us over there."

"Alright then. I think we're good to go."

"So when are we going to light this candle?"

"Once you see that video I think you'll be ready. There's nothing much to this that you haven't already done when you were at Fort Creech. Getting the electronics in place has been taken care of and getting the bird in the air and back down are things you can do. How about Monday?"

"Fine with me."

"Then we're good to go on Monday night. Anything else?"

"So can we talk about where my drone is going to be and who and what I'm looking for?"

"It's in the video, but it's what I've told you all along…you'll be our eyes in the air over Nuristan province. You'll be going over, around and through Gowardesh, Kamdesh and Kunar valleys…your old stomping grounds. This should be familiar territory for you. There are ten potential targets on your list, and you will know some of them and, possibly, most of them. That will make it easier for you to identify them."

"And if I see any of the targets, I call it in."

"That's right."

"Nothing else? What about if I see what looks like a terrorist training camp? Or if I see bad guys coming across the border in bunches, things like that?"

"Call it in. Be discreet. If you think it's worth a call, do it. I'd rather err on the side of maybe you're right, rather than maybe you're wrong. Remember, we pulled out of there. As far as anyone else knows, we're not there. You're not there."

"But they know that drones are up there. Plenty of their people have been killed by drones in the last several years."

"That's right, they do, but they can't see you. They can't hear you, and they don't know you're there, but you're right. They're trying to stay out of sight and that includes sight from drones, so it won't be easy. Just be patient and let's hope for the best. If this was easy, we'd have already done it. Got it?"

"Roger that."

I was beginning to get the big picture, and I didn't have a problem with what I was being asked to do. I wouldn't want to see my picture on the front page of a newspaper about it, either. Until I had a hellfire missile on a drone, I was nothing other than a lookout.

"So what do you think your neighbors have to say about we did out there?"

"Nothing yet. It looks like a big antenna. If anyone asks, we'll just say it's a new Dish Network satellite system. How's that?"

"Don't say Dish. Someone might call Dish and say they want one like yours. Tell them it's something you got off the internet, that's it's an experimental thing. That should do it. Looks kinda cool, don't you think?"

"Yeah. It's not bad. We live in a quiet neighborhood. I'm not sure the neighbors will even notice. We don't talk to them much."

"Good. The less they know the better. We don't want any snoopers."

"They couldn't see in anyway. There are no windows in this room, as you know. You blocked them all off. I don't think it will attract much attention at all."

"I hope not. You live in the suburbs of a small town in South Carolina. Hopefully this won't attract any attention from anyone. Anything else?"

"Not on my end. Is that it for today, Captain?"

"I think so."

"What are you up to today?"

"Fort Benning."

"Baby brother about out of paratrooper school?"

"He's got another few weeks of training, but I'll get to see him for a couple of hours."

"Tell him I said hello."

"No. I won't do that. Not even him. This is between you and me, Chris. I don't want anyone else knowing about this. You are hidden deep."

"Got it."

"2200 hours on Monday the curtain goes up. Have fun with it. Let's find some bad guys. Good luck, Sergeant."

The training video and enough money to keep me paid up for another month arrived an hour later.

CHAPTER FOURTEEN

The Targets

A S SOON AS IT arrived, I was in my "War" room, pouring through the materials provided to me. Most of the information was about the newer drones I would be working with, but the most important part concerned the procedure to be followed when firing a missile. There was a strict protocol to be followed but, for me, I was required only to obtain authorization from Captain McMullen. The list of targets was included in the materials provided.

As I viewed the video and read the accompanying materials, I noticed that they applied to the CIA, Homeland Security, the FBI, and all branches of the military involved with the use of drones. The protocol was the same for all. I had no idea who was making the ultimate decisions on whether or not to fire a missile, or if each entity was allowed to make its own decisions. The trail ended, as far as I was concerned, with my Captain.

The more I thought about it, the more convinced I was that I had no problem doing what my former LT was asking me to do. I was to find Afghans who were either Taliban or al-Qaida leaders, not just the lower echelon terrorists who had waged war against my comrades and me in the Gowardesh valley, and take them out. That was fine with me. I had no reservations about doing just that.

Much of the stuff I already knew. It still made me chuckle whenever I read the name, Predator, thinking that it was an apt description of a drone. That un-manned aircraft was like a lion, tiger, crocodile or other predator…it hunted and killed its prey. I looked forward to having the opportunity to hunt down and kill the people responsible for killing and wounding so many of my fellow soldiers. It made me feel like I was a soldier again.

I found it amusing how the bombs carried by the drones were called "hellfire" missiles. "Hellfire" is right, I said to myself, just like Toby Keith's song about lighting up the sky and putting a boot up their ass. Just reading the materials fired me up.

I was interrupted by a loud pounding on the door. It was Ingrid.

"Honey! Do you want dinner?"

I looked at my watch. It was now 6:00. I'd been inside that little room for four hours, totally engrossed in what I was reading. I snapped out of the semi-induced trance I found myself in, stood, and walked to the door.

"Yeah. Thanks. I'll be right there."

I made sure to lock the door on my way out.

"Pretty interesting stuff, huh?" Ingrid asked.

"Yeah, it is," I responded.

"You think you're going to be able to do what it is they want you to do?"

"Oh yeah. No problem. It's definitely something I can do, I'm sure, but I still have a lot to read and learn."

"You can't talk about any part of it with me though, right?"

"Sorry, sweetheart. I can't. I gave my word. It's better that way."

"Are you going back in there tonight after dinner?"

"No, I'm not. I'm going to spend the rest of the night with you and Darla. I'll have to be in there for ten hours a day starting on Monday, so that's soon enough."

However, the next morning, a Sunday, before my wife or child was awake, I was back inside my new office, reading more of the materials provided to me. I was still a little concerned about how take-offs and landings were going to work. At Fort Creech, I knew that there were always people on the ground to call upon if I ran into any trouble. Now, I'd be doing them myself and I'd have to call the Captain if I had a problem.

I also wondered who the people on the ground in Afghanistan might be, and if they would be soldiers or someone else, like me, a former soldier. I made a list of questions to ask as I was reading. I interrupted my studies for an hour once Ingrid and Darla woke up, but after breakfast, I was back in my room, studying and taking notes, as if I was going to be tested.

Later that day, after lunch, I received a phone call.

"Have you done your homework?"

"I have, but I haven't quite finished yet."

"So are you going to be ready?"

"I will be in an hour or so, but, I have a few questions…"

"Buck, once you're ready, after a few days of test runs where you'll just be doing surveillance, I'm going to put missiles on your drone."

"What happened? I thought I was going to be operating a surveillance drone for a while. What's up?"

"Things are happening fast. The Taliban and al-Qaeda are still going to be your only concern, but things are crazy around here. I need to get you to work and deal with other things on my plate. ISIS is now the main focus of the entire civilized world, although splinter groups, or copy-cats, are popping up all over the place."

"And then there are the lone wolves, too."

"That's right, and everyone in the world is concerned about terrorists these days."

"And for good reason. Things seem to be getting worse."

"That's right, and December, when most of the military will be out of Afghanistan, will be here before you know it. So we're going to pick up the pace a bit on this. What questions do you have?"

"Well, for one, do the birds fly out of the Air Force base there outside of Kabul? Or Kandahar?"

"Neither one. We have a facility in the middle of nowhere. Nobody is anywhere near it. I thought I showed you a picture of it. Didn't I?"

"That's right, you did. Sorry. So I won't be attached to a military base?"

"Well, that's a military base, just not one that many people are familiar with. Anything else?"

"I'm a little fuzzy on how those folks will get the missiles on the birds and the rest without me being able to have any direct communication with them. I'm not going to have to worry about that, though, right? I communicate with you, that's it? That's all I need to know?"

"That's right. I'll take care of all of that. Your drone will be serviced and well taken care of. You just launch it and land it. Don't worry about the rest, Buck. What else?"

"So what type drone will I be getting?"

"You'll be working with a Predator and, by the end of the week, your drone will have two hellfire missiles on it. Later on, you might get a Reaper, which can hold four missiles, as you know. You're orders are to shoot on sight, once you identify a target and follow the firing protocol. Anything else?"

"So when I see one of the targets, I am to fire, once you give me the green light. Is that it?"

"That's right, Buck. You've got a limited number of high profile targets who are hiding from us, so you may not see any of them or fire a shot for a month, but when you see a target, you fire. Got it?"

"Got it."

"You've got to follow the protocol, though. That is for your protection, and mine. I've got to be able to say that we did things right, and then be able to prove it, if necessary. Any problem?"

"No sir. I don't see a problem. The room you created for me is pretty much the same as it was at Fort Creech. The equipment is hi-tech and it has all the whistles and bells I had out there, with a few new ones. Except for the take-offs and landings, it's the same, and that part about how I am to do the take-offs and landings was pretty clear in the materials. I don't see any problems at all."

"And listen, as far as that protocol is concerned, I just want you to notify me so I can say we went through the process. You just send me a message and that's it. Unless you hear back from me immediately, and I mean within ten minutes, you have my authority to fire at will. Got it?"

"Got it. I'm a sniper in the sky."

"That's right. There are others within the military who will still be doing the normal military stuff, looking for terrorist cells, training camps, fighters on the move and those kinds of things. We are on a completely separate mission. Have you looked at your targets? Do you see who they are?"

"Not yet. I've been focused on the procedure, mostly. I should be getting to that shortly."

"These guys are important people. I want you to know these guys inside and out. After you review what I've sent you, you'll know everything we have been able to find out about them. I want you to be able to recognize them on sight without any uncertainty on your part. That's part of the reason for this program....to focus on a small, select group of targets and not be distracted by other targets, or other objectives, like those training camps, vehicles or rank and file terrorists."

"Understood."

"Great."

"I'm ready, Captain, but you have other guys in on this, right? I'm not the only guy involved with these drones, am I?"

"No, you're not. You're part of a team, but you're my number one guy. I know you better than any of the others. I trust you more than anyone else on the team."

"So once I get a few missions under my belt, I'm ready to rock 'n roll."

"Curtain goes up tomorrow night. This is no longer a training exercise. These are bad guys that we want to get, and we haven't been able to get them using conventional methods. I'll be around to make sure you get off to a good start. Call if you have any problems."

"Will do."

"You're on a fixed schedule now, Buck. No changes unless approved in advance, and I really don't like changes, so try to keep it exactly the way it's set up, okay? Nothing gets in the way. That's what you asked for and that's what you got. Only in an emergency, and I mean an emergency, are we to change this schedule. Got it?"

"Roger that, Captain. I'm good to go."

From this point on, don't call unless it's one of the emergency situations we discussed, and don't expect to hear from me all that often. You're on your own, cowboy."

"Roger that."

"Good luck, Buck."

Captain McMullen had been kind enough to make posters of each one of the targets, blown up to 36" by 36". I carefully placed them on the wall behind me. It was game time.

The inaugural mission went off without a hitch, as did all the ones that followed, but three weeks into my mission I was becoming impatient. I'd been spending hours and hours staring at screens, looking for my targets, with no success. I was feeling as if it was a waste of time.

I was afraid that these guys weren't going to come out in the open. They knew we had eyes in the sky. I began to think that this wasn't going to work.

Then, just as I was about to give up my post for the day, I spotted a familiar figure. It was Mullah Abdul Anayatullah. I knew him to be a leader in one of the villages in Kamdesh. I knew the man.

I knew that the Anayatullah family had been chased out of the area by 10th Mountain back before the Blue Platoon was at Checkpoint Delta years before. Seeing him back in the village was a clear sign to me that the Taliban was back.

He was number five on the "hit" parade. This man had been responsible for the deaths of several men in the 10th Mountain. I had known some of the men who had died because of him. This was why I was here. It was battle stations.

I zoomed in on the man to confirm identification. This was exactly why Captain McMullen wanted me for this job. There was no confusion about who he was. This was no innocent civilian. This was no goat herder who looked like Anayatullah. This was the man we were looking for.

Anayatullah was walking, alone, down a dirt lane between a group of houses in the small village. I watched as the man entered a cleared area and began bending over and moving about slowly. He was holding a basket in one hand and moving his other hand about. I figured he was in his garden.

It was getting dark, and the window of opportunity was closing, so I hurriedly armed my missiles and began going through the firing sequence. As I was nearing the final step, after obtaining authorization from Captain McMullen, preparing to launch a missile, several small children ran out of a house and circled around Anayatullah.

The children began putting things in the man's basket. I could see him smiling and engaging with the children. I backed off. I wasn't going to risk killing innocent children. I waited, hoping the children would leave and the man would be alone again.

I watched as Anayatullah and the children left the garden and entered one of the houses at the end of the lane. I eased back in my chair, exhaled, and said, "Damn!"

I debated whether or not I should continue to monitor the house, but it was late in Afghanistan. The sun was going down there whereas it was well up in Greenville. I decided against it, but I had found a target.

I was tired. I had worked a ten hour day, and I would be back at work later that night, so I entered the necessary commands to fly the craft back to base. I would have to make sure that the craft was safely on the ground, which would take half an hour or so to accomplish, before I could close up shop.

When I was finished, I stumbled out of my cave. Ingrid and Darla were up having breakfast. I quietly joined them.

"Well, hello, stranger! Welcome back to the human race! You look tired," Ingrid said, warmly.

"I am."

"So how did things go last night?"

"Good. Good. I had a good night last night."

"You don't seem to mind it too much. Is everything going well?"

"Yeah, it is. It was slow at first, but last night was the best night so far. I'm okay with it. It's a job and it pays well. As long as I get paid, I'm there."

"What's it like? Can you tell me that much?" Ingrid asked.

"It's like playing a video game or something like that."

"A video game?"

"Actually, operating a drone remotely is very much like a video game. The only difference is that these are real people. I read somewhere that people who were good at playing video games on computers were actually better than soldiers who had learned to operate drones through the military. I don't want to believe that was true, but that's what I read."

"I would think you'd get tired just staring at a computer screen all day." Ingrid said.

"I do, but so do thousands of other people all across the country and the world, and I get to do it from the comfort of my house. Not everybody can do that."

"That's true. I'm glad you're here," she said, as she gave me a kiss on the top of my head.

"The four day work week helps. I look forward to the days off when I can spend all my time with the two of you!"

I picked Darla up from behind and pulled her into my arms. She shrieked with delight.

Ingrid tried to engage me on some other issues, such as what was going on in her life that day, but my mind was still on my drone and Anayatullah. The thought of leaving my target for the rest of the day was still bothering me.

Even though I wanted to stay on task for a while longer, I thought that there were men on the ground in Afghanistan who were expecting me to land my bird at about the same time every day. I figured that if I stayed out longer than I was supposed to that some sort of bells would go off. I really didn't know, for sure, but this wasn't an emergency. I didn't think that it was justified in this case, but I was second-guessing myself. I had found a target and I knew where to look later that night.

"Do you mind if I run off to bed now? Let me get a few hours of sleep and I'll catch up to the two of you later, okay, sweetheart?" I asked.

"Of course! We're going to the park later this morning, if you wake up in time."

"I'll do my best to be there."

"You need the sleep. Hope you can join us, but that comes first."

"I'm off for three days after tonight. I can sleep then."

"Okay. We'll look for you."

"12:00, 12:30 or so? That'll give me almost three and a half, four hours…I should be good by then."

"Okay. See you then."

Later that night, I was back on the job, refreshed and encouraged by my recent success, even though nothing had come of it yet. Once the bird was airborne I re-directed my drone back to the village. I began circling around the house I had seen Anayattallah enter fourteen hours earlier.

Everything was ready. I was in the right place, at the right time, and with the right equipment. I waited patiently, like a predator stalking its prey, high above my target, so high that the sound of the drone couldn't be heard by the humans below, nor could it be seen by them with the naked eye.

It was early morning in Afghanistan. An hour later, a lone figure emerged and walked out towards his small garden. I zoomed in and confirmed the person to be my target. Without any hesitation whatsoever, after going through the protocol, and after receiving authorization from Captain McMullen, again, I pushed a button and unleashed two Hellfire missiles earthbound.

I stared intently at the screen and followed the flight of the missives through the air. I counted the seconds and, when the first Hellfire missile made contact with its target, I saw a miniature explosion occur. I slapped my hands in the air and, just as the second missile was landing on the target, yelled,

"Yes!"

I had accomplished my first kill.

I typed in the coordinates to direct the craft to another area of the region. I walked out of my room, proud of what I had accomplished, hoping to share a moment of joy with someone, but Ingrid and Darla were both sound asleep. What would I have told them anyway? Nothing.

There was no one to share the moment with. I knew that Captain McMullen would know, because he authorized the strike, but we hadn't talked about reporting kills. This was the first one. How should it be reported? I wasn't sure, so I did nothing.

I was delighted with what I had accomplished, but it was somewhat less than completely satisfying not to be able to share the moment with anyone. After a few self-congratulatory minutes, I settled back into my chair and went back to work.

The rest of the night went uneventfully. I returned the bird to its base and turned off all of the equipment. I had the next three days off.

Before I left the room, I used a black magic marker and drew an "X" across Anayattullah's face.

CHAPTER THIRTEEN

More Kills

ONE ITEM OF BUSINESS that I was required to do on a daily basis was to read the Stars 'n Stripes newspaper cover to cover, as well as the Washington Post.

"If something important happens in Afghanistan, both of those two newspapers will let the world know about it," Captain McMullen had told me.

I read in the Saturday edition of both papers reports of the killing of Anayattullah. The Post's article indicated that innocent women and children were also killed by the drone attack. The majority of the article questioned the efficacy of the usage of drones. The issue was a hot political topic in Washington and had been for quite some time.

The Stars 'n Stripes article said that there was a claim that innocent civilians had been killed in addition to Anayattalla, but that nothing had been confirmed. The thrust of the article was that another high ranking member of the Taliban had been brought to justice. The article discussed the number of enemy fighters killed by drones over the years.

Even though the article was wrong regarding anyone other than Anayattalla being killed, I was glad to see it in print. I now knew that Captain McMullen and the whole world knew about it. It made me smile. Ingrid saw me smile and asked,

"Anything interesting in the paper, Dear?"

"No. Same old stuff," I responded.

That Monday night, encouraged by the attention I was sure Captain McMullen was getting, and by my participation in it, I went back to work with a renewed sense of purpose.

I found myself studying the pictures of the men on my target list over and over, and from different angles. I had gone over them dozens of times already, but I wanted to make sure that I knew their faces well. I might only get a glimpse of a man. I wanted to feel confident in making a positive identification, and then be able to pull the trigger without hesitation.

There was Haji Usman from Gawardesh, a border village. I knew the man. I had heard rumors, which I was sure were true, that he was a timber smuggler and that he had many fighters under his command. Much of the forests in that part of the country had disappeared due to illegal logging.

Usman was suspected of killing a number of U.S. soldiers in the Gowardesh Valley. I'd heard stories of how men from the 3-71st Cavalry Unit had been killed because of him before I got there. Men I didn't know, but they were my brothers-in-arms. I would like nothing more than to find him and avenge those lives. I knew his face and I knew the area that he roamed. I was on the lookout for him.

Gul Mohammad Khan was another Mujahadeen fighter who was suspected of ties to the Taliban. He was a Mullah, or leader, of a large number of men who roamed the Gowardesh Valley. He was over in the area near Agasi and Urmul, and although that was less than thirty miles away from Checkpoint Delta as the crow flies, it was days away by foot. The Blue Platoon seldom strayed more than a day's march from its base, so we hadn't been in that part of the country, but I had heard of this man and I wanted to make sure his face was firmly imbedded in my brain.

Ahmad Shah was known to be an al-Qaeda operative. Everyone knew that he was one of a large number of Syrians who were operating out of the tribal lands in northwestern Pakistan and coming across the mountains to cause trouble in Afghanistan.

Shah was one of the men the Blue Platoon was on the lookout for at Checkpoint Delta. He had escaped detection for years. I had seen his face before and now I was planting it in my brain. I hoped to find him.

Another target was an al-Qaeda operative named Abu Ikhlas. He was linked to the deaths of soldiers at FOB Lybert and Lowell. He had been on the list of people to look for at the border crossings when I was at Checkpoint Delta. I had seen his face before, too.

It puzzled me how the United States Army could set up a checkpoint at or near the border of Pakistan, put a wooden bar across a dirt path in the middle of nowhere, and expect terrorists, like Abu Ikhlas, to simply walk up to the checkpoint. Perhaps the thinking was that U.S. soldiers couldn't tell one Afghan, Syrian, or Chechnyan, from another, and they could pass by undetected. I always figured that they simply took other routes, since they knew the terrain so well.

Regardless, even though Blue Platoon didn't ever capture many suspected terrorists at Checkpoint Delta, the Army brass apparently thought it worked as a deterrent, so the practice was continued for several years. As far as I was concerned, the use of drones was, by far, the best way to locate and eradicate known terrorists.

Better to be half way around the world in the comfort of my home, operating a drone, than lying on the ground with a rifle in hand, hoping to get one of the bad guys in my sights. I prayed that Abu Ikhlas, or one of the others, would come into my view one day.

Hakimullah Mehsud was also on the list. He had been identified by the United States as a known terrorist for his alleged involvement in an attack on Forward Outpost Base Chapman in Khost, Afghanistan. He was actually part of the Pakistan Taliban, but he did much of his dirty work in Afghanistan, too.

I didn't know him, because he operated further south from where the Blue Platoon was situated, but I knew of him. Hakimullah had become the leader of the Pakistani Taliban after his fellow clan member, Baltullah Mehsud, a relative, had been killed in 2009 by a drone strike.

As far as I was concerned, we didn't need any more justification for what we were doing with the drone strikes. They worked! We never would have found those guys without these drones.

I went through everyone on the list, every day, taking my time as I did so. The last person on the list, although he was said to be the number one target, was Mullah Mogabbi. He was the leader of the Afghani Taliban.

The U.S. had put a 10 million dollar bounty on his head shortly after September 11, because it was believed, and eventually confirmed, that Mullah Mogabbi had been protecting Osama bin Laden in the days and weeks after that horrific event. Yet, in the dozen years since, little more had been learned of the man and no one knew where he was.

It was strange to me how could it be that we know so little about this man? How was I supposed to find him if they couldn't? And all we had on this guy was one photograph? So all I knew was that he was tall and blind in one eye. Great. What was I going to do with that?

I had plenty of time to think about things while operating my drone. While in the Army, a soldier doesn't question command decisions as much as one does after leaving the Army, especially a low-ranking soldier, even a sergeant such as I had been.

But during those long nights, when Ingrid and Darla were sound asleep, in the quiet of the nice, suburban neighborhood just outside of the Greenville, South Carolina city limits, where we lived, I couldn't help but reflect back on my days as a soldier in the Nuristan province of northeastern Afghanistan and wonder why we had been there and whether or not we had done any good while there.

We only had one full fighting brigade in all of Afghanistan, whereas there were fifteen brigades in Iraq. There were four aviation brigades in Iraq but only one in Afghanistan. What was up with that? We were the ones doing the fighting.

We had been sitting ducks, fighting an enemy on its turf, basically hand-to-hand, giving them the upper hand and allowing them to throw the first punch! It just didn't make sense to me. I asked myself over and over why we didn't have more help. I couldn't understand the logic behind that strategy.

My most pleasant memories of my time there were of the incredible beauty of the area. The Hindu Kush mountains were majestic, and they spanned the horizon for as far as one could see. The Landay-Sin River, which flowed out of the Hindu Kush not far from us, was as beautiful as any river I had ever seen.

However, that beauty masked a poverty unlike any I had ever seen as well. In Nuristan province, only 2 percent of all households had access to safe drinking water. People lived in structures made of stone, some possibly dating back to when Alexander the Great roamed the area some twenty five hundred years earlier. The ground didn't yield much by way of vegetables and foodstuffs, and goats were the primary source for milk, cheese and meat.

The United States had tried valiantly to make sure that it didn't repeat the sins of its past, and not simply destroy everything in its path, kill innocent people and try to militarily beat the inhabitants into submission. The United States tried to win the hearts and minds of the Afghan people. That hadn't worked.

We had come into the area and built gravity-fed water distribution systems in Mandiga, Gawardesh, Urmul, Kamdesh and other places. We had built micro hydroelectric plants, improved roads, paid locals a lot of money to work on the roads, paid millions of dollars to build schools, provide training and improve the quality of life for those poor people. I, personally, had distributed tons of bags of rice, beans and flour, as well as hand out teacher and student kits.

I knew that the United States had tried valiantly to win the hearts and minds of the Afghans, but there was no way that was going to happen. Those people weren't in the third world, they were in a different world altogether. There was no way we were going to bring them into the 21st century in a matter of a few years. It was going to take decades, maybe generations.

At the time I left, there wasn't anyone in the Blue Platoon who felt any warmth coming from the Afghans. I was sure, deep in my heart, that there were those who appreciated what I and the others had tried to do, but we were outsiders. We were strangers in a strange land. Nothing had changed from the time the U.S. first entered Nuristan Valley until the time the U.S. pulled out, as far as I could tell.

I think we should have just picked up and left that God-forsaken place once we got bin Laden, but we were still there...and in Iraq...and now in Syria...and Egypt...and Libya...and Somalia...and Pakistan. The Middle East was fomenting in the midst of what had been called the Arab Spring. To some, that was democracy finding its root in areas that had been ruled by despots for centuries.

To others, it was the beginning of a Jihad, or holy war, by Muslims against all those who were not true Muslims, and that included others who did not believe in the same strain of Islamic faith that they did. The Sunnis would fight the Shi'ites with the same degree of ferocity as they would the Russians, or the Americans, or the English, or the Greeks, or anyone else who came upon their lands.

I understood that the problems were complicated, and that money was, as always, one of the underlying problems but, to me, the problem was simple...we didn't belong there. The natural gas and other resources in Afghanistan undoubtedly played a major role in the decision to stay in Afghanistan but, for me, that wasn't good enough. We weren't going to change their way of life overnight.

How could it be that we hadn't learned that lesson yet? And why were we continuing to be dependent on foreign oil, and on oil itself? The oil companies were making gigantic profits, and they were global companies, but now we were getting huge amounts of natural gas through a controversial process called fracking. Environmentalists were concerned, but the use of natural gas helped to bring the price of gas at the pumps down enormously, so little was done about it, although some States banned it entirely. I hoped that Elon Musk will help find the answer to some of those problems with his battery operated cars.

I had to keep my mind on the task at hand, and that was to find the enemy leaders. I was operating my drone at 50,000 to 60,000 feet above sea level, and about 40 some thousand feet above the crests of the Hindu Kush. I was able to scan a wide area from that height. I was focusing most of my attention that night, as I did on most nights, on the border areas, hoping to find some bad guys crossing over from Pakistan into Afghanistan.

But it didn't take much effort to turn my attention to the Kamdesh Valley at that altitude. Kamdesh was due west of Checkpoint Delta, whereas the Naray and the Kunar Valleys were due south of Checkpoint Delta.

Haji Akhtar Mohammad was number seven on my list. He was a local man from Kamdesh who received huge amounts of money from the United States for many of the building projects undertaken in that area. Many times, those Afghans who worked with the U.S., and took our money, were captured, tortured, mutilated and killed by the Taliban for cooperating with us, but nothing ever happened to Haji. He was, apparently, playing both sides of the fence.

I figured that the U.S. got tired of being used, which was why he was on my list. He might not even have known that he was on a kill list. I thought that he might be still walking about town like he was a big shot, with all that money he took from us, so I decided to make him my number one priority that night.

Kamdesh is a small village in Nuristan Province, but it is the capital of the Kamdesh District. The U.S. Army had several bases in the area, including Combat Outpost Keating, Observation Post Fritsche and Combat Outpost Lowell. In 2010, the U.S. and NATO commander in Afghanistan, General Stanley McChrystal, decided to abandon all of the combat outposts and focus more attention on the areas with more people in them.

The result was that the entire province of Nuristan had become a Taliban stronghold. There were no U.S. soldiers left in the area. The Afghan government had all but conceded the area as well, although a makeshift government continued to function as best it could.

Dos Mohammad was another man on the list. He was the leader of the 2009 attack on Combat Outpost Keating, and he was thought to be still in the area as well. The Battle for Camp Keating was a particularly stinging event. I knew all about the many soldiers who died and the men who received Medals of Honor for their bravery in repelling an assault on their base by an enemy that outnumbered them five to one, at least.

I had multiple targets right in the Kamdesh area, not far from where I had been stationed. I was to stay there in that part of the country and see what turned up. Those were my orders.

The good part of the withdrawal of U.S. forces from Afghanistan was that the bad guys were no longer as afraid of coming out in the open, though they were aware of the possibility of being killed by a drone, since several of its leaders had been killed by drones, but it wasn't nearly as likely to happen as it would, or might, if soldiers were there. Some may have felt safer, and less vulnerable, with no armed forces to oppose them anywhere close by. If they got the least bit overconfident, and showed themselves, I was going to light them up.

Sure enough, one late afternoon in Afghanistan, as the sun was coming up in South Carolina, a man who looked much like Dos Mohammad, showed up on my screen. I immediately zoomed in him. He was surrounded by several armed men. They had come out of a house in the village and were about to get in a vehicle.

I didn't see any women or children, and I believed this to be a confirmed sighting, so without any hesitation whatsoever, I went through the firing protocol and, after Captain McMullen gave me the green light, I fired two Hellfire missiles at my target. I watched as both missiles hit the vehicle at approximately the same time. I put a large "X" across his face on my poster.

A few days later, I was pleased to see a headline in the Stars and Stripes that Dos Mohammad was reported as having been killed by a drone strike in Kamdesh, Afghanistan. The article went on to re-tell the details of the Battle for Camp Keating and of the many soldiers who were awarded medals for their bravery in that battle.

I had been on the job for over almost two months and had not heard a word from Captain McMullen. I had killed two of the men on my target list in that time, and didn't know if that was good or bad. Was I performing to the Captain's expectations or not? I wanted some feedback, but I knew better than to ask for it, so I continued on.

A week later, while combing the valleys around Kamdesh, again, I saw a figure emerging from a house of worship. All Muslims are required to pray five times a day, and to prostrate themselves before their God. I had looked at people coming and going from those mosques on many, many occasions, in different areas, thinking that I might find one of my targets, without success, until today.

I zoomed in to confirm the sighting. It was definitely Haji. There was no mistake about it. His facial characteristics were unique, as was his rotund body, but the American-style horned-rim black glasses were the give-away. It was him.

But, since he was leaving a mosque, he was doing so with others, some of whom were older male children, too young to be called men, but too old to be called boys. I would have to be patient. I watched as Haji spoke with other worshipers. I waited as Haji strolled down the dirt streets of Kamdesh to the very last house on the block, and entered it.

Once Haji was inside the building, I had a dilemma. I had no idea who else was in the house, but I knew that Haji was there. Did I want to risk killing a woman or a child to kill a known enemy? Was there anyone else in the building? What was I to do?

"Fuck it!" I said to myself as I went through the protocol. Ten minutes later, when I didn't hear anything back from my Captain, I pushed the button to cause the Hellfire missiles to be released from the harnesses which held them and I watched them descend through from the sky towards their destination. I watched as the house exploded into a ball of fire as both missiles struck the target.

I wasn't quite as happy to read headlines in the Washington Post a few days later which lambasted the use of drones since two innocent children and his wife were killed, together with Haji, that night. The article indicated that the branch of the military responsible for the attack had not been identified.

I resented the criticism. This was a legitimate target. He was a bad guy. The press didn't jump all over Reagan when he sent missiles into Al-Gaddafi's house and killed his children and one of his wives. I didn't get it. I felt that the country should have been happy about that kill. Another Taliban bad guy bit the dust. I didn't know the wife and kids were in the house. Those things happen. That's war, and we were still at war with them.

A few days later, I received a call from Captain McMullen.

"When can I see you?"

"Is tomorrow soon enough?"

"10:00 sound good?"

"Usual place?"

"Yep."

"See you then."

We met at the Dillard House, again, and sat in the same general location as before within the wide expanse that was the dining room.

"You're doing a great job, Buck! I'm so proud of you!"

"Thanks, Captain…"

"Steve, please. We're in public now."

"Sorry. We're alone, and I didn't think anyone could hear us, but that's no excuse. Thanks, Steve. I wasn't sure if I was going to get chewed out today or get a pat on the back."

"You get a big pat on the back, Buck. You've taken out three of the targets on your list. That's great! Do you know how long we've been looking for these men? Dos Mohammad? Do you know how many men saw that? Some men were so happy they cried when they heard that news. The Battle for Keating was one of the worst days in our recent military history."

"And the best. Those men fought courageously and prevented a massacre."

"Yeah, and many died and many more were seriously injured. That was a huge victory for all infantrymen and the Army. That was huge, Buck. Are you kidding me? You thought I was going to be upset?"

"Well, the national papers gave us a bunch of shit over me getting Haji's wife and kids."

"Haji Ahktar Mohammad was a turncoat. We took him into our confidence. We gave him a ton of money, and all the while he was providing the Taliban with information about us. That man deserved to die for what he did to us. I, personally, met with that man on several occasions and, believe me, I was nothing but happy about that. I had no problem whatsoever with what you did. You were following orders."

"Even though you didn't actually authorize it?"

"I told you to fire if you didn't hear from me and that's what you did. I had no problem with that whatsoever."

"But all that business about killing innocent civilians…"

"Buck, this is war. Innocent people die in firefights, too. This is why we have the drone program. The criticism of what we do doesn't make a damn bit of sense to me, really, since we would never have found any of these guys through conventional means. Drone warfare is, I think, the best possible method of warfare for us right now. Do you think for one minute that I would rather have you out at Checkpoint Delta, living like a rat behind Helios barriers, unable to stand up for months and months without fear of being shot? And I'm an infantryman myself! No way, partner. No way. This is way better, and the death of innocents is called collateral damage. That is an unfortunate, but unavoidable, part of war."

"I'm glad to hear you say that. I feel the same way. When I was on the ground, if I had a good day, I would kill a bad guy or two. Sometimes those were just kids, or goat herders doing the Taliban's dirty work. I'm going after the leaders now. To kill a snake you cut off its head, right?"

"That's exactly right, Buck, and you're doing a great job."

"So what's up? Are you here just to congratulate me or was there something else?"

"I thought you might be worrying about the press, so I decided to come down and give you a vote of confidence, that's all. I could have talked to you on the phone, but I decided to come see you, so I'm here."

"Thanks, Dozer. I appreciate that. I'll admit it. I was a little concerned after I read those articles."

"Don't be. I've got your back. You know that."

"I do, and I thank you for that. So the press doesn't know who fired the missiles?"

"That's right."

"Who do they think did it?"

"They're thinking it's one of the operators from Fort Creech, but they don't know which branch of the military did it, Chris, and they want to know. It's like what went on in the Ukraine a while back. They know that the separatist rebels fired the missile that took down that Malaysian airliner, but all you hear on the television and talk shows is that they don't know who pulled the trigger, and that's the same situation here."

"Who cares? What difference would it make?"

"They just dig and dig and dig until they have gotten every last tidbit of information out of a story. They don't know and we're not going to tell them. Let them try to figure it out. Trust me, they won't."

"That's good. I'd rather nobody knows it was me."

"They won't. I've got things under control. Buck. No one will ever know about your involvement in this, I promise you."

I thought about that for a few seconds, and then responded,

"I'm good with that. I guess that's what a clandestine operation is, right?"

"That's right, and I've got a package to give you when we leave. I've added a few people to the list, now that a few names have been taken off of your list."

"Great. Anything else?"

"No, that's about it. I can't tell you how happy I am that this is working out the way it is. I just knew you were the perfect guy for this job, and you were."

"Thanks, Steve. I appreciate the vote of confidence."

"And the money is helping out?"

"Oh yeah. It's helping tremendously. I don't know what we'd do without it. Ingrid still isn't back to work yet, so this is allowing us to do things we wouldn't have been able to do, like plan a trip back to Germany, among other things."

"Do you have plans to go back to Germany now?"

"We haven't set a date yet, but we're hoping to go back sometime in the Fall for a short visit. All of Ingrid's family is there. We've got the money set aside so, when we decide to go, we'll make the reservation."

"I'm glad to be able to help, and there's enough money in that package to hold you over for another month, just in case I don't see you again for a while. I'll need at least two weeks' notice before you go off to Germany, once you decide."

"Oh, I'll be able to do better than that, I'm sure."

"Two weeks is good enough, but the more advance notice you give me the better, okay?"

"Okay, and thanks, Steve. I really can't tell you how much I appreciate this. I like doing this. It's almost as good as being back in the Army. I want to die with my boots on, not in some nursing home."

"Like the Vikings of old, right?"

"Or the Spartans. They were favorites of mine, too. Those boys were soldiers to the core."

"They were serious alright. I'm not sure I believe that story about three hundred Spartans versus tens of thousands of Persians, though."

"At Thermopylae?"

"Right."

"It's a great story, though. I would have loved to have been one of those three hundred men."

"Well, you'd have died with your boots on if you were, Buck. They all died in that battle, as I recall. So I'm glad to hear that it's working out well for you and your family. I'm happy with the way that it's going, too. Keep up the good work, Buck. Drone warfare is here to stay. I can see us doing this for some time to come."

"I'm glad I got the training when I did. I didn't want to be injured and unable to be an infantryman any longer, but it turned out to be a blessing in disguise, I guess. I can still fight."

"You have a skill that few others have. You may be the soldier of the future…a man with a computer instead of a rifle."

"By the way, how's your brother doing?"

"He's in Vicenza at the moment."

"Just like we were, though I wasn't there long. They sent me to Bamburg not long after I got there."

"I remember."

"So what's he doing?"

"He's being trained for a special unit that can be sent into hot spots at a moment's notice. He's a Ranger, but he works with Navy Seals and other elite units. He loves it."

"He just got out of Paratrooper school and now he's being trained to be a Ranger! That's great!"

"He's doing really well. I don't expect him to see any action for a while, but he will before too long, I'm sure."

"So you won't get to see much of him once that happens, will you?"

"Not as much as I want, but I'll see him every chance I can get, even if it means flying halfway around the world. Whenever he gets a few weeks off for R & R, I'll make it a point to meet up with him. I saw him a few weeks ago in Cannes."

"France?"

"Yeah, the kid wanted to go to the French Riviera before reporting to Vicenza, so we did. He wanted to see those French women in bikinis and gamble in Monaco."

"That must have been fun."

"It was. I don't really care much for the place, but it was great being with him. He's become a fine, fine young man. I just couldn't be prouder of who he is and what he is."

"I can tell. Congratulations, Dozer. You're responsible for that, to a large extent, since he didn't have anyone else to look out for him after your folks died."

"I know, but military schools aren't for everyone. That was the best I could do, and he didn't fight me on it. Some kids would have. A military life isn't for everyone."

"I'd say he seems to have taken to it pretty well."

"I just hope that's what he really wants from life, not just to follow in his older brother's footsteps because he had no choice."

"It sounds like he's having a blast."

"He's alive and well, thank God. Maybe someday you'll meet him."

At that, the Captain stood and said, "Buck. I've got to go. Good seeing you. I'd like to stay longer, but I've got a plane to catch. I hope to be reading more good news in the Stars and Stripes about your activities again soon."

That Monday night, encouraged by Captain McMullen's words, I was back to work, feeling much better about how I was doing.

I maneuvered my craft back into the Kamdesh District. I still had several more targets, plus some new ones. There were hundreds of villages in Kamdesh Valley and I was particularly enthused by the prospects of finding any of the four new people on my list. One of the other men on my list had been killed by somebody else.

Two of the new names on the list were Amir Khan Muttagi and Mullah Abbas Akhund. I had never heard of them before, but Captain McMullen provided some background information and I learned that they were two of the people in the Taliban who had governed Afghanistan prior to the time the U.S. and others entered the country. They had been in hiding since 2001.

I wasn't a foot soldier anymore, looking to defeat an enemy fighter with a gun pointed at me. My targets were the leaders, and the most prominent ones at that. We were out to kill snakes and, if I was successful, we were going to cut off some heads. I repeated that expression to myself several times a day.

CHAPTER FOURTEEN

Unrest throughout the world

I SAT IN THE KITCHEN early one morning, after completing my ten hour shift, eating my breakfast and reading my two favorite newspapers, the Stars 'n Stripes and the Washington Post, while Ingrid scurried after Darla, who was now running around the house. Both papers were summarizing the events of 2014 and discussing the prospects for 2015. The news wasn't good.

The biggest current event was the killing of Charlie Hebdo and his staff of cartoonists in Paris in early January. Four million people, including the heads of state of numerous countries, joined together in solidarity to support freedom of the press and to show their opposition to the terrorists. The whole world was on alert, fearful of more attacks.

Another article told how the problems in the Ukraine remained unresolved, and Russian separatists continued their acts of defiance, while the Russian military hovered along the border, menacingly, and, according to many reports, was already inside the Ukraine. I could understand the point that no one had discovered the identity of the person who actually pulled the trigger on the weapon that brought down the Malaysian airliner, but the entire world seemed to agree that it was one of the separatists within the Ukraine who had done it and he had done it with a weapon supplied by the Russians. Economic sanctions were being imposed upon Russia. Putin remained defiant.

Other articles discussed what was going on in Iraq, Syria, Egypt,

Libya and throughout much of the rest of the Middle East. The "Arab Spring" had become an opportunity for extremist Muslim groups to seize power, and Christians were being slaughtered. Chaos was rampant throughout the region.

Some of the rebel groups in Syria had become so bad that it now seemed as if the world community would prefer to see Bashar al Assad's government prevail. This was a seemingly complete turnabout since the United States, and many other nations, including France, had demanded that Assad resign months earlier, after the United Nations determined that Assad had, indeed, used chemical weapons on his own citizens. The more moderate rebels, who the United States openly supported, were losing the battle.

Christians in Iraq and Syria were being annihilated by a Muslim extremist group which called itself the Islamic State of Iraq and Syria, or ISIS. Things were so bad that even the Taliban denounced the horrific practices of ISIS, which, like the Taliban, had a fundamental goal of establishing Islamic States throughout the entire Middle East, beginning in Iraq and Syria.

ISIS had taken control of many cities in the north of Iraq and was mounting an offensive against Bagdad itself. Although the United States had pulled its combat troops out of Iraq, Nouri al-Maliki, the Prime Minister of the country, a Shi'ite, had asked the United States to provide military assistance, especially air power, to help combat the insurgents. President Obama was reluctant to re-engage and, therefore, refused, at first. Not long after that, al-Maliki was replaced because he was thought to be partly responsible for the rise of ISIS, which was comprised of Sunnis.

However, shortly thereafter, Obama reluctantly sent in a few hundred troops to save a group of Christians called the Hezzidis. The city of Queragosh, which had a large Christian community within it, had been overtaken by ISIS. Reports being circulated in the media indicated that children were being beheaded. Christians were told to convert to Islam, leave, or die.

The worst news out of Iraq, as far as the United States was concerned, was that journalists, four of whom were United States citizens, had been beheaded, and more such atrocities were sure to follow. Incredibly, the incidents were filmed and put out over the internet. In early September, NATO had agreed to form a coalition to eradicate the group, if possible, through air strikes, not troops on the ground. Air strikes had begun but little had been accomplished. By the end of December, some success had been achieved, but not even close to the degree desired.

ISIS wasn't backing down. It threatened to take the war into the United States. More journalists were beheaded, one a Brit, another a South African, a third was from France, and then a Japanese journalist was killed. ISIS threatened more killings if ransoms were not paid. The entire world was appalled. Air strikes into Syria became more frequent. More countries joined the coalition. The terrorists were to be bombed wherever they could be found. It became clear, fairly soon, that the air campaign, alone, was not going to be enough.

It seemed as if the entire Middle East was in armed conflict. What few countries in the region that were not torn apart by war were over-run with refugees from the war-torn countries. Every country was involved. Several countries in the region agreed to join with the United States and fight the extremists.

Most of the conflict centered around differences in religion. Radical Muslim groups, some Sunnis and some Shi'ites, were seen as the cause of all of the violence. There were splinter groups of Muslim extremists at work, as well. One group, called Boko Haram, had captured hundreds of young girls in Nigeria and were committing atrocities. Another group, called Al-Shabaab, was causing problems in other parts of Africa. There were other radical groups, too, in Yemen and Libya and elsewhere. More moderate Muslims pleaded that the extremists did not represent the true Islamic faith.

The article indicated that almost 25% of the world's population is comprised of Muslims. Christians are said to constitute nearly a third of the world's population, with Hindus at 15% and Buddhists at approximately 8%. About 10% were not affiliated with an organized religion. I was surprised to read that Jews constituted less than .2%. Many Arab states, most notably Iran, posed a threat to the very existence of Israel, which was of grave concern to the United States, as well as Jews all over the world.

In mid-2014, the Israelis and the Palestinians had waged deadly battles. After weeks of intense bombings, the problems in Gaza abated. A truce had been declared after thousands of people, mostly Palestinians, had been killed. The world community hoped for a permanent solution, though that still seemed to be unlikely, as an occasional killing, or a bombing, continued to occur.

One journalist wrote an article saying that, in Afghanistan, instead of defeating the Taliban and crippling al-Qaeda, as had earlier been claimed by the United States, it appeared that both movements were growing stronger and bolder as the date for the withdrawal of U.S. combat troops drew nearer. The Taliban offered assurances that military action would not be taken once the U.S. forces left, but refused to agree to allow elections to determine who would lead the country. I didn't believe a word of what the Taliban was quoted as saying.

The attack on the U.S. embassy in Libya in which our embassy was over-run and our Ambassador killed was still news, although no longer on the front-page, years after the event. That was, undoubtedly, due to the politics of the situation. Hillary Clinton had yet to formally announce that she was running for the presidency, though all observers were certain she would be a candidate. Because of that, the House of Representatives continued to investigate the Benghazi attack. Republicans sought to blame her, as Secretary of State, for failing to adequately protect the embassy.

Yet another article cited a recent poll which indicated that most people in the United States were tired of a dozen years of war and didn't want the U.S. to put "boots on the ground" anywhere in the world, whether it was in Syria, Iraq, Afghanistan or anywhere else in the Middle East. Many felt as if the painful lessons learned in Vietnam had been forgotten and were now being repeated.

In Somalia, a drone strike killed Ahmad Godane, the leader of a terrorist group with ties to al-Qaeda. I was pleased to read that. I wondered who had done the killing. Maybe it was Captain McMullen and his clandestine group, or maybe it was the CIA, or one of the other branches of the service. The article didn't say.

Letters to the Editor and the Op-Eds criticized President Obama for his handling of foreign policy on all fronts. One letter criticized President Obama for waiting so long to do anything in Syria, saying that he should have bombed the country, after threatening to do so, when it had been established by U.N. investigators that the Syrian government had used deadly gas bombs on its people. The man claimed that it was a fatal sign of weakness that would be impossible for Obama to overcome. He said that there was absolutely no reason why the U.S. should not have begun military operations in Syria sooner, Now, after the beheadings and the rest, much damage had been done which could have been avoided.

Another writer criticized Obama for waiting so long to get us out of Afghanistan and Iraq. She felt he betrayed a campaign promise made in the 2008 presidential campaign. She wanted all combat troops out of the Middle East immediately. She didn't want to see any further U.S. involvement in either country, despite the horrid actions of ISIS.

Most other writers wanted more action by the President due to the slaughter of Christians in Iraq, which was appalling to all Christians within the United States. Some, but not many, were calling for the return of troops to Iraq, saying aerial bombings weren't enough. To most, however, aerial bombings and drone warfare were seen as the best alternatives to putting combat soldiers back into the country.

None of those writing in, or the commentators, wanted to see a war with Russia, yet everyone wanted some sort of action to be taken against Russia. No one wanted U.S. soldiers on the ground in the Ukraine, even if they were accompanied by soldiers from other NATO countries, yet everyone wanted to see the separatists stopped and the Russians punished for the actions of the separatists. The European Economic Union backed the United States and imposed more serious economic sanctions, yet soldiers were still dying as the Ukranian military continued to battle the separatists.

NATO made it clear that it would back any NATO country threatened by Russia, but the Ukraine was not a member of NATO. Other countries which felt threatened by Russia's actions included

Lithuania, Estonia, Latvia, Poland, Romania, and even Finland, all of whom share a border with Russia. The mere threat of a military confrontation with Russia was alarming.

On the domestic front, more and more senseless killings were occurring at schools, malls and work-places across the country It seemed to me as if these horrific events were happening on a near-weekly basis. The debate for gun control raged on, with most Americans wanting more regulation of gun ownership, while the use of guns in places across the globe continued to escalate, causing some to say it gave even more reason why individual citizens in this country needed to be armed.

The most appalling and disturbing event on American soil occurred in late September when a man in Oklahoma beheaded a co-worker. The man was a recent convert to Islam. The man had been trying to convert fellow workers and had been fired from his job at the packing facility a day earlier. A fellow employee, who happened to be a reserve police officer carrying a gun, shot the man. If he hadn't had a gun on his person, others would have died.

The immigration problems raged on, with no end in sight, due to the elections in November of 2014 in which the Republicans gained control of the Senate. No one wanted to tackle the issue so the problem with children from Mexico in the United States without their parents languished, as did the problem of over eleven million people living here illegally. The Governor of Texas called out the Texas National Guard, claiming that he did it because the Federal Government wasn't doing anything and something had to be done.

Racial tensions were the biggest problem within the United States, though. A series of deadly encounters between police officers and African-Americans sparked demonstrations across the country not seen in decades. It was reminiscent of the sixties.

To add to the political unrest, there was an outbreak of the Ebola virus in Africa in 2014. The World Health Organization spread the alarm. When the care givers became the victims the world took notice. When the first Ebola patient arrived in the U.S., it quickly became a major news story and officials were doing all they could to assure worried Americans that an outbreak in the United States was extremely unlikely. When the patient died, near panic gripped the country for months.

As far as our foreign policy was concerned, it seemed to me that before any combat troops would be sent into action anywhere there would be considerable debate in the public forums as well as in Congress. The political scene in Washington had gone far beyond a stalemate position. It was now simply a stagnate situation. I didn't think the new Congress was going to help the situation. I thought it would only make the Republican opposition that much less likely to agree with Obama about anything.

I could see how a less publicized operation, like the one Captain McMullen and I were involved in, had advantages over a more transparent approach. If Congress became involved, nothing would happen. If the press got wind of it, problems could arise. If the Afghans, the Pakistanis or other world powers opposed our proposed actions too vigorously, the politicians might relent. The more I read, and the more I thought about it, the more convinced I was that Captain McMullen and I were going about this in the right way.

Ingrid walked in and around me, but I was deep in thought, absorbed by what I was reading, and I didn't notice her presence. I was reading an article about how a retired general was pleased with the military's job of "finishing" what remained of the conflict in Afghanistan. The general expressed his opinion that U.S. troops had successfully trained the Afghan Security Forces and the police. He argued that the Afghanistan military was now capable of withstanding an attack by the Taliban or al-Qaeda and that the Afghan forces would prevail. I shook my head in disbelief while reading that article, but I didn't say anything about it to Ingrid.

Buried on page six, I found an article which reported that U.S. casualties continued to mount in Afghanistan, even as the December date came and went and all of our combat troops were supposedly out of the country. My interest was piqued as I read that ten soldiers were killed when a helicopter crashed in Nuristan province. I hadn't seen or heard of any military activity in the area.

I hadn't read much of anything about U.S. soldiers being in Nuristan province in months, if not years. The article recounted how, after the near massacre at Outpost Keating in 2009, and after General McCrystal pulled all of U.S. soldiers out of Nuristan, that province had become a safe haven for the Taliban and its al-Qaeda allies. The fact that the U.S. had gone back into Nuristan was newsworthy. I was surprised to read about it.

Even while I was there, I had heard many soldiers openly refer to Nuristan province as the "dark side of the moon." It was such a poor, under-populated area, deep in the most remote parts of the Hindu-Kush mountains, that it was more like life on another planet. The U.S. had been out of the area for several years.

The article said that the proximity of Nuristan to Kabul, the capitol of the country, and the ease with which terrorists could enter Kabul, wreak havoc, and then escape back into Nuristan and on to Pakistan, had made it a most desirable location for the Taliban and al-Qaeda. The Army knew that the Taliban had been amassing a large number of fighters in Nuristan, and that those fighters came and went as they pleased from Pakistan. It feared that the Taliban would attack Kabul sometime in the near future, before winter arrived, and it had decided to do something about it. They struck the enemy before the enemy struck Kabul.

The article went on to say that the attack may have been retaliation for the August 5 attack on a military base in Kabul. A general in the United States Army had been killed. Fifteen others were wounded. The United States was surprised and embarrassed by the attack.

The Kamdesh area, where the small number of soldiers manning Outpost Keating had been attacked by over 300 insurgents in October of 2009, was the area chosen for this particular operation. The Taliban had over 1,800 fighters, plus massive amounts of equipment, vehicles and supplies in the area. I had seen them, and reported the information, but since I hadn't found any of the men on my list within that group, I did nothing about it. Those were my orders.

Many al-Qaeda fighters, most of whom were Pakistani or Chechens, were there with the Taliban, too, according to the article. There were nearly 2,500 enemy soldiers in a relatively small, well-defined, area. I had combed the area on a regular basis, searching for my targets, without success.

Despite the odds, with the element of surprise on their side, U.S. soldiers came down the mountainside and opened fire on the insurgents. Apache helicopters, A-10 Warthogs, F-15 jets joined the fray after the soldiers were in position, but they waited until the aerial assault had been completed before they began their attack. By noon, over 800 enemy fighters had been killed. Hundreds of vehicles had been destroyed, buildings where the enemy was housed were leveled, plus weapons, ammunition and mortars were blown up.

The mission was deemed a huge success, but not without a cost. Ten U.S. soldiers died in action that day. One Apache helicopter crashed as a result of an apparent mechanical problem, not as a result of enemy fire. Its crew of six were among those who lost their lives.

A company from the 1-12 Infantry Regiment, some of the finest soldiers in the Army, was air-lifted into Nuristan province. Under cover of darkness, just before dawn, four Chinook helicopters dropped the soldiers, who carried mortars, ammunition and heavy machine guns on their backs, high up in the mountains. The men had orders to locate and destroy all enemy fighters found in the area. A troop of Afghan soldiers accompanied them.

It saddened me to think that men were still dying over there. It surprised me to learn that there was a major military operation in Nuristan province and I wasn't told anything about it. I was disappointed that it took place on a day I wasn't working or else I could have watched the whole thing take place.

However, it made me wonder about my operation, and if things were being coordinated with central headquarters. If I had seen a target in that area and fired a weapon, it could have jeopardized the entire mission. I thought about asking Captain McMullen about it, but opted, instead, to say nothing.

CHAPTER FIFTEEN

Dissension within the Family

A FEW DAYS LATER, OVER breakfast with Ingrid and Darla, as I was browsing through the latest edition of Stars and Stripes, I read an article which told of more soldiers killed in Afghanistan. It saddened me whenever soldiers died. I muttered something which Ingrid heard.

"What? What's wrong?" she asked.

"Six more soldiers killed in Kabul by a road side bomb."

"I'm sorry to hear it, Chris."

"Me, too."

"I wish we'd just get out of there once and for all and let those people live whatever way they want to live. I don't want to see anyone else die over there."

I knew better than to broach the subject, but I was so dismayed by what I read, I made the mistake of asking her if she thought we should get completely out of Afghanistan and just let the Taliban take over.

"Yes, I do," she replied.

"But what about the women and the children over there? Aren't you concerned about what will happen if we get out?" I asked.

"You know how I feel. The United States needs to keep its nose out of other peoples' business."

"So we should just stand by and watch as girls aren't even allowed to go to school? They can't go outside except when every part of their body is hidden? They can't play soccer, or softball or anything. They can't even fly kites, for God's sakes!"

"Chris, what did the United States learn from the Vietnam War? Anything?"

"I don't want to talk about the Vietnam War. I'm talking about the Taliban here."

"What the U.S. should have learned from the Vietnam War is that it was up to the people of Vietnam and, in this case, it's up to the people of Afghanistan to fight for what they believe in. If they don't, they will lose and they will suffer the consequences."

"So those little girls and all the women should stand up and fight those men?"

"That's right, and all the good men of Afghanistan should fight with them. That's what I think."

"How can you say that! They don't have the power to fight the Taliban! They'll be massacred, and I mean, literally, massacred. You know that! They will! Anyone who stands up to the Taliban and opposes them dies."

"Unless they win. From what I read, and I read all of your Stars and Stripes magazines, too, the Afghan Security Forces and the police are getting stronger. They're getting better. They can win that fight."

"I don't think so. You didn't fight alongside them like I did. They'd run at the first sign of trouble, and some of them were on the side of the Taliban in the first place. They just wanted to get paid and learn how to use all of our guns and equipment."

"That was six years ago, Chris. They've received six years of training since then. There are hundreds of thousands of them now. They're better now."

"Maybe. Maybe you're right. I just don't think so. I think those people are going to have a blood bath if we pull out of there for good, and there's nothing we or anyone else can do to prevent it, and I think the Taliban will win. That's what I think."

"That may be true, but that's up to them, right? It's not up to the United States to decide."

"So you think we should just pull out and then stand by and watch as all that happens, like we did in Ruwanda? Or in Bosnia, until we, together with the U.N., finally stepped in to stop it? Or like in the Ukraine, where we're just standing by, making idle threats?" I asked, incredulously.

"Or how about in Syria? I continued, "where ISIS is beheading people and killing Christians? Should we just stand by there, too?"

"The whole civilized world is now fighting ISIS, and all the terrorist organizations. I agree with your President. I don't think the U.S. should put troops on the ground, Chris, and the U.S. is going to provide all kinds of support to the men fighting ISIS, as well as to the Afghans fighting the Taliban, you know that, from weapons to air support to food and supplies and all the rest. Let the Iraqis, and the Syrians, and the Afghani people decide their fate. That's what I think," Ingrid responded, emphatically.

"I think we should finish the fight, and we should win it," I told her.

Ingrid, who was facing the sink, doing the morning's dishes, stopped what she was doing, turned to face me, and said,

"Oh really? Do you really think that? If you were able to, would you want to go back up into those mountains and fight those people again, the same way as you fought them six years ago? I don't think so! From everything you ever told me about your time spent in Afghanistan you always said that it was madness, sheer stupidity, to fight the enemy in those mountains, on their turf, as sitting ducks at the bottom of deep valleys. Is that what you want to see U.S. soldiers do?"

"No. That's not what I think we should do."

I hesitated before speaking further, because I didn't want to let anything slip and allow Ingrid to get any idea of what I was actually doing in my "war" room, and then I continued,

"But I think we need to keep a military presence there. I don't think we should just let the Taliban take the country back after we leave. I think we need to keep up the fight, somehow."

"So let me ask you this…what's this all about anyway? To defeat the Taliban, isn't that it? Aren't you saying to the people of Afghanistan that their religion is a bad one and that they need to get a new religion? Christianity? Is that what this is about?"

I was dumbfounded, and asked,

"Do you really think that's what I believe, Ingrid? Really? I believe in God and in Jesus Christ, but I don't go around trying to convert people to Christianity. Why would you say that?"

"Because, while I disagree with everything I know about the Taliban and what they believe, I believe that there are good Muslims in Afghanistan and that they don't agree with what the Taliban has done and wants to do."

"I agree with that!" I told her, "But those 'good' people aren't strong enough to beat those 'bad' people! That's what I'm talking about! We need to help those good people win!"

Ingrid was silent for a few seconds before responding, and then said,

"Chris, you know what I mean. I say that the U.S. should get out of Afghanistan and stay out of Afghanistan. I also believe that the U.S. needs to stay out of a whole lot of places in the world. The government here wants you to believe that it's doing the right thing, and that if it didn't do all the things it does all hell would break loose. There are those in the world who think that the United States is a big part of the problem…that the United States is acting like an imperialist country, trying to export its values, morals and the rest upon the world….all for M-O-N-E-Y!"

"You don't believe that, do you? That the United States is in Afghanistan for money?"

"Yes, I do! Money is a big part of it, and it's about oil and gas, just like in Kuwait and Iraq. Yes, I do believe money is a big part of it. I admit that, at first, it was all about getting bin Laden, and I don't blame the United States for pursuing him to the ends of the earth to bring him to justice for what he did on September 11, but…"

"And for what he did before and after 9-11…"

"I have no problem with that, but he's dead now and it's time to get out. I was serious when I asked about the religion issue. We, and that includes the whole Western world, are basically telling the people of Afghanistan that the interpretation of Islamic law by the Taliban is wrong and, although I agree with that, I'm not sure the world should do what it is doing to address that problem, which is a religious issue to a large extent."

"You don't think we need to stop the Taliban from getting back in power?" I asked. I could feel myself getting all excited and raising my voice as I spoke. I was angered by the things Ingrid was saying.

"Those people, and I mean the Taliban, believe with all of their hearts, minds and souls that what they are doing is good, that they are doing the will of Allah, their god. They gladly die for their beliefs every day! Who am I to tell them that they are wrong, even though I disagree with them as much as I possibly can?"

"If we don't stop them, who will?" I asked.

"That's my point...maybe it's not up to us, and by that I mean the United States of America, to tell them what they can believe and what they can't believe."

"I can't believe I'm hearing this...are you kidding me!"

"No, I'm not kidding you," Ingrid responded. "How is that any different from the Spanish Inquisition when they killed anyone who didn't believe in the teachings of the Catholic church? Or what Catholic priests did in the name of Christ to all of those people in Mexico, Central America and South America hundreds of years ago? They burned their temples, made it illegal for them to worship their gods or practice their religion. They killed people who continued to worship their gods. How is that any different from what we're doing now?" Ingrid asked.

"That was hundreds of years ago...I think we've learned something in the past five hundred years..." I responded, "And there are a number of countries who support what we're doing in Afghanistan! It's not just the United States doing this!"

Ingrid stopped what she was doing, turned and said,

"Listen to you...six more U.S. soldier die and you want to send in more young boys to the slaughter? You said it was like slaughter for those camps to be placed at the bottom of the valleys, where you were just waiting for the enemy to fire on you. Do you hear what you are saying? Are you listening to yourself speak?"

At that point, I decided that things were getting a little out of hand

and that it would be best for me to be quiet for a few moments, and I was, but then I said,

"I don't know…maybe you're right. I just know that the Shi'ites, who number less than a quarter of the population, are probably going to lose and that the Taliban, and the Sunnis, who number well over half of the population, are going to get back in control over most of the country within a week or so after we're gone. I don't want to see that happen. It will be back to the way it was in 2001, before we went in over there."

Ingrid walked over to me, put her arms around my shoulders, and said,

"Chris, you fought that battle. You received permanent wounds as a result of those battles…let it go! You did your part. Now you've got a job trying to help this country remain safe and protect it from terrorists who would come to this country and do us harm. That's a good thing. Do you remember what happened in Oklahoma a while back?"

"You mean the beheading of that woman at a packing plant?"

"Yes."

"I remember. That's still hard to believe, isn't it?"

"ISIS says it is bringing the war to the United States. Chris, keep doing what you are doing…protect us from terrorists in this country. Keep us safe," she said, earnestly, giving me a kiss on the top of my head when she was finished.

After that, I kept silent as Ingrid spoke. She had no idea what I was really up to, and I wasn't about to tell her. She continued,

"Think of Napoleon, or Hitler, or any tyrants in the history of the world, or tyrants in today's world, like Putin…you can't fight every battle and right every wrong. The United States isn't the world's police force. You, as a country, must choose what battles to fight. Do you think the United States is going to go to war with Russia? I don't think so. So why go to war in Afghanistan? Especially after Russia went in and lost! I say it again, in my opinion, now that bin Laden is dead, there is no further reason for the United States to remain in Afghanistan. That's what I think," she said, matter-of-factly.

"Maybe you're right. It just makes me mad to think that if we pull out now, as we're planning to, that U.S. soldiers died in vain. What will we have accomplished? We kicked the Taliban out of office for over twelve years but did we change anything?"

"Probably not. Those people have a way of life that has been their way of life for centuries. That is not your fault. There isn't much anyone can do to change that. That's the way their culture is. You can't have it both ways. Unless you're willing to sacrifice the lives of hundreds, even thousands, of soldiers every year, to fight a battle the Afghanis don't want to fight themselves, then you've got to get out."

Again, I remained silent. I was fighting a battle for democracy and for those good people in Afghanistan. I believed that. I believed in what I was doing, but Ingrid continued,

"But Chris, I love you, and I need for you to let it go. I know how it tears you up. I know how hard it was for you to watch the movie Lone Survivor. I know what your counselor says...let it go! Please!"

"I'm trying," I responded, but Ingrid kept on,

"And don't forget what Hitler did in my country seventy years ago! He told the people of Germany, and the rest of Europe, that they couldn't practice the Jewish religion, or the Catholic religion...and the communists in Russia did the same thing. How is it different? I am just asking...I am not telling you that this is what I truly believe in my heart of hearts, but it troubles me. You don't know what it was like for my family under Hitler. You have no idea."

At that point, I stopped. I knew better than to get started on what things were like in Germany under Hitler. I wanted to ask Ingrid if she thought the world should just stand by and let the Taliban, or al-Qaeda, breed and export fear, violence, murder and mayhem, all in the name of its interpretation of Islamic law, as Hitler had done in the name of Arian supremacy. I wanted to ask what it would have been like in Germany and the rest of Europe if the United States hadn't entered the war in 1941, after being bombed at Pearl Harbor, but I knew better than to do that, and I didn't. Instead, I just told her that I needed to get some sleep and that we could talk about this later. Then I just got up and walked towards the bedroom.

"I'm sorry for your soldier friends, too." Ingrid said, softly.

There was no way I wanted Ingrid to know of the plan Captain

McMullen and I were working on. My orders were to find the leaders of the Taliban, the men who had instituted Sharia Law, the men who sent so many young men to war, all of whom believing that they were doing Allah's will and would be going to heaven if they died, when it was the will of the leaders of the Taliban that had sent them to their graves. No, I would never tell her of the things that I was involved with. I would have to keep that a secret until I went to my grave and beyond.

Despite our occasional differences of opinion on various things, including politics, Ingrid was reasonably happy with the way things were going. With me at home all the time, even though there were times when I was unavailable, because I had to sleep so much during the day so often, it allowed her to get out and be more active. She was able to do the food shopping and shop for clothes and other things whenever she wanted, and she was able to spend much more quality time with Darla. The additional money in the house made things much easier for the family as well.

Things were better, except for our time together. Our love-life suffered from the strange hours I had to work and the odd hours I slept. The Hoffakers hadn't found another location to open their restaurant and it appeared more and more likely that they wouldn't get back into the restaurant business. She was still thinking about finding a job at another restaurant but she felt as if her heavy German accent, which was such an asset at the Hoffaker's restaurant, was a real detriment to her chances of finding another job.

The thought of moving back to Germany came up in conversation on a regular basis, but as long as I could continue to make the kind of money I was making we would be staying in Greenville. If it was up to her, she had decided that she would prefer to move back to Bamburg.

She respected my wishes and stayed out of the private room we had created, and though she wanted to know more about what I did, she didn't ask too many questions.

She kept track of the books and we were making much more money than we were spending, even without her income, and we were able to save a sizable amount of money for our planned trip to Germany. She didn't know that I had been stashing away some money, too.

However, I didn't like conversations like that with my wife where we disagreed with one another so heatedly. This conversation disturbed me more than most, since I was actively involved in doing exactly what Ingrid was so vehemently opposed to. Despite that, I continued to believe that what I was doing was the right thing to do.

CHAPTER SIXTEEN

The Afridi Tribe

A FEW DAYS LATER, AS I sat in my War room scanning the area around Kamdesh, hoping to find some remnants of the terrorists who had been attacked by the Army days earlier, I was startled to receive a phone call at around midnight. It was Captain McMullen.

"Chris, can you talk?"

"Sure. I've got all night. What's up, Captain?"

"I've got a man on the line who is in Pakistan, and I'd like for you to hear what he has to say. His name is Mitch Urbanek, and he's one of us. Mitch, can you hear okay?"

"Loud and clear, Captain."

"Chris, can you hear him okay?"

"I heard that just fine."

"Good. Mitch, go ahead and tell Chris what you were just telling me. Chris, this is extremely important...."

"Okay. Well, let's start off with a little background information... first of all, we're talking about a tribe of people called the Afridis who, according to myth and folklore, are descendants of the lost Jewish tribe of Efraim. Twelve Hebrew tribes were expelled from the area now known as Israel when the Assyrians conquered the Hebrews in 723 BC. The Afridis fled east to the area between what is now Pakistan and Afghanistan, known as the Tribal Lands.

"They have inhabited the area in and around the Khyber Pass for centuries, dating back as far as at least five centuries before Christ walked the earth. All are now followers of Islam, though Mohammad didn't arrive upon the planet until the sixth century after Christ. The Afridis were Hebrews until they converted to Islam.

"All Afridis are fiercely independent, and that's an important part of this...they have demonstrated their willingness to fight any and all who would seek to subdue them, including the Taliban from Afghanistan who have been living there since 2001. No one, since the Assyrians, has been able to subdue them again.

"Now, a man named Haji Ajab Afridi is an elder in the Afridi tribe. Before the U.S. arrived in Afghanistan in 2001, and before thousands upon thousands of Taliban fighters fled Afghanistan and began living in Pakistan, Haji lived, with his large and happy family, in the village of Shalutar. He was the oldest member of a family which prided itself on its heritage. He and his wife, Bakhtawara Bibi, had seven children, three sons and four daughters.

"Their children married and had children. The entire Afridi family stayed in Shalutar, as it had for generations. Most of the Haji Ajab Afridi family lived together in a cluster of four houses surrounded by stone walls. The three sons lived in three of the buildings, and Haji and his wife lived in the fourth inside the confines of eight foot high walls. It was like a fortress within the village. Members of the Afridi family inhabited the area for as long as anyone could remember, and probably since the earliest days the tribe settled there. There was peace and tranquility in Shalutar...until the Taliban arrived, and this is where our story really begins....

"So here's what we think....and this is why we're talking....not too long ago Mullah Mogabbi and his followers came upon Shalutar. I guess they were on the move and getting away from what the Pakistan government is doing to the Pakistani Taliban in Northern Waziristan. I assume you read about the hundreds of children killed in an attack upon a school by the Pakistani Taliban not long ago, right?"

"Yeah. I read about that," I responded.

"I'm well aware of it, too," Captain McMullen added.

"Well, that's the Pakistani Taliban, and they're a completely different group from the Afghanistan Taliban, though they are similar in many ways. We think Mullah Mogabbi found Shalutar to be an ideal place to hide from those who sought to capture them, most notably the United States of America, and that is where he is now, and here's why we think that...

"One evening, several months ago, while Haji and his family slept, they were awakened and forced to leave their home at gunpoint. They were allowed to take with them little more than the clothes on their back.

"Other families who lived in the houses surrounding the Afridi compound were also evicted. Their homes were apparently needed to house the hundreds of soldiers who accompanied Mogabbi. I'm sure that there are hundreds of other Taliban fighters living in camps outside of the village, in the mountains surrounding the town, to protect against any possible attacks upon their leader. He is, as you know, the number one guy in the Taliban. He is the Supreme Leader. He is the guy who started all this."

"So I'm told," I interjected.

"That's a fact, Chris," Captain McMullen added.

"So the Afridi family took refuge in the homes of other family members scattered around the village, but by early morning the entire community was apparently in a state of rage. People gathered in the streets, at the market places, at their places of worship, and at every gathering spot in the village to voice their concerns for Haji and his family, who were their friends, to no avail. The Taliban didn't ask for, nor did they care about, the approval of Haji and his family, or from any of the people who lived in the village.

"Mullah Mogabbi is a recluse. He rarely left his home in Kandahar, even when he was the leader of the country, before the Twin Towers were destroyed by Osama bin Laden and his followers in September of 2001. He immediately became public enemy number two after it was confirmed that he had been hiding and protecting bin Laden for months, or years. The United States and its allies entered the country and forced him out of power, as you know.

"Even in exile, Mogabbi has continued to be the spiritual and military leader of the Taliban. He rules with absolute power, which is, apparently, never questioned by anyone within his ranks.

"Unfortunately for those who lived in Shalutar, their lives changed when, in late August of last year, Mogabbi came upon Haji's quiet, little village and decided to stay. Not only that, he was ensconced within the safety of what had been Haji's fortress, waiting for the Americans to leave Afghanistan. Once we're gone, there is no doubt in my mind that he intends to return to his homeland, regain power and, finally, establish it to be the pure Islamic state he so fervently wants it to be.

"Within days Mullah Mogabbi saw to it that Sharia Law was implemented in the community. Anyone who failed or refused to follow his commands or to obey Sharia Law was beaten, or worse. Taliban members attended services at every place of worship and saw to it that all Muslims were to practice their faith in a manner as proclaimed by Mullah Mogabbi.

"Mogabbi immediately transformed the village of Shalutar into his own personal refuge. Visitors were diverted. What little commerce there was continued, but trucks were stopped at the outskirts of the town and no one was permitted to enter the village, except when escorted by the Taliban warriors who guarded the city. Supplies were brought into the village by members of the Taliban.

"Though he has never been seen by anyone, other than his most trusted associates, the people in Shalutar knew that someone of great importance had taken refuge in Shalutar. No one knew who that was, however. Everyone knew of the Taliban. They just didn't know how important the person who had taken over their village was.

"People began to disappear. Haji lost two of his sons within a week of the initial invasion. They had complained too much. They were killed.

"Within months, Haji's other son was nowhere to be found and presumed dead. That son had continued to complain about what had been done to his family. Haji's wife died soon thereafter, unable to cope with the sorrow of losing all of her sons.

"No one was allowed to leave the village without permission. Anyone who escaped the village was captured and some were killed by Taliban fighters. The once vibrant village was silenced by the overpowering strength of the Taliban military might.

"So this man, Haji, was a broken man. His whole life crumbled before him in the span of months. I guess he must have walked the streets of his village, ranting and raving. For whatever reason, the Taliban didn't kill him, they just ran him out of town. They just sent him on his way, telling him never to come back. I'm sure they thought he was a lunatic.

"For months, this guy has been wandering about, apparently feeding himself only with whatever food he could find on the bushes along his path, or the crumbs given him by passers-by who pitied this poor, old, raving, mad man.

"So that brings you up to where we are now...and why I called you tonight, Captain...earlier today, Haji wandered into the path of a truck headed back towards Pechawar after the driver had dropped off vegetables and supplies at the Afghanistan border to the Khyber Pass. The man slammed on his brakes to avoid hitting this guy. Although he did his best to avoid a collision, he hit the man and knocked him to the ground.

"The driver was a man named Ali Malihabadi. He's been a good contact of mine for years. He leapt from his truck, thinking that he might have killed the man, and started yelling at the guy for causing the accident.

"This man, Haji, supposedly started wildly waving his hands over his head, and said things like 'Leave me alone! Go away! I want to die! I have nothing to live for.'

"And then this guy tells Ali that the Taliban had killed his family and taken everything he owned."

"He said it was the Taliban, right, Mitch? You're sure of that?" Captain McMullen asked.

"Yes, I'm sure of it, but let me go on and I'll tell you why in a minute or two.....so Haji told Ali how the Taliban had killed his sons, his wife, took his home and everything he had, leaving him with nothing, and when the guy told Ali that his name was Afridi, Ali became extremely interested. He knew the name. Everyone does. It was one of the most well respected names in the entire area.

"So Ali put the guy in his truck, gave him some food and water, and coaxed whatever information he was able to get out of the man, and then he called me. He knew all about the Afridi and its history. He also knew Shalutar to be a remote, little village, rarely visited by outsiders. He immediately realized how important this could be.

"On his way back to Peshawar, Ali gives me a call. He knew that there must have been some truth to what this man was telling him. With a last name of Afridi, he knew the man must have been a person of some importance in his village. We all know it's not unlike the Taliban to kill people, take property and completely take over a village. They did that for years before we went into the country in 2001 and sent them into hiding.

"So who is this guy anyway? Captain McMullen asked.

"You mean Haji?"

"No, Ali."

"Ali is an interesting guy. He is a distant relative of a man named Josh Malihabadi. Ever heard of him?"

"No," I responded.

"Me neither," Captain McMullen chimed in.

"Well, Mr. Malihabadi was a renowned Indian born poet who emigrated from India to Pakistan in 1958. Like his famous relative, Ali is a lot more intelligent than the average man driving a truck in these areas. He worships his relative, though he had never met him, and he dreams of a better life. He dreams that he, somehow, some way, is going to make his way to the United States, London, Paris, or Sydney, and follow in his relative's footsteps. He is looking for a way out of where he is, which is why he is working with us.

"During the Soviet invasion and occupation, which was between the years 1979 to 1989, Pechawar had been one of the main venues for CIA operatives to train the Afghans who fought the Russians. Ali was born in 1988. His father, a Muslim, had fought the Russians as part of an Islamic Jihad.

"Mullah Mogabbi was one of those who fought the Russians, too. Many of Mogabbi's fighters right now are Pakistani Muslims. Ali's father had been one of those trained by Americans. For all I know, he might have known Mogabbi, or bin Laden. He fought the Russians, too. Ali's father died shortly after Ali was born, just before the Russians pulled out of Afghanistan entirely.

"Though he is a Pakistani, and a Muslim, Ali has good feelings towards Americans. To him, America had helped Afghanistan, and Islam, rid itself of an unwanted enemy, but that was twenty five years ago. Now America is the enemy, at least to some, but not to him.

"Ali speaks English. He frequents the bars and coffee shops where English speaking foreigners hang out. He befriended such people over the years. I think he might even have an English girlfriend right now. I'm not sure of that, though. He's had a few English speaking girl friends over the years I've known him. He's not the most devout Muslim, by any means."

"How long have you been over there?" I asked.

"Off and on for the last twenty five years or so," Mitch responded. "I'm retired CIA. I spent much of my career here. I helped to train a lot of these guys we're now fighting."

"We've known each other for a long time, Chris. You can believe everything Mitch is telling you. I do." Captain McMullen added.

"So as soon as I heard the story, I drove over to Ali's place to meet the man, and I talked to him for an hour or two."

"And that's when he called me, and that's when I called you, Chris. And now we're all up to date. So tell us where we are with this guy, Mitch. Where do we go from here?"

"Well, I don't think we're going to get much more out of him."

"No chance of him getting back into his village?"

"When I asked, he became extremely agitated and started yelling things like…'No! No! They will kill me. They told me never to come back again! I do not want to go back there ever again.' But he's sleeping now, maybe he'll be different when he wakes up. He was in really bad shape when Ali found him, but he was better after he got some food in him. We'll see. I'll try."

"So what do you think, Mitch?" Captain McMullen asked.

"I think Mullah Mogabbi is in Shalutar. That's what I think."

"It sure sounds that way. What do you suggest we do now?"

"I'm at home now. I didn't want to talk about this in front of him, but

I'll call Ali and see if he thinks anyone can get in or out of Shalutar. He knows a few of the men who drive trucks to Shalutar. Maybe he can get us some more information."

"I'd like to get some confirmation on some of the things he told you."

"I can ask. This man was delirious. It was obvious that he's distraught over what has happened to him. I don't think he's crazy, just so completely overwhelmed by what has happened to him and so upset that there's nothing he can do about it."

"How soon do you think you can get me some more information about what's going on in Shalutar?"

"I'll ask Ali if he can go see some of those men who drive to and from Slalutar tomorrow morning. They all usually gather at the market in the morning, waiting for their trucks to be loaded. Hopefully, he'll be able to find someone who can give us some more info."

"Let's talk tomorrow night about this time and see what you've been able to come up with. Thanks for calling, Mitch. This could be a very big deal."

"You're welcome. You're the first person I thought of when I learned about this man. It's a miracle Ali didn't kill him. I'll call tomorrow. Until then, take care, guys, and keep your fingers crossed.

"Until then, stay well. Chris, I'll call you in a few minutes so we can chat about this."

CHAPTER SEVENTEEN

A breakthrough

"**M**ULLAH MOGABBI! No SHIT! He's on my list and I have absolutely nothing to go on...I mean, no pictures, no description, and absolutely no clues as to where he might be. I saw that and asked myself what I was supposed to do with that."

"Well, now we've got something," Captain McMullen replied.

"I don't know much about him, other than that he's the prince of fucking darkness. From everything I've heard, he's the one responsible for all of the shit the Taliban is doing. He's the head of the snake."

"That's right, and I'm going to tell you a whole lot more."

"Great! Lay it on me...."

"There's been a ten million dollar bounty on his head since 2001 and we haven't had any solid leads as to where he is or where he has been for years."

"Nothing? How can that be?"

"Believe me, we've been trying. We've been doing our best to piece stuff together on him, about like what we did with bin Laden, and it's been harder because at least bin Laden would show himself on Al Jazzeira television every now and then and we'd get some clues, plus his face was so well known that he'd be recognized wherever he went in the world. After all these years, we still have very little on him, but this activity in Shalutar may be the breakthrough we've been waiting for."

"So what do you know about Shalutar?"

"We've known, or suspected, that he's been in Pakistan for years, but we thought he was in North Waziristan ever since he left Afghanistan in 2001. Now that things are changing and we're getting out, we think he's getting ready to come back in. We don't want that to happen. We want to find him and stop him before he can do that."

"So as soon as the U.S. gets out he'll be back in power, right?"

"Yeah, that's what we think. Maybe not right away, but it won't be long. That's the big issue right now. What's going to happen when we get out."

"But we're still going to have 10,000 soldiers there for another two years, right?"

"Not combat troops. Karzei wouldn't sign the treaty that would have allowed us to keep troops in the country."

"But the new leader signed it, right?"

The election was in early April of last year, and the two men fought over the results for over six months, but finally came to a compromise, and one of the very first things they did was to sign that treaty with the U.S."

"But we're not going to be completely out until the end of 2016, just before Obama leaves office, right?"

"All combat units are out now. The 10,000 still there are military personnel and they're supposed to be advisors and to provide support to counter terrorist activities, but on a limited basis."

"Does that include the Taliban? Aren't they still considered a terrorist organization?"

"I'm not sure. Obama is now distinguishing terrorists from armed insurgents and it isn't clear what category the Taliban falls under, but from what I'm hearing, and this was just announced not long ago, we're supposedly going to continue to go after the Taliban. Now, that's become a bit of a problem for us because the new leaders of Afghanistan don't want us to do that. They are trying to come to terms with the Taliban, and they want us to stop attacking the Taliban, at least for a while."

"But if the Taliban is going to take over the government, then why wouldn't they want us to eliminate the Taliban leaders?"

"It's a touchy situation. If that's what the Taliban intends to do, then they're going to need our help, but they think they can work with the Taliban. We don't. So things could change in a hurry."

"So what about my targets who are members of the Taliban? What am I supposed to do?"

"They're still on your list. Until we get orders to the contrary, nothing changes as far as you're concerned, and the last orders I received were that all of the Taliban leaders are still considered to be terrorists and we are to continue to hunt them down and eliminate them, if possible."

"Those guys are kidding themselves. Everybody knows what will happen as soon as the U.S. leaves...the Taliban will take over again, and those newly elected leaders might be dead men right now, don't you think?"

"I think so. Karzei wouldn't sign the treaty because he was afraid of what was going to happen to him after we're gone, when the Taliban comes back."

"I think Karzai's a dead man, don't you?"

"Maybe. He's hoping that he saved his life by not signing the agreement, but who knows? I'd say he's scared, and I don't blame him. I would be, too, if I was him. But in Afghanistan, there are so many lies, deals, unkept promises, bribes, pay-offs...who knows what's going to happen once we're gone. I'll bet he's out of the country before too long, if he's not out of there already."

"What do you think, Dozer? Do you think Mogabbi is going back in right away?"

"We're not sure. The new president, Ashaf Ghani Ahmadzai, is appealing to the U.S. for a chance to reach agreement with the Taliban and to bring peace to the country. The new Prime Minister, Abdullah Abdullah, is doing what he can to make that happen, too. Mogabbi says he won't agree to democratic elections, although he also promises that he won't use military force to take over the government. I don't believe him."

"Nobody can stop Mogabbi, can they?"

"That's right. There is no group in Afghanistan that can successfully oppose him from a military point of view. The Taliban never went away. Look, it wasn't but two or three years ago that the Taliban attacked Kandahar and damn near re-took it. We had to fight like hell to prevent that from happening, and they're still pulling shit every day. Just a few months ago they attacked one of our bases and killed a general!"

"I read about that."

"The Taliban is here to stay, unless and until the people of Afghanistan stop him. They've been in hiding the last dozen years, but they have never gone away. The Afghan people are going to have to beat them, not us, but we're going to do what we can to them before we leave. I guarantee you that much, Chris," Captain McMullen stated emphatically.

"So we know this, and we're just going to let that happen? It will go back to what it was in 2001, before we entered this god-forsaken place?"

"That's right. We're basically telling the Afghan people, and the world, that we're not going to fight the Taliban anymore. The Afghanis think they can handle their own problems and they want everyone out of Afghanistan, not just us, but the way I see it, taking out Mogabbi would solve a lot of problems."

"What a mess!"

"But there's still a major power struggle going on behind the scenes, and it's not a complete slam dunk for the Taliban. Some people think the Afghani military can stand up to them, but I don't. And you've still got the Shi'ites in eastern Afghanistan, who have the backing of Iran, plus what's left of the Northern Alliance, and whatever is left over from all the rest of the minority groups in the country, so this place is still fucked no matter what we do.

"I don't think it's going to happen right away, though. I think the real battleground will be after we are completely gone in 2016. I don't think anybody expects the 10,000 troops we leave behind at the end of this year to do very much other than protect our air bases and other facilities, like our Embassy, but it still gives us a military presence, and I think the Taliban is going to be satisfied to just wait for a while."

"So everything we did was for nothing..."

"I'm afraid that's about right, but we got bin Laden, and I know that we wouldn't have if we weren't here like we were."

"The Afghan troops won't be able to stand up to the Taliban! You know it, and I know it, and everybody knows it."

"That was definitely the truth when you were there, but we, together with the British and our other allies have been training them for years. They are better, and there are a whole lot more of them now. At some point, they're going to have to fight for themselves."

"Either way, it's gonna be a blood bath."

"That's right, but it won't be the blood of U.S. soldiers or our allies. These people have feuds that date back centuries. The Sunni's and the Shi'ites hate each other, and the Sunnis have been the big, bad bullies for years. They are either going to have to learn to get along or they're just going to have to kill each other off, one of the two. Something's got to give, but we don't want one more U.S. soldier to lose his life for these people."

"As the saying goes, 'Frankly, I don't give a damn if they do,'" I told him.

"What we're really worried about now, Chris, is that this thing escalates…If Saudi Arabia and Iran decide to fight, and I mean really decide to join the fight, then we're talking about something that could become WW III, and that is something you, me and everybody else in the world does not want to see."

"So what do you want me to do, Dozer?"

"You're gonna find him for us, Chris. Once he's gone, there's a chance a much more moderate leader will emerge as the head of the Taliban. I think it's the Sharia law that Mogabbi imposed that is the root evil in all of this."

"So how am I going to find him?"

"I need for you to find out for me exactly where he is within that village. I need information on who he is with and what his daily life consists of…all of that."

"We still don't have any pictures of him, though, right?"

"No. No pictures. Nobody in that part of Waziristan has a camera. Anybody who did would be killed on the spot. Photographs aren't allowed by the Taliban. Plus, they know how much we want him. They see anything suspicious and somebody is dead."

"But this is in Pakistan, yes? I've been in Afghanistan the whole time. No problem with that?"

"No, we've been operating in Pakistan for years now."

"But I've never been there, and Pakistan doesn't want us there, right?"

"That's right, and they've complained about it the whole time, but nothing has ever come of it. It's like with bin Laden…we were gonna get that son-of-a-bitch wherever he was on the planet. If he was in the Tribal Lands of Pakistan and we found him, we were gonna take him out, as we did, no matter what they, or anybody else, said about it. Same thing here. They can complain all they want. Unless and until I hear otherwise, we're doin' it!"

"Okay with me. So I wait until you get more information?"

"No, we don't wait. I'm giving you your orders today."

"Fine with me."

"You're to keep a close eye on Shalutar, and I'm talking about observing that little village 100% of the time. We might get some more intel from our source tomorrow, or later today, whatever the fuck time it is over there now, and I'm hoping that you're going to be able to provide me with some additional information, too.

"So you want me to monitor the area, and see if I can find a tall, thin man who looks anything like this Mullah Mogabbi?"

"No. I want you to monitor the area and get the lay of the land. Forget about everything else you've been working on and watch this village and the surrounding area. We've been told he's inside a walled area which has four houses in it. I'm hoping you'll find that spot for us."

"I'll see what I can do."

"Good. I've got a package on its way to you which will give you everything we know about him. It's the best I can do."

"So if I see another bad guy on my target list, am I to take him out?"

"No, but keep your eyes open. If you see someone else on your list, mark him, but don't shoot him. Like I said before, what's happening right now is bigger than anything else you've ever done in your life. I want you to just concentrate on this. I don't want to scare our main target away. Once I know more from our source on the ground I'll be back in touch."

"Got it. Anything else?"

"No, that's about it. We've got a chance to do some real good here, Buck. This is the most important mission of my career. It's as big as it was for us to find bin Laden. Find him, Chris."

CHAPTER EIGHTEEN

Waziristan

LATER THAT DAY, I received a package, which included a disc and some money. I found two tightly wrapped packets of hundred dollar bills. Most of the money went to Ingrid, but I kept some for myself, too. My savings continued to grow.

I focused all of my attention on the village of Shalutar. I gathered maps of the area and learned to identify, from the sky, the various villages and towns in the area. I hadn't been given much to go on, but I followed orders and waited for further instructions.

While watching over Shalutar, some 65,000 feet in the air, I spent time learning about the Federally Administered Tribal Lands, called FATL, that were in Pakistan, but were part of Northern and Southern Waziristan. With only one town to watch, I had plenty of time to study.

The Khyber Pass was the major landmark in the area. From my viewpoint high above the earth, that was my guide post. The whole world knows of the Khyber Pass. It was the closest major area to Shalutar.

The Pass, which is a long, winding road, with a series of "S" turns, is within the Spin Ghar Range of mountains. It is well-known to be a particularly treacherous road in a land of treacherous mountain roads. Those winding roads made it difficult for invading armies to penetrate and easier for defending armies to defend.

The Pass is of great historical significance because armies led by Alexander the Great and Ghengis Khan, among many others, travelled through the Pass on their way to conquer distant lands. It was of greatest importance at this time in history because it's the road which connects Kabul, the capital of Afghanistan, with Pechawar, a major city within Pakistan. Over a million and a half people live there, while another million live in the surrounding rural areas. It has been a hub for commerce for centuries. It was important to me because that is where our contact, Ali, lived.

Once I got a visual on Shalutar, I saw that it was a remote little place, with less than 5,000 residents, it seemed. I only saw two roads leading into and out of the town, and both of them were extremely narrow and had foreboding walls as high as 600 feet on either side. It was an ideal spot for defenders to see an enemy coming and attack them from above, much like the Pass.

I was looking for a walled fortress containing four houses in Shalutar. I found a few places of interest, but one looked particularly promising. I watched it as closely as I could.

The next night, at about the same time, Captain McMullen called.

"You should be receiving a fax right about now. Are you?"

"A fax is coming through as we speak."

"Go get it."

I walked to the far corner of the room and picked up a sheet of paper off the fax machine, and then returned to my chair.

"Got it."

"If you look in the lower right hand corner, you'll see an area where we believe Mullah Mogabbi may be."

"I recognize the village. That's Shalutar alright. And I've seen that grouping of houses. In fact, I'm looking at them now. So what, exactly, is it that I'll be looking for within that area," I asked.

"The specific house where the big man himself is living."

"Okay. I've been watching that complex all day. What, specifically, am I to be looking for that's going to tell me that?"

"He's going to have people around him. I'm pretty sure he'll have at least one wife with him, and some children, so I want you to keep an eye on that compound and tell me what you see. Did you notice anything of interest today?"

"Not really. I definitely didn't see anyone who I thought might have been him."

"From what we know about him, he doesn't come outside of his house too much, so you're going to have to look for other clues."

"Anything other than look for a wife and kids?"

"Well, we know that there are negotiations underway between the Afghani government and the Taliban right now and he's the only person in the Afghanistan Taliban who will make any decisions, so he should be getting a lot of visitors these days. You're to monitor all the comings and goings. You might see people you recognize."

"Roger that, Captain. So where, exactly, is Shalutar? Is it in Northern Waziristan, or Southern Waziristan?"

"You know much about Waziristan and the Tribal Lands, Chris?"

"Not much, other than what I was able to find on line today. I found out that Waziristan is in the Tribal lands, or maybe it is the tribal lands. I'm not sure which."

"Well, to understand how this came about, you'd have to know something about the area."

"Okay, tell me what you think I should know."

"You want to short answer or the long answer?"

"I've got all night, and I'm watching the monitors while talking to you, so lay it on me."

"Okay, here we go…Waziristan is right on the border between Afghanistan and Pakistan, and it's broken up into two parts, a Northern Waziristan and a Southern Waziristan. It's named after the Wazir tribe and that tribe has been around for centuries. It is called Pakistan's Federally Administered Tribal Area. The southern part of Waziristan is big, over 5,800 square miles…it's about the same size as Connecticut, so it's not a small area. The northern part is a little smaller, but not by much.

"It was its own country until 1893, when it became a part of India, but then, in 1947, it became part of Pakistan when India and Pakistan were divided up, after the British pulled out. Pakistan couldn't control it any better than the British did, so they made it into a "Tribal Area," whatever the hell that means.

"There are over 350,000 people in Northern Waziristan and about

450,000 people in Southern Waziristan, and they're mostly Sunni Muslims. They're all part of the Wazir tribe, too, and they all speak the same language, called Wazirwola. A large number of them speak Pashtun, also."

"So why are they two separate areas?" I asked.

"I'll be damned if I know...doesn't make a lick of sense to me, but those folks are known for their blood feuds, and they are fighters. There are clans in there, so many I'm not even going to begin to tell you the names and whatever differences they have. It doesn't matter to you or to me.

"Those boys fought the British tooth and nail and they never were actually beaten. They are an independent lot.

"In 2001, when the U.S. and its allies went into Afghanistan, a whole bunch of the Taliban, including this Mullah Mogabbi, we believe, went into Northern Waziristan, and they caused a whole lot of trouble for the Wazirs.

"Things got so bad that the Pakistani Army, in the early part of 2002, not long after Bora Bora, went into Waziristan to stop what was called the 'Talibanization' of the area. Pakistan said that was its contribution to the global war on terror. They put a lot of soldiers in the area and, supposedly, they were looking to find bin Laden for us. We don't believe that entirely, but they spent a lot of money and lost a lot of soldiers and supplies in the process, so things have been bad there for a long time now.

"These people are so independent they refuse to allow police departments to exist and the Pakistan Army isn't welcome there. They don't want anybody governing them, but things got so bad that the local tribesmen called upon the Army for assistance."

"So how does that help us?" I asked.

"I'm not finished...you said you wanted the long version, right? I'm just getting started...."

I laughed, sat back in my chair, took another sip of my coffee, and said,

"I'm listening."

"So the Tribal leaders wanted everybody out of their lands and they signed an agreement with Pakistan saying that all foreign fighters had to go, they were no longer welcome in Waziristan. The tribes captured many al-Qaeda fighters, most of whom were from Chechnya, Uzbekistan and Tajikistan, and either killed them or put them out of the country."

"Then in 2007, things took a turn for the worse. In both North and Southern Waziristan these terrorist groups were gaining the upper hand, not only on the Pakistani Army, but on the Tribal warriors as well. Al-Qaeda was made up almost entirely of foreigners, and they were the ones causing the problems. The Taliban from Afghanistan were there, too, but we think the Pakistani government wasn't as interested in ferreting them out. They wanted to work with the Taliban, primarily because so many Pakistanis were a part of Mullah Mogabbi's group, but they did want the foreigners in the country, so it was like they were trying to weed out the bad guys from the guys who were even worse.

"In 2008, President Musharraf was defeated and the new government, under the newly-elected President Zardari, basically declared war against all of the foreign insurgents. They launched another military style attack on the area. Unfortunately, it caused about 200,000 people, over half of the population of Southern Waziristan, to flee.

"Later that year, over 30,000 tribal warriors fought the foreigners and they began to win the battles. Because they were locals, they could identify the people who didn't belong there. The U.S. backed them as much as we could, and we made hundreds of drone strikes.

"We wanted the tribal leaders to win, but it wasn't easy. The foreign militants captured and then beheaded four tribal leaders who opposed them. That caused a bit of a stir all over the world.

"The bad part of all of this was that the Taliban was the beneficiary of good will! The Pakistani people and the people of Waziristan wanted peace and they wanted the foreign fighters out of their country, but they weren't doing anything to go after the Taliban.

"So the U.S. wasn't happy about the Taliban being seen as 'good guys' but it was happy to see al-Qaeda and the other terrorist groups lose ground in the area, and remember, we still hadn't found bin Laden and that was part of the problem as far as we were concerned."

I wasn't seeing how any of this affected me and what I was being asked to do, so I asked,

"And where does all of this fit in with what I'm going to do, Captain?"

"I'm getting there....so the Pakistani government basically agreed to allow them to remain in Waziristan and impose Sharia Law while there, which caused problems, especially when a young girl was publicly flogged for refusing to agree to enter into a marriage forced upon her by an older brother.

"But the terrorists weren't done. They launched counter-attacks and captured cities and fought back, which caused the Pakistani government to put more soldiers in the area and win back whatever had been lost.

"In 2008 and 2009, the Pakistani Army was fully engaged with these foreign fighters and, remember, that was when you and I were in Gowardesh Valley, so they were helping us in a way. Otherwise, many of those terrorists would undoubtedly have been coming our way."

"We had our hands full as it was."

"But it could have been worse. So, anyway, by 2010, the government felt like it had control of Southern Waziristan and was ready to move into Northern Waziristan, but it was a slow process. The same type of fighting as we experienced was going on over there. The fighting was in the mountains, in rugged terrain, with a lot of minor engagements and not many major battles...constant fighting, every day, like what we went through."

"I remember those days all too well," I responded.

"It was so bad that supposedly as many as 300,000 people from Northern Waziristan, almost two thirds of the population, were forced to relocate. Many civilians were killed, or had their houses and their lives destroyed.

"We now think that when the Pakistani Army, under the new president, started to have some success, and began to move into Northern Waziristan, that this Mullah Mogabbi started to feel a little pressure, and that is when he started to move around some.

"So it continued that way until 2013, just last year, and the fighting was still fierce and unrelenting, but things started to happen in other parts of the world, like Syria, Iran, Somalia, Yemen, Egypt and other places, so many of the foreign insurgents left Pakistan and went to fight in those other places."

"Which brings us almost up to where we are now?"

"Almost. As those displaced people are going back to their homes, and as the U.S. and others throw money at them to help them rebuild their homes, there are a growing number of people coming forward saying they want their lives back and they want everybody, including any members of the Afghanistan Taliban, who are not Wazirs, out of their country. The Pakistani Taliban is an entirely different story, but we're not going to get into that tonight."

"So is Ali one of them?" I asked.

"Not quite. He's more of an independent. He wants to cash in on the $10 million dollar bounty, I'm sure, and if this little village is where Mullah Mogabbi is, I believe he'll get it. Once we know, for certain, that Mogabbi is there, then I turn it over to my superiors and they will tell us how to handle this. I don't know what they're going to tell us to do, Chris, but once we find him, then it's up to them."

"So what are my orders?" I asked. As I understand it, I am to watch that walled compound, see who's coming and going, look out for women and children and let you know what I see? And I'm not to fire my weapons even if I see someone who I think looks like Mogabbi, right?"

"That's right. And this guy is going to have fighters protecting him, so you should see guards, too. There should be plenty of signs that tell you where the leader of this group is. I'm hoping you can provide me with some convincing evidence of where Mogabbi is. I want to know exactly where he is."

"Is there anything else going on that I should know about? Any plans to put some boots on the ground?"

"I doubt that, but I don't know of any. This is all breaking news, Chris, and it's real hush-hush. That might happen, but I'd say probably not. Maybe we'll send in some Seals, like we did with bin Laden, but I doubt it. That's a decision that will be made after we firm things up a bit, and then the decision will be made at the highest level."

"You mean Obama?"

"Yeah."

"Do you think he'd do it? Pull the trigger, I mean?"

"I'm not sure, Chris. Personally, I don't think he has the balls to do it, given what the leaders of Afghanistan are saying, but he'll be getting advice from a lot of people, so I hope somebody in that group has the guts to do it. Did you listen to the President's State of the Union message?"

"I did."

"Then you heard him say that he wanted to curb the 'irresponsible' usage of drones."

"I heard that."

"Now, he didn't say we weren't going to use drones anymore, but it sure sounded like we aren't going to use them as much, so I'm not sure exactly what he meant by that, but it concerned me."

"Who else will be involved in making that decision, Dozer?"

"The Joint Chiefs of Staff will be involved, and they won't be afraid to do it. I'm sure of that."

"Really? This will go that high?"

"Absolutely. Remember how Obama, Hillary Clinton, who was our Secretary of State at the time, The Secretary of Defense and a bunch of other people from the White House, the FBI, Homeland Security and the CIA were sitting in a room watching the whole thing happen when we took bin Laden out?"

"I do remember that."

"The Joint Chiefs of Staff were in there, too. They'll definitely be involved in this, if we can find him."

"That was big."

"This could be exactly like that, or bigger. Taking this guy out will affect the entire Muslim community, and about one fourth of the people in the world are Muslim, so it's a big decision to make…bigger than my pay grade level, Buck."

"I understand. It would be like killing the Ayatollah ali Khamenei in Iran."

"That's true. He's the leader of the Shi'ites, by the way."

"Or the Pope."

"That's true, too, I guess, if you think of it that way. I don't. The Pope is Catholic. All these other people are Muslim. I think that's the main problem here."

"But you know what I mean."

"I do. I'm hoping that between the additional information you are able to give me, and whatever else we can get from our source over there, that we have enough to convince me, and the people above me, that we've got the right guy and we know exactly where he is before we alert the President of the United States, the Secretary of State, the Joint Chiefs of Staff and everybody else who is involved with making that decision once we've found him."

"Roger that."

"So for now, you keep your eyes open and tell me everything you see going on inside that little complex, and remember, we're looking for a tall man who is extremely secretive and, apparently, he rarely comes out of the hole he lives in, so I doubt that you'll see him, but you might. More than anything else, though, I think the activity that you observe is going to give me a whole lot of additional information and, hopefully, that will be enough."

"That's not much to go on, Captain, is it?"

"We didn't have much when we sent Seal Team 6 into that compound to kill bin Laden. There were only a few shadowy pictures of him coming out of that building at night, never during the day. Positive identification wasn't made until the moment the bullet went through his head. That's what we may be dealing with here."

"Understood."

"Alright, that's enough for now. I'll be back in touch once I hear from Mitch."

An hour later, I got another call from Captain McMullen. Mitch was on the phone, too. After pleasantries were exchanged, Mitch began to tell us what had happened that day in his world.

"This morning, when Ali woke up, Haji was standing over him asking Ali to take him home. Ali tried to talk him out of it, but Haji would have none of it. He wanted to go home, even if it meant getting killed."

"He wanted to go back to Shalutar?" Captain McMullen asked.

"Yes."

"But he knew they would kill him if he returned?"

"That's right."

"So what happened?"

"Ali decided that his only option was to comply with Haji's demands, so he took him home."

"Back to Shalutar?"

"No. Ali was too scared to do that, but here's what he did do.... after he finished making his deliveries, he took Haji as close as he could, using back roads, mountain roads, following Haji's directions, and he got within eyesight of the village."

"So what was he able to see?"

"Haji was able to show him where his home was within the village, and then Haji drew the map that I sent to you."

"So Haji confirmed that these four houses down in the corner were his houses and that is where the main Taliban guy is staying."

"That's right."

"Any chance we'll be seeing him again?" Captain McMullen asked.

"I don't think so."

"I think you're probably right. Anything else?"

"No. I told Ali that he was a lucky man. I don't know that I would have done that. He could have been killed today, and I'll bet he would have been killed if the Taliban discovered him to be with Haji drawing a map of Shalutar."

"If this is who and what we think he is, I'm sure you're right."

"Do you agree with me, Captain? It sounds like him, doesn't it?" Mitch asked.

"It sounds that way to me," Captain McMullen responded.

"Mullah Mogabbi in Shaltuar! Wow! Wouldn't that be something!" Mitch said.

Captain McMullen chuckled and said,

"It sure would."

"Do you think they'd give Ali the $10 million if it's him?" Mitch asked.

"I don't see why not. I'd back him, and how about you? Can't you collect a part of that?"

"I'm not so sure about that. I'm not a government employee anymore, but they might not see it that way. Besides, it might not be too good for me to get the attention."

"You're not an employee of the United States Government anymore. I don't see why you aren't entitled to some of that money, Mitch."

"If I collected any of it, I'd be a dead man, for sure, if they found out. You know that, Captain."

"That's probably true, but you'd have enough money to hide for a long time."

"Maybe, but we'll need to get Ali out of here if it's him. He couldn't continue to live here if he gets any money at all. Somebody would find out that he was the one who turned him in and he'd be dead in a matter of minutes. Could you guarantee him safe passage out of here?"

"I promise you that I will make sure my bosses know that Ali is the one to get the reward. I will do that, if we get Mullah Mogabbi, that is. I promise you that I will do everything within my power to make sure Ali gets that reward, and a safe passage out."

"Thanks, Captain. I hope like hell it's him."

"I'll let you know when I know, Mitch. Good job. If you weren't there, Ali wouldn't have known who to pass that information on to and we likely never would have known about this. Well done, Mitch. Thank you."

"I'm just doing my job, Captain. I'm happy to oblige. You know how it is…sometimes days, months, even years go by, and then something like this happens and makes it all worthwhile. I'm glad to help."

After Mitch hung up, the Captain and I talked about the map Ali had drawn up.

"So we know exactly where Mullah Mogabbi is hiding, and it's in one of these four houses in the lower right hand corner of this map, and that's about as good a confirmation as we're going to get, Buck. It's the best shot we've had in years. It's the only shot we've had in years.

"You'll be receiving another package in an hour or so. In it, you'll find a disk which will tell you everything we know about Mogabbi. Chris, I want you to work overtime on this. I'd like for you to stay on him every day for a while. I'll make it up to you later, but let's find him!"

CHAPTER NINETEEN

Mullah Mogabbi

A s soon as the tape arrived, I went into my war room and began to listen. Captain McMullen was doing the talking.

"Chris, Mullah Mogabbi is the leader of the Afghani Taliban. The only picture we have of him is over ten years old and it is a very poor picture at that. We know that he is tall, blind in one eye, and about 50 years old, but little else is known of his physical appearance. To many Afghans, he is a heroic figure.

"The U.S. put a 10 million dollar bounty on his head shortly after September 11, once it confirmed that Mogabbi had been protecting Osama bin Laden in the days and weeks after that horrific event. He immediately went into hiding. We haven't had many clues as to where he's been in the dozen years since then."

I still thought it was strange to think that we knew so little about this man if he was such a huge target for us. If we wanted him so bad, I was sure we'd have gotten to him by now. I couldn't believe it. I thought that maybe there was a reason why we hadn't found him. I doubted that many people in the United States had ever heard of this guy. I never had.

"Mogabbi is believed to have been born in the village of Nodeh in the Rahwod District of Urozgan Province to a poor, landless family. He is a Pashtun-speaking Sunni Muslim, which is, as you know, Chris, the dominant ethnic group in Afghanistan.

"Wikipedia and various news reports tell us that Mullah Mogabbi was born in 1959 or thereabouts, and his given name is Mohammad Mogabbi. He is the founder of the Taliban. He was the leader of Afghanistan, once the Taliban seized power in the mid-1990s, until the United States deposed him within a few months after the events of September 11.

"His official title is 'Head of the Supreme Council,' and 'Commander of the Faithful of the Islamic Emirate of Afghanistan.' Pakistan, Saudi Arabia and the United Arab Emirates recognize him as such.

"Mogabbi gained a degree of fame and recognition among his fellow Afghan Mujahadeen in the 1980s during the fight against the Russians. He was, reportedly, an excellent shot.

"He sustained at least four serious injuries in battle and it was during a battle over Jalalabad in 1989 that he lost his right eye, although others said he lost the eye in 1987 at the battle of Arghandab.

"Once the fight with Russia ended, he studied and taught at an Islamic seminary in the Pakistani border city of Quetta for a short period of time, but it was near Kandahar, in a small village just outside of it called Singesar, that his meteoric rise began.

"Mogabbi became a pastor in that small town. He taught young boys what it meant to be a Muslim. He was the headmaster of a school for those boys and young men, which is called a 'madrassa.'"

"It was from a pulpit in that small village where Mogabbi became a mullah, or holy man, and led the Taliban to take over the country.

"Once the Soviets withdrew their forces in 1989 and the Soviet-backed regime of Najibullah crumbled, the country became embroiled in sectarian violence as several factions vied for power. Warlords ruled parts of the country, while several political groups fought against each other to win control of the rest of the country. There was no central government to control things for several years.

"It was in 1994 when Mogabbi gained more fame within Afghanistan, and that was as a result of a few successful military uprisings which captured the imagination of the Afghan people. He became, almost overnight, a mythical figure, likened by some to Robin Hood of medieval England. It's really hard to believe how it all came about.

"The funny part about this, Chris, is that he's not a charismatic leader, like you might think he would be. From all reports, he's a shy, reticent man, not known for public speaking or giving any speeches at all, nothing like what Hitler was famous for.

"He's known to be a deeply religious man who leads by example, and his beliefs are extremely orthodox, some would say they are not what the prophet, Mohammad, intended. He wants the entire country of Afghanistan to become a pure Islamic state, and he began with his little community.

"Legend has it that in the spring of 1994, one of the warlords had taken two teenage girls and allowed his men to rape them repeatedly. The families of the two girls went to Mogabbi to plead for help. Mogabbi supposedly went, with 30 of his students, to free the girls.

"Mogabbi had military training, and experience, but the myth is that the 30 men who went with him to fight the ruthless warlord and his gang of thieves only had 16 rifles. Against all odds, Mogabbi's group prevailed and the girls were freed. Mogabbi hung the commander from the barrel of a Russian tank.

"Mogabbi received quite a bit of attention in the Kandahar area for that heroic rescue effort, and he captured arms and munitions. He was quoted, at the time, to have said,

"How could we remain quiet when we could see crimes being committed against women and the poor?"

"The story spread like wildfire through the local Islamic community.

"A few months later, so the legend goes, the leaders of two bands of heavily armed thieves quarreled over which one had the right to abduct a young boy from his family for the illicit purpose of sodomizing the boy. Again, the family went to Mogabbi seeking his intervention. Mogabbi and his men freed the boy, killing the two commanders and their men in the process.

"His prestige grew, especially since he took no plunder, or reward, and sought only to establish some order to the Afghanistan Islamic community.

"The name "Taliban," is the plural form of the word 'Talib,' which means one who seeks knowledge of Islamic faith. Mogabbi and his group were called, by others, the Taliban, and the name stuck. The name and the reputation of Mullah Mogabbi grew, but this time it spread across a wider swath of Afghanistan.

"Armed with the notoriety achieved by those two successes, Mogabbi reached out to other like-minded Muslims from other parts of the country to join him, and they did. His ranks grew larger.

"In early October of 1994, Mogabbi and his men, which had grown to number over 200 fighters, were called upon to assist with another problem in the area. One of the Kandahar warlords had created a business for himself by requiring anyone who travelled the road from Pakistan into Afghanistan to pay heavy tolls. Since there were few roads available for use by commercial truckers, it had become quite a lucrative business.

"Mogabbi defeated the men who were operating the border scam and, in so doing, opened up the roads for Pakistani merchants, who promised to give him a considerable amount of money to keep the roads open. Mogabbi accepted the money and he agreed to keep the border open. That incident took place in a village called Spin Baldak, not far from Chaman. It was little more than a truck stop in the middle of a desolate part of Afghanistan.

"In less than a year, Mogabbi had elevated himself dramatically in Afghanistan political circles. The number of people who chose to follow him began to grow exponentially. To some, he was a tool for their purpose. To Mogabbi, his purpose was always clear...cleanse Afghanistan and create a pure Islamic state.

"Right from the beginning, as the intervening years clearly showed, he wanted to purify the Islamic way of life. He saw an Afghanistan that was corrupt and impure. Under his leadership, he vowed that would change.

"A few weeks after that incident at Spin Baldak, a large convoy of trucks from Pakistan, which was accompanied by at least 80 drivers, many of whom had been in the Pakistani army, was stopped inside of Afghanistan, not far from Kandahar, by other warlords, who demanded a huge ransom. Pakistani officials turned to the government in Kabul for assistance, but there was no way they could help as they were under attack and fighting for their lives, so the Pakistani government asked the Taliban to assist.

"Mogabbi and his group routed the warlords, freeing the convoy in the process. Heartened by their success, the Taliban marched into Kandahar and destroyed whatever and whoever was in their way. The Taliban, under Mogabbi, had captured the second largest city in Afghanistan. The entire world took notice.

"Mogabbi demonstrated his mettle immediately. Pakistan thought of the Taliban as its ally after that incident, and hoped it would be able to work with him. They expected Mogabbi would be glad to reap financial benefits by so doing, but Mogabbi made it clear that the integrity of Afghanistan was his top priority.

"He cleared the roads for commercial traffic, but insisted that Pakistani goods would be transported only by Afghan trucks once inside Afghanistan, which was a major departure from the way business had been done prior to that, much of which was illegal and run by a mafia-like group. It was good for Afghanistan, but not so good for the Pakistanis.

"The next harbinger of things to come was what Mogabbi did as the de-facto ruler of Kandahar…he immediately instituted Sharia law. And Mogabbi's brand of Sharia law was the strictest interpretation of Islamic law ever seen in the Muslim world, even harsher than what the Saudis have had in place for years.

"He closed girls' schools and banned women from working outside the home, smashed TV sets, ordered all men to grow long beards, stopped any and all sporting activities which did not suit his interpretation of what a Muslim should participate in.

"And Mogabbi continued to march. His men, and the thousands of men who joined him, proceeded to militarily take over a third of Afghanistan's 31 provinces. In less than three months after capturing Kandahar, Mogabbi was at the outskirts of Kabul, the nation's capital, ready to take it over, too.

"At the time, no one quite knew what to make of Mogabbi. He had come out of nowhere and had, quite literally, risen to the top of the Afghan world. Later reports indicated that most of his followers, who numbered in excess of 20,000 fighters, were between the ages of 14 and 24 and many of those came from madrassas in Pakistan. This was truly a jihad…a religious revolt…and it really was like a wild fire, scorching everything in its path.

"There were, however, some other political groups at work in Afghanistan who were trying to gain control of the country. They opposed what Mullah Mogabbi had accomplished and what he wanted to accomplish, for a variety of reasons. The most significant opposition came from the Hekmetyar group, which controlled most of the northern part of the country. Its forces had Kabul surrounded and were shelling the city on a daily basis. Despite that, the Taliban moved into the area, either unaware of, or unafraid of, anyone or anything in their way.

"The Taliban then engaged in fighting Hekmetyar's group, and they won, sending Hekmetyar's fighters in retreat. Kabul would not be as easy to capture as Kandahar had been, however. President Rabbani had a capable and loyal group of followers himself. Though they were under siege, entrenched within the confines of the city, they weren't going to be easily defeated.

"Ahmad Shah Masud was the military leader of the Rabbani government, and he fought all comers. He was the most able fighter the government had. He, by his sheer will and determination, prevented Kabul from being captured.

"Yet another group vying to capture Kabul was the Hazzaras, who were Shi'ites, under the leadership of the Hizb-e-Wahadat party, which had the support of Iran. Masud defeated the Hazzaras in Kabul, but the Hazzaras then gave their support to the Taliban when it arrived at the party.

"The fighting in and around Kabul was not the pushover the Taliban had become accustomed to, and these were more powerful forces to deal with than the undisciplined warlords he had been fighting. For some reason, the Taliban killed the leader of the Hazzaras, probably because he was a Shi'ite, and, when they did, the Hazzaras then became the sworn enemies of the Taliban.

"The Taliban movement continued to grow in popularity and, in February of 1995, while continuing to battle for Kabul, it sent forces to capture other, less populated and more defenseless provinces, including Herat, another of the largest cities in Afghanistan.

"Ismael Khan was the leader of Herat and the two provinces around it at the time, but it became clear, very quickly, that he could not hold off the Taliban forces, so General Masud came to the rescue by sending in air support and air-lifting in 2,000 of his elite paratroopers.

"By March of 1995, a scant five months after the first major military victory of the Taliban, the Taliban remained on a riotous path to gaining control of all of Afghanistan. Despite opposition, some of which was formidable, the Taliban was relentless and undeterred, and it was gaining new fighters daily.

"However, what the Taliban forces had in terms of sheer passion and purpose, they lacked in organization. The troops soon ran out of supplies…much needed supplies…things like food and ammunition. The Taliban suffered its first major defeat in March of 1995 in the eastern provinces of Shindand and Herat. More defeats followed, and the Taliban withdrew from the north, east and west and went back to Kandahar and the south, where it continued to control eight provinces.

"The Taliban licked its wounds and then, a few months later, took the offensive again. In August of 1995, after the Taliban had replenished its supplies, re-armed itself, and attracted tens of thousands of new recruits, most of whom were still coming from the madrassas' in Pakistan, it began another offensive to gain control of the western part of Afghanistan, including Herat and Shindand.

"Despite receiving continued assistance from the government in Kabul, Ismael Khan was unable to withstand the onslaught and he abandoned Herat and the other two provinces in the west, and fled to Iran with several hundred men. When he did, it allowed the Taliban to gain control of the entire west of the country, which had not been Sunni territory. The Taliban were merciless victors and they branded the area with Sharia law. To the Shi'ites who lived there, this must have been pure hell.

"Flush with victory, the Taliban again turned its sights on Kabul later that year. The Rabbani government still controlled five provinces surrounding the city, but it had been under constant siege for years. This time, the Taliban were more successful in their military efforts, because they were winning over the religious community of the country, including many within Kabul itself.

"In March of 1996, Mullah Mogabbi hosted an enormous gathering of religious leaders, said to number in excess of 1,200 mullahs. Most of the Afghanistan Islamic community attended the event, called a shura. At the conclusion of the gathering, several weeks later, a Jihad against the Rabbani government was declared.

"Mullah ,was anointed as leader of the Islamic community. His supporters were calling him the 'Commander of the Faithful.' Perhaps even more importantly, he donned the cloak that was allegedly worn by Mohammad himself.

"The cloak was kept inside the Mosque of the Cloak of the Prophet Mohammad in the city of Kandahar. Legend had it that whoever retrieved the cloak from the chest would be the leader of all Muslims, or the 'Amir al-Mu'minin.'

"Incredibly, Hekmetyar and others, including the Hazzaras, decided to join forces with the Rabbani government in an effort to defeat the Taliban and prevent them from taking Kabul. Now that was as unholy an alliance as the world may have ever seen. They had all been fighting each other the year before, but now they banded together to fight the Taliban. Incredible.

"Hekmetyar, remember, was head of the group which had been shelling Kabul for months. He was allowed to return to Kabul by the Rabbani government. He hadn't been allowed into the city for over a year, and then, all of a sudden, he was welcomed into the city as an ally. Hard to believe.

"Another group, this one from the northern part of Afghanistan, mostly Uzbeks, led by General Rashid Dostum, which hadn't been involved in the fight to take Kabul before, and hadn't been attacked by the Taliban yet, decided to join forces with the Rabbani government in an effort to defeat the Taliban, too, since he could see that the juggernaut would be coming his way soon.

"Saudi Arabia and Pakistan favored the Taliban, because both countries were governed by Sunnis, and they provided arms and supplies to them. Iran favored the Hekmetyar group, because the Iranians were also Shi'ites. Iran provided arms and supplies to them and to anyone else who was willing to fight against the Taliban.

"While the battle for Kabul raged on, the Taliban continued its effort to gain control of the entire country by capturing the three eastern provinces of Nangarhar, Laghman and Kunar. The Taliban now controlled the south, west and east of the country, and it had forces to the north of Kabul as well, but there was fierce opposition in that part of the country.

"Kabul was encircled on all sides. The Taliban was focusing all of its military might on Kabul. The Rabbani government, with its new-found allies, continued to defend its turf as long as it could.

"However, on September 26, 1996, Mullah Mogabbi and his followers seized Kabul. The Rabbani government, the Hekmetyar group, the Hazzara, and all others avoided capture, but they fled the city in haste.

"Except for the few provinces in the north that were not under his control, Mullah Mogabbi and his Taliban warriors controlled Afghanistan. Mogabbi continued his efforts to conquer every city and every province in the country.

"Within 24 hours of taking Kabul, the Taliban again imposed the strict Islamic laws, as it had in every city it conquered. Even though one fourth of Kabul's civil servants were women, as were most of the people who delivered health care to citizens, and as were virtually all of the people who taught at the schools, the Taliban banned women from working. All girls' schools and colleges were closed down and women were required to wear veils which went from head to toe.

"TV, videos, satellite dishes, music and all games, including chess, soccer and kite-flying were banned. Consumption of alcohol was forbidden. Anyone caught committing adultery was stoned to death. Anyone caught stealing anything had their hands and feet cut off. All photography was banned as well.

"Mogabbi claimed he wanted to cleanse Afghanistan of all sin and debauchery and create a pure Islamic state. The Taliban tortured and/ or killed anyone who used drugs. Since opium was the main source of income to the country, a problem soon developed.

"At that point in time, Mullah Mogabbi offered the United States and the United Nations a deal…if the U.N. and the U.S. would recognize the legitimacy of the Taliban government, meaning allow it a seat in the U.N. General Assembly, the Taliban promised to eliminate the production of poppy, which the U.S. and the U.N. were reluctant to agree to, although they favored the elimination of poppy.

"However, Mogabbi quickly realized that he needed the income from poppy cultivation to continue to wage war and do what little he did to run the government. So, instead of curbing the growth of poppy, Mogabbi decided to increase it tenfold, and to impose a 20% tax, called a Zakat, or Islamic tax, on those who were involved in the opium business.

"At the time, Afghanistan, together with what was then Burma, were the world's largest producers of raw opium. Mogabbi did all that he could to stimulate the opium industry. It was estimated that over a million Afghan farmers then became involved in the production of opium. Within a year or two, they were earning hundreds of millions of dollars per year, of which 20% went to the Taliban.

"The apparent inconsistency did not seem to be of concern to Mogabbi. He didn't want Afghanis to use heroin, but he didn't mind if the rest of the world did. Not long after, Afghanistan became the undisputed leader in the world in the production of opium.

"The Taliban controlled over 90% of the country, but Ahmad Shah Masud, who had defended the Rabbani government for so long in Kabul, became the leader of all those who opposed the Taliban. Masud was alive and well and continuing to fight.

"Masud was known as the Lion of Panjshir because he had been an acclaimed hero in the fight against Russia. He had done all that he could, and much more than anyone else could have done, to defend Kabul, but he retreated with his men to the north. The Taliban pursued him, but they were no match for Masud in the mountains, which were his home.

"Not long after the fall of Kabul, Masud joined forces with the Hazzara leader, Karim Khalili, and the deposed President Rabbani, together with General Rashid Dostum, the leader of the Uzbeks, and they formed a "Supreme Council for the Defense of the Motherland," which was to become known as the Northern Alliance. They were the last of any opposition to Mullah Mogabbi and the Taliban.

"Masud launched a counter-attack, which was initially successful, but by January of 1997, the Taliban was firmly in control of Kabul, and the rest of Afghanistan. Masud and the Northern Alliance were safely embedded in the mountains and they continued to successfully defend that territory.

"Mogabbi remained confident that he and his followers would eventually rule all of Afghanistan. The city of Mazar-E-Sharif was the last stronghold in northern Afghanistan which was not under control of the Taliban. 60% of Afghanistan's agricultural resources and 80% of its mineral and gas resources are in the north.

"In the spring of 1997, fighting began in earnest. The same groups were at each other's throats, but this time there was some dissension in the ranks of the Northern Alliance. The Shia Hazzaras in the west quarreled with the Sunnis who were part of the Alliance. It was a serious issue which divided the group.

"All of the former Russian states, Uzbekistan, Tajikistan and Turkmenistan, beefed up its borders at every point. Iran was on high alert, protecting its border with Afghanistan, as was Pakistan, which was heavily involved in the political and military donnybrook on several levels. The entire world looked on, unable or unwilling to become involved in the fray.

"Madeline Albright, our Secretary of State at the time under President Clinton, declared that the United States was opposed to the Taliban because of their position on human rights, their despicable treatment of women and children, and their lack of respect for human dignity. However, the United States, and everyone else in the world, did nothing to stop them."

"Mogabbi responded by saying that all aid agencies should be thrown out of Afghanistan because they were spies and enemies of Islam. At times, Taliban officials refused to even talk to a woman unless she was behind a screen of some kind, so he could not see her face. None of that fazed the Taliban who were determined to conquer the north and gain control of all of Afghanistan. The battle appeared to be a stand-off.

"Saudi Arabia and Pakistan continued to back the Taliban. Iran and Russia continued to back anyone who opposed the Taliban. To a large extent, the battle was and is totally along religious lines, since the Taliban were Sunnis and those who opposed them were Shia's, for the most part, though there were some, such as Masud, who was a Sunni, but he opposed the Taliban because of its extreme and outrageous interpretation of Sharia law.

"Mogabbi named the country the Islamic Emirate of Afghanistan in October of 1997. His interpretation of Islamic law involving Sharia Law was contrary to the Shi'ites interpretation of Islamic law. Many other moderate Muslims around the world objected strenuously to the image Mogabbi was presenting to the world of Islamic law. They pleaded with world leaders to realize that Mogabbi was a zealot who did not represent the views of the overwhelming majority of Muslims throughout the world.

"The Taliban wished to eradicate all Shias from the country. Shias were told they had three choices, convert to Sunni Islam, leave for Shia Iran, or die. The Shia were not allowed to perform religious services in Afghanistan.

"In September of 1998, Taliban fighters dynamited the head of the two Buddha colossus, blowing their faces away. The two Buddhas were considered by the world to be Afghanistan's greatest archaeological treasures. They had stood for 2,000 years. Buddhists were not welcome in Afghanistan, nor were Christians or any other religious group. Only Muslims, and Sunni Muslims at that, were to be allowed to live there.

"Less than 1% of the population of Afghanistan was Buddhist, but those two statues were truly of great historic significance to the entire world, especially the Buddhist community. There are about 350,000 million Buddhists in the world, comprising about 6% of the people on earth. They were extremely unhappy with what had occurred, but they did nothing, and neither did anyone else.

"Iran's Supreme Leader, Ayatollah Ali Khomeni, threatened to take strong military action against the Taliban. He said that Saudi Arabia and Pakistan, who supported the Taliban, were largely to blame. The world feared escalation. If Iran, Saudi Arabia and Pakistan joined the fray, that would have been a major war. Russia might have joined in and who knows what might have happened, though I doubt that it would want any part of Afghanistan after what it went through from 1979 until 1989 when it pulled out.

"To skeptics, much of the interest in what was taking place in Afghanistan was due to a desire on the part of many, including the United States and Russia, as well as Iran, Saudi Arabia and Pakistan, to gain control over the supply of oil and gas in Afghanistan, which is plentiful."

I was dismayed to learn that oil and natural gas deposits might have had something to do with the decision by the U.S. to intervene. A U.S. company, Unocal, had been competing with an Argentinian company, Bridas, for years, trying to convince the Taliban to grant it the rights to build the pipelines. I thought to myself that someway, somehow, money was at the bottom of things, again.

"While Masud continued to successfully defend his territory, by the end of 1999, he had only one province left under his control, and it was embattled. The Taliban remained on the attack.

"Mogabbi was determined to gain complete control over the country and create the Islamic state he envisioned when he created the Taliban in 1994, but his efforts to defeat Masud and accomplish that goal were repeatedly thwarted. Up until September 11, 2001, the Taliban continued to defy pressure from any and all outside influences, and it continued its refusal to alter, amend or ameliorate Sharia law in any respect whatsoever. It was not, however, able to militarily subdue Masud.

"In fact, two days before September 11, two al-Qaeda operatives, posing as journalists, assassinated General Masud. The timing of the event was undoubtedly linked with what followed two days later. Presumably, bin Laden and al-Qaeda feared that somehow Masud would learn of the planned attack on the United States and warn us of it.

"After September 11, Mogabbi got the attention of the United States when he refused to turn over Osama bin Laden, despite hard evidence that bin Laden was in Afghanistan, and had been since at least 1996, with the blessings of Mogabbi and under Mogabbi's protection. Not only that, but Mobabbi was allowing bin Laden's terrorist group the opportunity to grow. Al-Qaeda was able to have training sites throughout the country.

"Within a few days after the September 11 attacks, bin Laden acknowledged that the destruction of America was his goal and that he wished to extinguish America and make it fall to the ground. Despite that, Mogabbi refused to cooperate with us and turn him over.

"That's when the $10,000,000 bounty was placed on Mogabbi's head, and that's when the United States basically declared war on Afghanistan.

"When President Bush promised the country, and the world, that the United States would find Osama bin Laden, and said that there was no place on earth where Osama bin Laden can hide that we won't find him, Mullah Mogabbi defied us and continued to protect bin Laden."

"We found bin Laden and we'll find you, you bastard!" I said to myself.

"Not long after the September 11 tragedy, the U.S. bombed the house in Kandahar in which Mogabbi had lived prior to September 11. Mogabbi's 10 year old son and his step-father were killed in the attack.

"The given reason for the engagement was to ferret out all of the havens for al-Qaeda and other terrorist organizations that were known to operate in the country. We knew they were in Afghanistan. We were determined to get Osama bin Laden. We knew he was there and we weren't going to let this guy prevent us from getting him.

"On October 7, 2001, the United States began the invasion of Afghanistan. It started with comprehensive air strikes at numerous strategic targets, aimed primarily at known terrorist camps and training sites. The U.S. would eventually commit all branches of the military to the effort, but it began with the Air Force.

"The U.S., Great Britain, Australia and Canada, among others, joined us and we allowed the Northern Alliance and the forces of General Masud to take the lead in the fight against the Taliban, since the Northern Alliance knew how to fight the Taliban, especially in the rugged terrain of the Hindu Kush. The United States and the others provided the necessary muscle, and huge amounts of technical support and supplies, including boots on the ground, to assist them and do what the Northern Alliance could never have done without that assistance.

"Despite the fact that the Northern Alliance had lost its leader, with the support of the United States and our allies, it made relatively quick work of the Taliban and the al-Qaeda terrorists. They all went into hiding.

"The bulk of al-Qaeda operatives were from Syria, Chechnya, China, Soviet Central Asia, from Algeria, Egypt, Kuwait, and some were from the Philippines. All were either mercenaries or soldiers of Islam, fully committed to jihad on a world-wide scale.

"The United States Army arrived in November of 2001, with 1,300 soldiers, including many Marines. That number grew to 2,500 in December. Most of those troops were sent to the mountains near Tora Bora, where bin Laden was thought to be. A battle ensued and, it now appears, we had bin Laden surrounded. We now believe that he escaped with the help of both Afghanis and Pakistanis who sympathized with bin Laden.

"A tribal leader, Hamid Karzai, was sworn into office as the chairman of the interim government. The United Nations Security Council established the International Security Assistance Force (ISAF), which included 46 countries, to oversee military operations and to train Afghan National Security Forces. In early 2002, Karzai formally became the leader of the interim administration when elected as such by Afghan leaders."

Internally, the country was in complete disarray. Statistics indicated that 1,700 women out of 100,000 died giving birth. The life expectancy for men and women was at about 43 years of age. The world average was 61. Only 12 percent of the population had access to safe water, compared to close to 80 percent worldwide. 90 percent of the girls and 60 percent of the boys were illiterate.

"The Karzai government inherited an educational system that had completely collapsed; a health care system that was virtually non-existent; and an infrastructure of roads, bridges and buildings that had been badly damaged during the many years of war with Russia, dating back to the 1979 invasion. The Russians sought to subdue the Afghanis by destroying all that stood in the way of their tanks, cannons and airships, but that strategy didn't work out too well for them, as we know.

"The process of rebuilding the country was a daunting one for all involved. It was disrupted, as much as possible, and as often as possible, by the Taliban and al-Qaeda. By March of 2002, 7,200 U.S. soldiers were in the country as part of Operation Anaconda.

"The Taliban and al-Qaeda forces re-grouped and began guerrilla attacks, much like had been done in the 1980s when the Russians invaded. Most of the raids came in towns along the Afghanistan-Pakistan border. The enemy would cross the border, fire rockets at coalition forces and bases, or ambush convoys and patrols, and then retreat back across the border with impunity.

"In September of 2002, the Taliban called for jihad, or holy war, by all Muslims, against the United States and its allies. Its ranks began to grow again. Most of the recruits continued to come primarily from the madrassas of Pakistan, much as they had during the years 1994-2001, when the Taliban originally came into power. The number of U.S. soldiers increased to 9,700 by December of that year.

"In January of 2003, the coalition forces instituted Operation Mongoose to combat the Taliban strategy of having groups of up to 50 fighters attack bases, convoys, patrols and basically any and all foreign military personnel, and then disperse into small groups and disappear before being caught, captured or killed. By December of 2003, U.S. troop levels were up to approximately 13,000.

"Throughout all of 2003, Taliban insurgency continued and the fighting continued into 2004 with no end in sight. There was little room for negotiations. The Taliban was waging a holy war to oust infidels from their country. As far as the United States and the forces from the 46 countries comprising the United Nations' delegation were concerned, al-Qaeda and the Taliban were remorseless terrorists. The Taliban had no intention of abandoning their stated goals and aims.

"By April of 2004, there were over 20,000 U.S. soldiers in Afghanistan. The guerrilla style warfare continued. There was no way that a band of al-Qaeda operatives or Taliban fighters would ever stand toe-to-toe with U.S. soldiers, who did most of the fighting. The only way the Taliban and al-Qaeda could wage war with the U.S. was by sneak attacks and hit-and-run techniques.

"Many of those killed by the Taliban and al-Qaeda were non-governmental organization and humanitarian workers, as well as Afghan government soldiers, and that was by intent. They saw humanitarian aid as doing nothing more than aiding their sworn enemies in their efforts to win over the hearts and minds of the Afghan people.

"In 2006, the primary role of the forces from the United Nations was to build what were called Provincial Reconstruction Teams, or PRTs. Their purpose was to help better the lives of the Afghan people. Together with Afghan leaders in small, rural villages across Afghanistan, as well as in the larger metropolitan areas of Kabul, Kandahar, Jalalabad, Herat, Mazir-el-Sharif and other communities, they built schools, roads, government buildings and other such things.

"The Taliban and al-Qaeda sought to undermine those efforts and they destroyed anything that was built and killed those Afghans who worked with the U.S. or U.N. forces. Again, they would kill aid workers and undermine construction projects, as well as attack our soldiers.

"That year was the deadliest of years for the United States and our allies to date. Over 100 soldiers died during the year. There were military engagements taking place all over the country. Both coalition forces and U.S. soldiers were dying in disturbing numbers, but we were taking the fight to the enemy.

"Although the number of Taliban and al-Qaeda fighters killed was significantly higher than U.S. soldiers lost, it was a slow process of attrition, similar to what took place in Viet Nam. There were many small battles involving a relatively small number of combatants, nothing like the battles of World War I or II, or the Korean War. Ho Chi Minh had once said, 'Even if you win all the battles, and you kill ten of our people and we kill only one of yours, we will win the war.' To many in the U.S., history was repeating itself.

"In 2008, the primary military focus, as far as the U.S. was concerned, was still Iraq. Afghanistan was second fiddle. From January to June, however, U.S. troop levels in Afghanistan increased from approximately 26,600 soldiers to over 48,000, which is when you and I went in, Chris.

"In June of that year, the Taliban successfully attacked the Kandahar jail, where over 1200 Taliban fighters were held as prisoners. Those men were freed to fight again. It was a major embarrassment for the United Nations forces, who were their captors.

"In September, Operation Eagle Summit brought electricity to Helmand province, which was a significant event in a country where supposedly less than 6% of the people had electricity.

"For the year, we experienced an increased loss of life for U.S. soldiers from any prior year. More British soldiers died than ever before, too. The French suffered a large loss of life when a remote NATO base in Kunar province was ambushed. Men and women from many countries in the world were dying or were injured in the ongoing battles.

"The Taliban increased its guerrilla warfare and began destroying supply depots, cargo trucks and Humvees. It hijacked a NATO convoy carrying supplies in Pechawar, Pakistan, too. The war was not being won.

"Problems with Pakistan were worsening. Reportedly, the Pakistan military had received orders to 'open fire' on any American soldiers who crossed the border in pursuit of militant forces. It said that it would protect its sovereignty with vigor. On September 28, 2008, Pakistani troops fired on ISAF helicopters. There were 140,000 Pakistani soldiers along the Afghanistan border to guard it from intrusion."

I listened with particular interest to the portion of Captain McMullen's report in which he said that drone attacks were up 183% in 2008, which included attacks in Pakistan. So even though Pakistan was trying to prevent soldiers and planes from entering Pakistan, they weren't able to prevent the drones from doing their work. Good to know, I thought to myself.

I was surprised to hear that the Taliban supposedly broke ties with al-Qaeda at the end of 2008. Since most, if not all, of the terrorists in al-Qaeda were from countries other than Afghanistan, it made sense. If the Taliban was truly interested in having a pure and holy country, according to the strict standards set by Mullah Mogabbi through his interpretation of Sharia Law, al-Qaeda would not be a part of that society.

But al-Qaeda was the enemy of the Taliban's enemy, so it was hard for me to understand exactly why the Taliban, and Mullah Mogabbi, decided to do that. The only reason I could figure was that Mogabbi truly was a zealot and he believed, with a fervent passion, in what he was doing.

As long as the Taliban philosophy didn't spread to other countries that was one thing, but if it spread, he was a terrorist, like bin Laden.

"In May of 2009 the number of U.S. military personnel in Afghanistan grew to 50,000, a slight increase over what it had been the previous year. Then U.S. Commander in Chief Stanley McChrystal said, on September 23, 2009, that 500,000 more troops were needed and that it would take 5 years to rid the country of the Taliban insurgents.

"On November 26 of that year, 2009, President Karzai asked the Obama administration to begin negotiations with the Taliban. He could see that there would be no end to hostilities unless some sort of diplomatic resolution of the conflict was reached. Aghans were weary of war.

"The Obama administration was opposed to such talks. It considered the Taliban, and Mullah Mogabbi, untrustworthy, given their stated agenda and their history of failed diplomacy, or no diplomacy whatsoever, to be more accurate. There was no middle ground for Mullah Mogabbi, it appeared.

"The Taliban became more emboldened. It hijacked more trucks in the Kunduz province and, in the process, killed 179 people, including over 100 civilians. In December of 2009, an internal report prepared by a top U.S. intelligence official revealed that incidents were up 300% since 2007 and the number of Taliban fighters continued to increase.

"Commander McCrystal said that the Taliban had gained the upper hand. He called them a very aggressive enemy. He asked for a 'surge' in commitment, much like what had been done in Iraq.

"Despite efforts by the Taliban to disrupt or prevent the people of Afghanistan to elect its leaders in a democratic fashion, Hamid Karzai was again elected President, with 54% of the popular vote.

"There were more insurgent attacks in 2009 than in any prior year. There were over 1,500 incidents that year, over four every day of the year, even though the U.S. now had over 100,000 troops in the country."

I was particularly interested to learn where, beginning in May of 2010, NATO and the U.S. began to concentrate its efforts to either capture or kill Taliban leaders. Reportedly, over the ensuing year, or less, over 900 low to mid-level Taliban commanders were killed, many of which as a result of drone strikes. Yet there was no sign of Mogabbi. It was hard for me to understand how that could be.

"By the middle of 2010, as part of the surge in commitment, there were more U.S. soldiers in Afghanistan than in Iraq for the first time. The CIA, which had its own set of drones, increased its attacks on al-Qaeda within Pakistan. There were reportedly 115 drone strikes in Pakistan in 2010, as compared to 50 in 2009.

"There were 700 air strikes by conventional jets and planes in the month of September alone, compared to only 257 in all of 2009. As was done in Iraq, a "surge" in the commitment of U.S. troops in Afghanistan was accompanied by a marked increase in the number of aggressive military actions on the part of the U.S.

"On July 25, Bradley Manning, now Chelsea, apparently, gave 91,731 documents to Wikileaks, which published them. Included in the documents was evidence of how Pakistan had been a major accomplice to the Taliban over the years.

"In late September, a U.S. piloted aircraft that was pursuing Taliban forces near the Afghan-Pakistan border opened fire on two Pakistani border posts. The Torkham border was then closed by Pakistan. Relations with Pakistan were worsening.

"At the beginning of 2011, the Taliban began its annual spring offensive by attacking government buildings in Kandahar. Their goal was to regain control of the city. They came close to succeeding. It was another major embarrassment for the Afghan government and those who backed it, including NATO forces and the U.S.

"On May 2, 2011, Osama bin Laden was killed by a team of Navy Seals. President Barach Obama announced a plan to withdraw troops from Afghanistan shortly thereafter. By July, Canada had withdrawn all combat troops. Great Britain declared it would do the same, but no time-table was given. By September, 23,000 troops were withdrawn, leaving 77,000.

"Later that year, on November 26, an accidental attack by coalition forces, not U.S. personnel, on Pakistan's armed forces caused the death of 24 Pakistani soldiers. NATO Secretary General Anders Fogh Rasmussen said the attack was 'tragic' and 'unintended.' Pakistan did not accept the apology well.

"At the end of 2011, with the announcements that the U.S. and other countries were withdrawing troops and would be leaving Afghanistan shortly, the Northern Alliance regrouped. It did not want the Taliban to return to power and it feared that would be the result. It called itself the National Front of Afghanistan.

"2012 saw the Taliban continue its attacks at a greatly increased rate from 2011. Instead of slowing down, given the news of countries leaving the fight, it decided to fight harder. There were over 2,800 Taliban initiated attacks during the year, double the amount of the previous year.

"On May 2, 2012, President Obama made a surprise, unannounced visit to Kabul on the first anniversary of Osama bin Laden's death. He and President Karzai signed a U.S.-Afghanistan Strategic Partnership Agreement, called the "Enduring Strategic Partnership Agreement between the Islamic Republic of Afghanistan and the United States of America.

"It provided for a long-term basis for the relationship between the two countries once the U.S. began to reduce the number of soldiers in Afghanistan. It took effect on July 7, 2012 and, as part of the agreement, the United States designated Afghanistan as a non-NATO ally. The two countries began negotiations for a bilateral security agreement."

I didn't quite understand why, even though the Taliban wasn't in control anymore, the country still called itself the Islamic Republic of Afghanistan. I guess the battle was an internal one between the various Muslim leaders, both Sunni and Shi'ite, as to what it means to be an Islamic Republic. Maybe it was all about the Sharia law imposed by Mogabbi. Who knows? I didn't, and I didn't really care. I just wanted to find and eliminate the bad guys who had killed and were continuing to kill our guys."

"On May 21, 2012 the leaders of the NATO forces formally endorsed an exit strategy by which the command of all combat missions in Afghanistan would be transferred to Afghan forces. NATO and the U.S. would continue to advise, train and assist Afghan forces. Most of the 130,000 ISAF troops were to leave by the end of 2014.

"At that same time, and as part of that agreement, President Obama ordered that all but 9,800 troops would be withdrawn from the country, and that all U.S. soldiers and military personnel would be out of the country by the end of 2016, when his eight years as President of the United States would come to an end.

"By June of 2013, the transfer of security responsibility for the country to Afghan forces was complete. NATO leader Rasmussen was quoted as saying that ten years earlier there were no Afghan national security forces, now there were 350,000 Afghan troops and police.

"Raids and suicide bombings initiated by the Taliban continued relentlessly. In February of 2014, a restaurant in Kabul was attacked. The owner and a U.N. staff member were killed, along with 21 other people. In March, the Serena Hotel in Kabul was attacked by the Taliban.

"The United States plans to keep a presence at the Bagram Air base, located just outside of Kabul, from the December, 2014, pull-out until 2016, when Obama leaves office. The Taliban is now focusing much of its terrorist activities in Kabul, as well as in Kandahar. They're not in the mountains or remote areas anymore, Chris.

"Despite the continuing terrorist attacks, plans for the withdrawal of troops were going forward. Afghanistan is going to have to deal with its problems on its own before long. Unless something dramatic happens, that's still the plan."

It seemed to me that the main thing the U.S. was going to do for Afghanistan was to provide them with help from drones, which was exactly what I was doing. Granted, we were still supplying them with training and support, but they were to do the fighting, not us.

"Despite the best efforts of the Taliban to disrupt the government and prevent it from functioning effectively, the health care system was greatly improved, girls were allowed to go to school again, and roads, bridges, buildings and facilities had been constructed. We accomplished a few good things, Chris."

As I was listening to Captain McMullen, I thought to myself that even though we were leaving Afghanistan without the job being finished, we had done some good there, but I still didn't quite get it...in 2000, before we went into the country, when the Taliban was in control, it was producing 75% of the opium for the entire world, and now, with the U.S. and NATO watching, it was at 90%, or higher. What was up with that?

I guess we just looked the other way. That just wasn't right, but it wasn't my problem. I had a bigger fish to fry.

"Ironically, Chris, the United States backed the Taliban during the Clinton years, which were from 1992 until 2000, in their efforts to gain control of the country. Iran was our enemy in the region at the time, and the enemy of our enemy was our friend. Although President Clinton and his administration publicly denied supporting the Taliban, the U.S. had a strong interest in a gas pipeline and it wanted someone other than those with ties to Iran to obtain control over that pipeline.

"So that's about where we are, Chris. Mogabbi has done what he set out to do in 1994. He wanted to purify his country, make it an entirely Islamic state, and impose Sharia Law on the people. Actually, he had accomplished most of his goals by 1997, within three years or so. Unbelievable story, isn't it?

"It is extremely important for you to realize that he and his followers believe in what they are doing and that it is ordained by Allah. If they die pursuing this goal, they believe they will go to heaven. This is a fierce, fanatical foe that cannot be underestimated. Its objectives are now being copied by other extremist groups throughout the entire Middle East.

"It is my personal belief that if we can eliminate Mullah Mogabbi it is possible that more moderate leaders can prevail. There are many who disagree with me. Some say it will have repercussions globally that will be far worse than we can imagine.

"I don't think things can be worse in Afghanistan than they are now, under Mogabbi's leadership. I hope those in power agree with me that we should take him out, if we find him. For now, our goal is to find him and let them decide his fate.

"Again, as I told you when we last spoke, you are not to take him out, unless and until I tell you to do so.

"So there you have it, Chris. That's about as much as I think you need to know about Mullah Mogabbi, maybe more than you wanted to know. Now, let's find this guy!"

After hearing all that Captain McMullen had to tell me about the Taliban and Mullah Mogabbi, I reflected on the task I had been assigned to do. I was still a sniper. For months, I had been an assassin. My job had been to find bad guys, and then kill them, but now my only job was to find Mullah Mogabbi.

Whether or not I would receive orders to kill Mogabbi remained to be seen. That was a decision someone else would make, maybe our President. It was a big decision, likely to have enormous consequences for the entire world. I was ready to do whatever I was told to do.

CHAPTER TWENTY

Allan Richard McMullen

That Sunday night, Ingrid and I were watching 60 minutes, as we usually did, and we watched the segment during which the names of the soldiers who had recently died or been killed were put on the screen, I watched as eight soldiers were listed as having been killed during a routine training mission in Vicenza, Italy, when a helicopter crashed.

I shuddered, groaned and said,

"Oh God!" as I read where Allan Richard McMullen was one of the soldiers who died in that tragic accident.

"What? What's wrong?" Ingrid asked.

"That's the kid brother of Captain McMullen. He died yesterday."

"I'm sorry to hear it, Chris."

"You have no idea how much that young man meant to my Captain."

"You haven't told me much about him, but I remember you telling me that he had a brother."

"He was a great kid, not even twenty years old yet."

"That is so sad."

"I can't imagine what is going through my Captain's mind right now."

"As I've told you before, I wish we'd just get out of there once and for all and let those people live whatever way they want to live. I don't want to see anyone else die over there."

"He wasn't in Afghanistan. He was in Italy, in Vicenza, where I was stationed for a little while, before they moved me to Bamburg."

"Well, that's different, but that doesn't make it any better."

"I'm sure my Captain is absolutely devastated."

"I'm sure he is. Does he have a big family?"

"No. That young man was all he had."

"That makes it worse."

When his picture came on the screen, I told Ingrid, "That's him. That's my Captain's brother!"

"Such a handsome young man..." she said, "Did you know him?"

"I never met him, but I heard all about him. He was pretty much raised by his brother after their parents died."

"Really?"

"Yeah. My Captain loved his brother so much. He's gotta be suffering big time right now. He wasn't married and his brother was the one person in the world with whom he was closest. His baby brother was following in his footsteps. The only reason he joined the military was to be like his big brother. I'll bet my Captain feels responsible for his death."

"I hope he's going to be alright."

"Me, too."

I didn't hear from Captain McMullen for several days.

When Captain McMullen called three days later, few words were exchanged, and a telephone conference was arranged for later that night.

"I am so sorry to hear about your brother, man."

"Yeah. I just came from the funeral. I'm pretty tore up about it."

"Mechanical problems? Bad weather? Pilot error? What happened?"

"They don't know yet. They're doing an investigation. It could have been any of the three or a combination. It was pretty nasty weather on the day of the crash, and the pilot was a young, inexperienced soldier. We've had these problems with the Blackhawks before, so I don't know, but it doesn't matter. He's dead and gone and a part of me died with him, a big part of me.

"So what are you going to do now, Dozer? Do you need some time off? That's a pretty tough pill to swallow."

"I can't, Buck. What you and I are onto can't wait. It's all coming together right now. I can't let any more time pass by. We've got to stay on this."

"Just tell me what to do, Dozer."

Captain McMullen said, with a quiver in his voice,

"I'm sorry I've been away the last few days, but...."

There was a long pause, and then he continued,

"I just couldn't do it, but I'm back now, so tell me, what have you found out since we last talked?"

"I've been hovering over Shalutar every day, just like you said, and I've seen people come and go from that complex, but not many. It's a small group of people in there."

"How many do you think?"

"It seems like each of those four houses has a separate purpose. In one house is a group of men, with guns, and..."

"How many men?"

"I've seen at least a dozen men go in and out of that one house every day."

"Okay, and the others?"

"One of the other houses seems to be used for prayer. I don't think anyone stays there at night, but five times a day, everybody in that complex goes into that building. It doesn't seem to be used for any other purpose."

"Everybody?"

"I think so. It looks that way."

"And the other two?"

"The third house is mostly used for visitors, it seems. It isn't used all the time, but a few people have come and gone and, as best I can tell, they spent a night and left, so I think they were just visiting."

"And the last house?"

I smiled a bit, knowing the reaction I was about to get, and told him,

"That fourth house seems to be for one family."

"Really? What have you seen?"

"I've seen a woman and some children come and go and," I purposefully hesitated for a moment or two, and then continued, choosing my words very carefully,

"I've seen a tall, thin man come out of that house five times every day at prayer time, and go back into that house after prayers are over."

"Really." Captain McMullen said, knowingly. "So what else?"

"When people come to visit, they go into that one house, presumably to see that one man. He never goes out to greet them. He never goes out to see anybody. They all come to him."

"Anything else?"

"Men guard the entrance to the complex, and they guard that one house, it seems. They gather around it, and there are always men positioned around that house, and at all four corners of the compound, on top, like guard houses."

"That's interesting."

"Plus, there are guards walking around the outside of the compound, too. There isn't any foot traffic anywhere close to that place."

"Nobody gets close?"

"Nobody gets in except whoever the guards allow into the compound. There's nobody wandering around anywhere close to that area, and I mean no cars, no kids, no people...nothing and nobody, for blocks."

"So we aren't going to get anybody in to take a closer look, are we?"

"You mean like a spy? Like a soldier on the ground?"

"Yeah."

"No way. Not from what I've seen."

"It doesn't sound that way to me, either. Okay, can you think of anything else you've seen in the last few days that I should know?"

"I saw a couple of guys on my hit list."

"Really? Who?"

"I saw Amir Khan Muttagi and Mullah Abbas Akhund come and go. They stayed one night each and left the next morning."

"Muttagi and Akhund! You're sure?"

"As sure as I could be. If you hadn't told me not to fire at them, I'd have killed them. I was that positive."

"They were in Mogabbi's government before we kicked him out of the country...."

"That's what you told me."

"How often do the women and children get out of the house?"

"A couple of times a day, at least. The kids are about ten or so, and the mother lets them out of the house every day for a little while."

"What do they do outside? Do they kick a soccer ball around? What?"

"No, that's against the law. They just stand around and talk. They don't stay out too long."

"Does the mother stay outside with the kids?"

"Yes, but most of the time she's out there she's talking to the guards."

"Does she ever leave to go shopping or anything?"

"She hasn't ever left the compound while I've been watching. She seems to be telling the guards what to do, so I assume they go to the store for her."

"So will you have enough time to hit our target when the women and children are outside of the home?"

"I should be able to, as long as she stays outside with them as long as she has been doing."

"Is that usually at the same time every day?"

"For the last three days it has been. It's usually sometime in the morning and then again later in the afternoon. I've seen her outside of the house twice a day for the last three days."

"And this man…describe him to me as best you can."

"He's tall, he's thin, he wears a hood, so I haven't been able to get a good look at his face, but from what I have been able to see, he's not a young man, but he's not an old man, either. I'd say he's a middle-aged man."

"That may be the best we're gonna be able to do….so what do you think, Buck? Is that enough as far as you're concerned?"

"I don't know, Captain. It seems to all add up, but can we be sure? No way. Do I think it's him? I'd say it sure could be. If it isn't, it's somebody else who's really important, and either way, he's a bad guy."

"Remember, when we sent Seal Team 6 to get bin Laden we really didn't know if it was him or not. We did it on our best guess."

"That's true."

"I think we have more to go on with this than we did with bin Laden."

"That's your call, Captain, or maybe it's the President's call."

"Okay. I've heard enough. I'll make a few phone calls. Hang tight for now, but keep your eyes on that place until you hear back from me."

CHAPTER TWENTY ONE

Game time

THE NEXT DAY, AS I was beginning my shift, I received a phone call from my Captain.

"We're doing this thing."

"You want me to hit the compound?"

"I want you to blast the shit out of that one house."

"You got the green light?"

"Yeah, I did," Captain McMullen told me.

"Really? The President got involved?"

"That's what I'm told."

"Really?"

"Yeah, Chris. This is it. This is what we've been waiting for. We've got the man we want in our sights. He's the guy who's responsible for the deaths of thousands of our soldiers, and hundreds of thousands of innocent people."

"And the President, the Chiefs of Staff and the others agreed with you. How about that! Good for you, Dozer! That's gotta help your career some. This would be a big feather in your cap, Captain."

"Let's not get ahead of ourselves, Chris. We haven't done anything yet."

"So what are my orders, Captain. Let's get this right."

"I am ordering you to blast the shit out of that house the first time you see the woman and the two kids out of the house with our guy inside. Got it?"

"Just that one house, nothing else?"

"Yep. He's our only target. I couldn't care less about any of the others. Take him out!"

"Will do, Captain."

"Alright. You've got your orders, soldier. That's all for now."

"How will we know if it's him? If we didn't have a video showing it was bin Laden, people might not have believed it. I think they even did DNA testing on him, if I'm not mistaken."

"That won't be a problem, I assure you. There will be such a racket that you'll know, trust me."

"I can't wait."

"I'm counting on you, Chris. The country is counting on you. The whole civilized world is counting on you. This guy's got to go!"

"I'm ready."

Just as I was about to hang up, I heard Captain McMullen say,

"And Chris, one more thing...call me just as soon as it's done, no matter what time it is. I'll be sitting by the phone, awaiting your call."

"Roger that, Captain."

Later that night, as soon after my shift began, I maneuvered my aircraft into position above Shalumar and watched all that was taking place in the compound below. When the wife and the two children were out of the house, I pushed the button and sent two hell-fire missiles into the house, praying that I would not miss.

I watched with pride as the missiles exploded upon contact with the target. I immediately called my Captain.

"Mission accomplished, Captain!"

"Great job, Chris! By morning, it will be all over the news, the TV, the radio, the internet, the papers, twitter....everything! The world will know he's dead, and the world will be glad! Way to go, man! I am so proud of you!"

"Thanks, Captain. I appreciate the confidence you've shown in me."

"He called the United States the great white devil. As far as I'm concerned, we just killed the devil, or at least one of them. The world will be a better place without him."

"Afghanistan will be, for sure."

"Chris, are you a religious man?"

"Not really. My wife and I have been going to church for the last year or so, but it's more of a social thing."

"Do you read the bible much?"

"No, I can't say that I do."

"Well, if you take a look at Revelations, you might find some passages that suggest the world is going to come to an end with a destructive war in the Middle East. That's what some people believe is going to happen, and we may find out pretty soon if there's any truth to that."

"You think? Because of what we did?"

"Yeah. I do. The entire Muslim community might be up in arms over this. We rocked the world, Chris."

"It's big. I know that. I don't know that it's that big, but I'm sure it was the right thing to do."

"My brother would be proud of both of us."

There was a pause, and I could hear the Captain weeping as he said,

"We avenged his death."

I wasn't sure how to respond, and offered,

"And the deaths of a lot of other good men, too, Captain."

"That we did. That we did. Now Chris, you might not hear from me for a while."

"Really? Why is that, Dozer?"

"I'm gonna take some time off. I need it. With my brother gone and all, I just need to lay low for a while."

"That's understandable."

"I've got plenty of leave time available to me, so now's a good time to take it, and listen, this mission is now officially ended. We are shutting her down. You have done your job, soldier."

I was a little taken aback by what Captain McMullen told me. I was enjoying all the money I was receiving, and I was getting better and more confident in my abilities to operate drones every day, plus I had just achieved a major accomplishment. I was hoping for a raise, not a termination.

"Shutting her down, Captain?"

"Yep, and I want you to box up everything in that room of yours, and I'll come get it first chance."

"The antenna as well?"

"Especially the antenna, and I want that done first. Just put it in that room with everything else, but get it down right away. Can you do that?"

"I'm sure I can, but it will take a little doing."

"Well, you figure it out, Chris, but get it done ASAP, okay?"

"No chance we'll do something else like this again, Dozer?"

"Not for now, Chris, and if we do, we'll just rebuild it.

"And it might not be a bad idea for you to take that trip to Germany you've been talking about."

"We're thinking of going next month. I was going to ask you about that, but I guess that won't be necessary now."

"Nope, you're back to being a full-time civilian. Stay as long as you want. If I need you, I'll find you."

"If you say so, Captain."

"You'll be receiving a package from FedEx in an hour or so. This will probably be the last package you get from me for a while, Buck. You deserve every dime you get. You earned it and then some."

"Thanks, Captain."

"Alright, Buck. That's it. God bless!"

"I'll miss our meetings, our conversations, our breakfasts.... everything," I said with a laugh.

"I'll miss you, too, Buck. We did a great service for our country, and for the good people of Afghanistan. Believe that!"

"I do, Captain. I do."

"Get that antenna down and everything boxed up as soon as you can, Chris. They're gonna come looking for who pulled that trigger and we don't want them to find him. Got it?"

"Got it."

"Take good care of yourself, Chris, and that wife and daughter of yours, too...."

At that, the line went dead. I stared at the receiver for a few moments before putting it down. I spent the night in the war room, so as not to alert Ingrid to anything unusual happening. I couldn't sleep, though. Captain McMullen's last words kept running through my mind. "Who was going to coming looking for me?"

CHAPTER TWENTY TWO

The Aftermath

THE NEXT MORNING, I walked into the kitchen and saw Ingrid reading the paper. I kissed the top of her head and read over her shoulder. The morning headline in the Washington Post read,

MULLAH MOGABBI KILLED BY DRONE ATTACK

Pakistani officials confirmed today that Mullah Mogabbi, the founder of the Taliban, head of the Supreme Council, and Commander of the Faithful of the Islamic Emirate of Afghanistan, was killed yesterday when missiles fired from a drone, presumably controlled by a branch of the United States military, struck the home in which he was living in the village of Shuristan, South Waziristan, in the Tribal Lands of Pakistan.

The newly-elected President of Afghanistan, Ashaf Ghani Ahmadzai, expressed remorse at the news and asked his countrymen to remain calm until all the facts surrounding the event are made known. He, and his Prime Minister, Abdullah Abdullah, both stated that if the killing was perpetrated by the United States that such action violated the spirit, if not the written terms of the Treaty entered into in early October of last year.

Both feared that his Taliban followers might react violently to the news.

Nawaz Sharif, Prime Minister of Pakistan condemned the attack and angrily claimed that the United States has, once again, violated the sovereignty of his country. "Mullah Mogabbi wore the cloak of Mohammad. He was the spiritual leader of all Muslims in the world. This is a shameful, sacrilegious act, which will surely cause an equally harmful response from the Muslim community."

President Obama denied any knowledge of the incident and maintained he had not authorized the attack. He urged all concerned parties to exercise restraint while the incident was investigated. He confirmed his commitment to remove all troops from the country by the end of his presidency and that it was his fervent wish that Afghanistan would resolve its internal problems in a peaceful fashion.

He speculated that the perpetrator may well have been a rogue operator seeking to collect the $10 million bounty on Mullah Mogabbi's head, which had not been withdrawn and was not a part of the Treaty entered into with Afghanistan. He stated that the Treaty which he signed did not include any provisions by which the United States agreed to cease targeting Taliban leaders, although he acknowledged that he was aware of the fact that the new Afghani regime sought to establish peaceful relations with the Taliban.

He also stated that any attacks on U.S. personnel by Taliban forces or others in response to the killing of Mogabbi would not be tolerated and would be responded to in kind.

John Kerry, the United States' Secretary of State, also denied any knowledge of the incident and expressed regret that attempts to diplomatically resolve the problems in Afghanistan had been unsuccessful, stressing that armed conflict and killings are not the desired method of resolving disputes. He confirmed that the United States would continue to withdraw all troops from the country by the end of 2016, as promised, and that this recent incident would not have any effect on that policy.

Representatives from Saudi Arabia and the United Arab Emirates, both of which, together with Pakistan, recognized Mullah Mogabbi as the leader of the Muslim world, expressed outrage over the incident.

Leaders from countries which had participated in the United Nations' sanctioned military action initiated in 2001 after the September 11, 2001 attack on the United States were not available for comment.

In July of 2002, the Taliban was identified as a Specially Designated Global Terrorist Organization by Executive Order issued by then President George W. Bush. That Order had not been rescinded as of this date. A $10 million bounty was offered by the United States at the time for information leading to the arrest of Mogabbi.

It is estimated that there are 1.6 billion Muslims in the world today, comprising 23% of the world's population. Mullah Mogabbi was recognized by Sunni Muslims to be the chosen leader of the Muslim world. He has worn the cloak of Mohammad since 1996, after he and his Taliban followers gained control of Afghanistan.

Shuristan is a small village located approximately twenty miles from the Khyber Pass. It is unknown how long Mullah Mogabbi had been residing in the village. His followers expressed immense sadness and anger at the news.

Mullah Abdul Ghani Barada, the second in command for the Afghanistan Taliban, was unavailable for comment, but it is expected that he will assume the responsibility of leading the Taliban until a successor can be chosen.

Amir Khan Muttaqi, the former Minister of Cultural Affairs and Information, who has been in hiding for over a decade, issued a statement condemning the attack and vowing that the entire Muslim world would join together in a jihad to avenge the death of their leader.

The Taliban was formed by Mullah Mogabbi in 1994. It enjoyed many military successes in a short period of time and by 1996 had gained control over most of Afghanistan, until the months after the bombing of the World Trade Center, when the United States and its allies entered Afghanistan and drove the Taliban from power. A democratically elected government, headed by Hamid Karzai, replaced the Taliban at that time.

Many diplomats from across the globe, who spoke on condition of anonymity, expressed hope that a more moderate leader would emerge and that the harsh Sharia Law, which Mullah Mogabbi implemented immediately upon gaining power, would be revisited.

Arrangements for a funeral have not been announced.

When I read the news, I was happy. I was proud of myself. However, I knew that I had to curb my enthusiasm. I knew that Ingrid would have a different reaction.

"Look here! The United States killed the leader of the Taliban! Just think what trouble that's going to cause. Muslims all over the world are going to seek revenge against the United States for that!" Ingrid said.

When I didn't respond, Ingrid pressed the issue.

"So what do you think? Don't tell me that you approve of it? Do you?"

Reluctantly, I acknowledged that I did, and added,

"And I think you, as a woman, should feel the same way. You know how much he repressed women and their rights."

"I don't agree with what he did or what he stands for, but I don't think it's the place of the United States to kill him, which is what they did."

"Somebody killed him. We don't know who. Everybody says it was the United States, and it probably was, but we shouldn't jump to conclusions, should we?"

"Don't give me that! You know who did it!"

"That's what Mullah Mogabbi said after Osama bin Laden attacked the United States in 2001. He said 'prove to me that he did it,' while he was hiding him from us the entire time. Did you know that there was a $10 million dollar bounty on his head? Someone seeking to get that bounty might have done it. You don't know."

"Don't give me that, Chris! You know it was the United States."

"Say, can we talk about something else, like when we're going to go back to Germany? I think this would be a good time for us to get out of this country and get over there. What do you think?"

"Are you trying to change the subject?"

"Yes."

Ingrid fumed for a few seconds, and then decided that she'd rather talk about going to Germany, too, and she responded,

"I'm ready when you are. How soon do you want to go?"

"Check the airfare and see what you can get us for a deal."

Ingrid seemed to be mollified by my willingness to take Darla and her back to Bamburg, and asked,

"So when can we leave?"

"Whenever you want. I'll need to give some notice to my Captain, that's all."

"So how long should we stay?"

"How long do you want to stay?"

"I don't know, maybe forever. I think the Taliban and al-Qaeda are going to bring the fight to this country after what just happened."

"Well then, get an open-ended ticket for us."

Ingrid stared at me and said,

"This is so unlike you, Chris. What about your job?"

"I told my Captain several weeks ago that we had plans to take a trip to Germany. He had no problem with me taking some time off."

"That was before the leader of the Taliban was killed."

"That's true, and I expect that there will be some repercussions. Security within the United States is going to go on high alert and, as a result, I expect the Army, or the CIA, or the FBI, or somebody else to take over this operation from me before too long. They're not going to let a civilian be in charge of that much longer. So as far as I'm concerned, we're good to go whenever you say."

"So you think you may lose your job?"

"We knew it wouldn't last forever."

"You don't seem all that concerned about it, Chris."

"I'm not happy about it, but I am happy that I was able to do that job for as long as I did. I really didn't like working the graveyard shift, so I won't miss that part of it at all. I will miss the money, though."

Ingrid was puzzled by my apparent indifference to the prospects of losing my job, and she asked,

"And you can stay away as long as you want?"

"If necessary, I can fly back by myself, but I think I can take at least a month off, if you want me to," I told her.

Ingrid remained suspicious and eyed me skeptically, but she was pleased with what she was hearing, so she went along with it.

"I'll look into it today."

That night, I began the process of tearing down the war room and boxing things up. It would take some time, but I didn't want to make Ingrid suspicious and decided to keep my normal schedule.

I avoided watching the news, but Ingrid had the television on and was glued to the set. Despite continued denials from the administration, world opinion continued to be that the United States was the responsible party.

The news out of Afghanistan was mixed. The broadcasters indicated that there was no clear indication as to who would replace Mogabbi as the leader of the Taliban, and plans were being made for the funeral. It was anticipated by pundits that little would happen until after Mogabbi was buried.

I listened, with interest, to the news reports about the threats made by various extremist groups and how the United States would pay for what it had done to Mogabbi, but others in the region seemed to feel as if the death of Mogabbi would have a calming effect on Afghanistan.

There were those, including the new president, who believed that the possibility of a compromise of some sort between the various competing groups was more likely without Mogabbi's steadfast resistance to anything short of a pure Islamic State ruled by Pashtun-speaking Sunnis with Sharia Law in effect. He didn't say it that way, but he was expressing his hope that whoever was chosen to replace Mogabbi would be willing to discuss a peaceful resolution of the problems in Afghanistan.

A reporter for one of the nightly news broadcasts had interviewed a spokesman for ISIS who issued a statement saying that its ranks were swelling with new recruits from across the world and that a global jihad was imminent. ISIS said that its efforts to recapture the Mosul Dam in Iran would be intensified, and that Baghdad would soon fall. He denied that the Air Strikes by the United States and other members of the 60 nation coalition would prevent them from taking over Syria, as well as Iraq.

Other news reports indicated that the death of Mogabbi had done nothing to slow the fighting in the two countries. To the contrary, the fighting had intensified. In Syria, the main beneficiary of the bombing campaign seemed to be the Assad administration, which asked the United Nations to rally behind it and defeat all rebels in his country. The Syrian town of Kobani, just across the border from Turkey, was still under siege by ISIS fighters, but Kurdish reinforcements from Turkey were helping to turn the tide of battle.

It made me laugh to read the reports out of Russia that President Putin, who continued to deny that he had anything to do with the downing of the Malaysian Airliner in the Ukraine, called President Obama a hypocrite because of his denials that the United States was involved with the death of Mogabbi. He said that everyone in the world knew that the United States had killed Mogabbi.

The part of the world I was most worried about was in Israel and the Gaza Strip. I was afraid that Muslims would unite and attack the Jewish state. Surprisingly, things remained calm there, though Israeli authorities said that security would remain on high alert. Benjamin Netanyahu, the Prime Minister, said that Islamic extremists such as the Taliban, ISIS and others were no different from Hamas and he continued to request that Hamas be declared a terrorist organization. He hoped that the coalition of Arab states fighting ISIS would be the beginning of an alliance which would include Israel in an effort to stop terrorist groups from wreaking more havoc in the Middle East.

Though Ingrid and the entire world expected death and destruction to follow, no major incidents of violence were reported in the days immediately after the assassination.

"I'm surprised," Ingrid said. "I would have bet my bottom dollar that there would have been more violence than what has taken place so far."

"There still might be, but have you ever heard the expression 'If you want to kill a snake, cut off its head?'" I asked.

"I have, and I've also heard the expression 'Don't kill the sheep, kill the shepherd,' so maybe nothing will come of it, but I'll be surprised if nothing happens."

"I hope you're wrong. I think a more moderate person will become the leader of the Taliban, and the world will be better off with Mogabbi dead."

"We'll see, but I think this is definitely a good time for us to go back to Germany."

"Does it scare you that much?"

"Yes, it does, and since the Hoffaker's haven't found another site to open their restaurant yet, and your job may be ending, this is definitely a good time for us to go. I would feel much safer there, and you promised, remember?"

"I remember. So let's see if we can find a house in Bamburg that you like while we're there. We'll keep our options open."

Ingrid liked the sound of that and she spent the rest of the day looking into making travel arrangements while I continued to take down the War room at night. I counted the money I had saved while working with Captain McMullen and was pleased to see how much we had saved.

When Ingrid took Darla to the doctor's office that week, I got out my ladder and took down the antenna as fast as I could. It was down and in the war room before they got back.

I continued to read the Stars and Stripes on a regular basis and was delighted to see nothing but positive reactions to the killing of Mogabbi from my fellow soldiers.

However, I was devastated to read an article in the obituaries of both the Washington Post and the Stars and Stripes several days later where Captain McMullen had died as a result of an apparent suicide. He was found by security personnel in his personal vehicle in the parking lot at the Pentagon with a gun in his hand and a gunshot wound to his temple.

The article recited his accomplishments during a stellar 25 year career that saw him rise from an enlisted man to a well-respected and high-ranking officer in the Army. Funeral services were to be held at Arlington National Cemetery. He was to be buried next to his brother.

My first reaction was that it was made to look like a suicide. My Captain wouldn't have done that. I figured that someone had traced the drone back to him and they'd made it look like a suicide, and that they'd be coming after me. I brought my pistol out of storage, cleaned it, loaded it, and put it in a safe place. If they found him, they might come looking for me, just like he had warned me.

Given all that I had heard over the television and all that I had read in the newspapers following the killing of Mogabbi, I wondered whether or not President Obama had, indeed, authorized the assassination. I didn't know and I didn't want to know. I was proud of what Captain McMullen and I had accomplished. I would go to my grave believing that we had done what our country asked us to do, and there was no way I would ever say or think anything but the best of him. He was my hero.

I wasn't happy with the fact that my career as a covert drone operator was over. My time back in the saddle as a soldier made me feel like the warrior I wanted to be, and still considered myself to be. I still had fire in my belly. I was still a young man. I had just turned thirty and, with luck, I might live another fifty years, or more.

There's no telling what the future holds for me. I'm sure that there will be more battles to fight. Terrorists weren't going to go away, and I was a damn good drone operator. If a terrorist, or a Muslim extremist, came looking for me, and found me, he'd have a fight on his hands. Maybe I'll die with my boots on after all. Only time would tell. For now, Valhalla would have to wait.

THE END

Appendix A

A Decree from the Taliban dated November, 2006, announced by the General Presidency of Amr Bil Maruf and Nai Az Munkar (Religious Police):

Women, you should not step outside your residence. If you go outside the house you should not be like women who used to go with fashionable clothes wearing much cosmetics and appearing in front of men before the coming of Islam.

Islam as a rescuing religion has determined specific dignity for women. Islam has valuable instructions for women:

Women should not create such opportunity to attract the attention of useless people who will not look at them with a good eye;

Women have the responsibility as a teacher or co-ordinator for her family. Husbands, brothers and fathers have the responsibility for providing the family with the necessary life requirements (food, clothes etc).

In case women are required to go outside the residence for the purposes of education, social needs or social services they should cover themselves in accordance with Islamic Sharia regulation.

If women are going outside with fashionable, ornamental, tight and charming clothes to show themselves, they will be cursed by the Islamic Sharia and should never expect to go to heaven.

All family elders and every Muslim have responsibility in this respect. We request all family elders to keep tight counsel over their families and avoid these social problems. Otherwise these women will be threatened, investigated and severely punished as well as the family elders by the forces of the (Munkrat).

The Religious Police (Munkrat) have the responsibility and duty to struggle against these social problems and will continue their effort until evil is finished.

Appendix B

RULES OF WORK FOR the State Hospitals and private clinics based on Islamic Sharia principles, Ministry of Health, on behalf of Amir ul Momineen Mullah Mohammed Mogabbi.

1. Female patients should go to female physicians. In case a male physician is needed, the female patient should be accompanied by her close relative.
2. During examination, the female patients and male physicians both should be dressed with Islamic hijab (veil).
3. Male physicians should not touch or see the other parts of female patients except for the affected part.
4. Waiting room for female patients should be safely covered.
5. The person who regulates turn for female patients should be a female.
6. During the night duty, in what rooms female patients are hospitalized, the male doctor without the call of the patient is not allowed to enter the room.
7. Sitting and speaking between male and female doctors are not allowed, if there be need for discussion, it should be done with hijab.
8. Female doctors should wear simple clothes, they are not allowed to wear stylish clothes or use cosmetics or make-up.
9. Female doctors and nurses are not allowed to enter the rooms where male patients are hospitalized.
10. Hospital staff should pray in mosques on time.

11. The Religious Police are allowed to go for control at any time and nobody can prevent them.

Anybody who violates the order will be punished as per Islamic regulations.

Appendix C

General Presidency of Amr Bil Maruf, Kabul, December, 1996.

1. To prevent sedition and female uncovers (Be Hejabi). No drivers are allowed to pick up women who are using Iranian burga. In case of violation the driver will be imprisoned. If such kind of female are observed in the street their house will be found and their husband punished. If the women use stimulating and attractive cloth and there is no accompany of close male relative with them, the drivers should not pick them up.

2. To prevent music. To be broadcast by the public information resources. In shops, hotels, vehicles and rickshaws casettes and music are prohibited. This matter should be monitored within five days. If any music cassette found in a shop, the shopkeeper should be imprisoned and the shop locked. If five people guarantee the shop should be opened the criminal released later. If cassette found in the vehicle, the vehicle and the driver will be imprisoned. If five people guarantee the vehicle will be released and the criminal released later.

3. To prevent beard shaving and its cutting. After one and a half months if anyone observed who has shaved and/or cut his beard, they should be arrested and imprisoned until their beard gets bushy.

4. To prevent keeping pigeons and playing with birds. Within ten days this habit/hobby should stop. After ten days this should be monitored and the pigeons and any other playing birds should be abolished.

5. To prevent kite-flying. The kite shops in the city should be abolished.
6. To prevent idolatory. In vehicles, shops, hotels, room and any other place pictures/portraits should be abolished. The monitors should tear up all pictures in the above places.
7. To prevent gambling. In collaboration with the security police the main centers should be found and the gamblers imprisoned for one month.
8. To eradicate the use of addiction. Addicts should be imprisoned and investigation made to find the supplier and the shop. The shop should be locked and the owner and user should be imprisoned and punished.
9. To prevent the British and American hairstyle. People with long hair should be arrested and taken to the Religious Police department to shave their hair. The criminal has to pay the barber.
10. To prevent interest on loans, charge on changing small denomination notes and charge on money orders. All money exchangers should be informed that the above three types of exchanging the money should be prohibited. In case of violation criminals will be imprisoned for a long time.
11. To prevent washing cloth by young ladies along the water streams in the city. Violator ladies should be picked up with respectful Islamic manner, taken to their houses and their husbands severely punished.
12. To prevent music and dances in the wedding parties. In case of violation the head of the family will be arrested and punished.
13. To prevent the playing of music drum. The prohibition of this should be announced. If anybody does this then the religious elders can decide about it.
14. To prevent sewing ladies cloth and taking female body measures by tailor. If women fashion magazines are seen in the shop the tailor should be imprisoned.
15. To prevent sorcery. All the related books should be burnt and the magician should be imprisoned until his repentance.

16. To prevent not praying and order gathering pray at the bazaar. Prayer should be done on their due times in all districts. Transportation should be strictly prohibited and all people are obliged to go to the mosque. If young people are seen in the shops they will be immediately imprisoned.

About the Author

Pierce Kelley received an undergraduate degree (B.A.) from Tulane University, New Orleans, Louisiana, in 1969. He received a Doctorate of Jurisprudence (J.D.) from the George Washington University, Washington, D.C., in 1973. He now practices law in Cedar Key, Florida.

Printed in the United States
By Bookmasters